Nevil Shute Norway, which he shortened to Nevil Shute, was born in England on 17 January, 1899.

Shute was educated at Shrewsbury, then at Balliol College, Oxford, where he studied engineering. He went to De Havilland Aircraft as an aeronautical engineer, then joined Vickers in 1924 to work on the airship R100 in competition with the British Air Ministry to develop the R101. Shute's first published novel, *Marazan*, came out while he was working on the airship. It was then that he shortened his writing name to protect his engineering career.

After the crash of the R101, airship design was written off as a lost cause and the Vickers team was disbanded. Shute decided to set up his own company, Airspeed Ltd., in 1931. While doing this, he wrote his novel *Lonely Road*, which was published in 1931. He was bought out of the company in 1939 by the other directors following a dispute. He served in both world wars, although he did not serve overseas in the First World War in which his elder brother had been killed in France. Shute was a commander in the Royal Navy Volunteer Reserve in the Second World War, working on secret projects.

Shute flew his own aircraft to Australia in 1948–49 to do research for his novel, *On the Beach*, published in 1957. He settled there permanently in 1950 living in Langwarrin, in Victoria, Australia. His knowledge of engineering and the aircraft industry was often woven into his novels.

He died in 1960.

NEVIL**SHUTE**
Slide Rule

HOUSE OF
STRATUS

First published in 1954 by William Heinemann Ltd.

This edition published in 2000 by House of Stratus, an imprint of Stratus Holdings plc, 24c Old Burlington Street, London, W1X 1RL. UK.

www.houseofstratus.com

Typeset, printed and bound by House of Stratus.

A catalogue record for this book is available from the British Library.

ISBN 1-84232-291-5

Cover design: Marc Burville-Riley
Cover image: Camera Press

AUTHOR'S NOTE

My full name is Nevil Shute Norway. Readers will find on pages 44–45 an explanation of the reasons that made me use my Christian names alone when writing my books.

NEVIL SHUTE
Langwarrin, Victoria, Australia. October 1953

ACKNOWLEDGEMENT

The poem by E F A Geach on page 11 is quoted by kind permission of Messrs. Basil Blackwell Ltd.

To travel hopefully is a better thing than to arrive, and the true success is to labour.

R L STEVENSON

CHAPTER ONE

A YEAR OR so ago I was driving on the coast road near Mornington, forty miles south of Melbourne in Australia. I was going to see some friends to return an unwanted kitten that they had wished on to my children while my back was turned. Maybe the kitten had a malignance that I did not fully understand, because I was driving along between the red cliffs and the blue sea and thinking no evil when I was stabbed suddenly by an intense pain in my chest. It was so sharp and so agonizing that I could not go on; I was alone in the car but for the kitten, so I pulled in to the roadside and parked to sweat it out. Ten minutes later I was rather better and went on, but two miles farther on I had to park again. Finally I got to the house of my friends but I didn't get out of the car; it hurt too much to move. I stayed in the driving seat and hooted, and when the wife came out, 'Look, Joan,' I said. 'I'm sorry, but we can't cope with this ruddy kitten. It's come home. Apart from that, I think I've had a heart attack. Will you get in and come with me to Mornington? I'm going to see the doctor, but I'd just as soon have someone with me in the car.'

It wasn't the first time that I had had this thing. It happened to me first in 1939, in Grand Central Station in New York, at midnight. I had been in America for about a month and in a few days I was to sail for home; during that month I had been lavishly entertained by all manner of Americans as is their way. I had travelled a long distance, I had made the first public speeches of my life, I had met a great number of interesting and important people, and I suppose I was very tired. That night I dined and danced with a charming lady in the Rainbow Room, who introduced me to mint juleps. We refuelled on mint juleps from time to time, and when at last I took her to Grand Central Station to put her on the train to her suburban home we found that she had missed it,

1

and had three quarters of an hour to wait. The prudent course was clearly to turn in to the station bar for a mint julep, and after that, 'I know a lovely drink,' she said. 'It's called a Bebeda Commodore.'

'What's in it?' I inquired.

She was a little vague about that, but said it was delicious. So I called the waiter and ordered two Bebeda Commodores.

The waiter raised his eyebrows. 'On top of a mint julep?' he inquired.

If there weren't any fools in the world there wouldn't be any fun. 'On top of a mint julep,' I said firmly. He raised his eyebrows again as if to say, 'It's your body,' and brought two of these things.

When I got up to take her to the ticket barrier to catch her train the pain shot me through, as if the bullet had gone in in front and had come out behind. It was difficult to walk or to breathe, but I got her to the barrier. She was concerned to leave me so, but I made her go, and found a seat, and sat down very motionless till the pain eased. Finally I got myself to a taxi and went back to the Hotel Chatham.

In the morning the hotel doctor told me how silly I had been, and sent me to have a cardiograph taken. The report was that I had strained my heart, not very badly; if I took things easily for a few weeks I should be as good as new. I did so and I was, but it was six weeks before the pain entirely disappeared.

The second time it came was during the London blitz, early in 1941. I had joined the Royal Naval Volunteer Reserve as an 'elderly yachtsman' in the official phrase, thinking to spend the war in charge of a drifter or a motor minesweeper. But Their Lordships had other views: I had only been in training for two days when I was pulled out of the squad and asked some awkward questions about my previous career and technical experience, and I was sent up to an Admiralty office to work on the design of unconventional weapons. And there I stayed for most of the war, living in my club and going to the office every day, with occasional excursions to sea to attend trials of my toys. By the middle of the war I had attained the dizzy rank of lieutenant-commander, in the executive branch to make it worse, so that I ventured on board little ships wrapped in a secret terror that I might find myself the senior naval officer on board and have to do something. I think I must have been the only executive lieutenant-commander in the Navy who had never attended Sunday Divisions, and didn't even know what happened at that ceremony.

However, all that is by the way. It was in a train coming back to London after some trial in a ship or at a port that the pain shot me through again; perhaps it had to do with hard work in the middle of the bombing. I went to the Admiralty doctor, a temporary officer who had a Harley Street consulting room, and told him about New York and the

Bebeda Commodore. He took a lot of trouble over me, and at the end of it he said, 'You've not got a heart attack, and what's more you've never had one. What you've got is wind. Take these six powders, and if you get any more trouble come and see me again.' I never did.

So when I got to the consulting room again, at Mornington in Australia, the score was one all, so to speak. By that time I was well known as a writer and the doctors took me very seriously. They put me to bed and got me a specialist, and took cardiograph after cardiograph in the hope of finding something wrong with me, with results that were ludicrously negative. Finally they ordered me to stay in bed for three weeks, and not to do it again.

That didn't worry me, of course, because three weeks in bed is a light sentence to a man who can work a typewriter upon his knees in the morning and dabble with an oil painting on his knees in the afternoon. More serious was the matter of my pilot's licence.

Most of my adult life, perhaps all the worthwhile part of it, has been spent in messing about with aeroplanes. Kenneth Grahame once wrote that 'there is nothing – absolutely nothing – half so much worth doing as simply messing about in boats'. With that I would agree, yet for a fleeting period in the world's history I think that aeroplanes ran boats very close for sheer enjoyment. For about thirty years there was a period when aeroplanes would fly when you wanted them to but there were still fresh things to be learned on every flight, a period when aeroplanes were small and easily built so that experiments were cheap and new designs could fly within six months of the first glimmer in the mind of the designer. That halcyon period started about the year 1910 and it was in full flower after the First World War when I was a young man; it died with the second war when aeroplanes had grown too costly and too complicated for individuals to build or even to operate. I count myself lucky that that fleeting period coincided with my youth and my young manhood, and that I had a part in it.

Sitting in bed for three weeks at the age of fifty-two I had time to speculate on what would happen if this thing came a fourth time, while I was flying my Proctor. I could probably fly again because it was clear that the doctors had found no real reason for this pain, and nobody but I knew quite how incapacitating it had been. I could probably bluff them into a renewal of the medical certificate of fitness for my pilot's licence. If it came a fourth time, and came while I was flying? I very seldom have another pilot as a passenger. I would probably grow tired very quickly with the pain; I would have to land as soon as possible. If I were on a long flight over mountains or sea, that would be just too bad. Like many men today, after two wars I have been in danger too often to bother very much about being killed, and when it comes I would prefer that it should happen in an aeroplane, since aeroplanes have been the best part of my life. It would be bad luck on any passenger who happened to be flying with me, though.

If I went on flying, I should have to fly alone. My four seat Percival Proctor that had carried me across the world and back would have to go lest I should be tempted to take passengers, and to replace it I should have to find a single-seater aeroplane for my enjoyment. Finished for me were the days of cruising from country to country with my wife or friends, the cheerful comradeship of perils shared. Flying alone, when the clouds dropped down to touch the mountain range ahead of the long nose of the machine, there would be nobody to turn to with a grin and say, 'Stuffed clouds. What the hell'll we do now?' There would be nobody with me to enjoy the chasms of the sunlit cumulus, nobody to share the look out for a training plane upon the circuit as you came in to land, nobody to plot wrong courses on the map for me, nobody to share with me the joy of the first landfall after a flight over sea. All that was over; if I went on flying I should have to fly alone.

I didn't want to fly alone, of course. As you grow older you learn that everything comes to an end, and you accept that phlegmatically as just one of those things. In England no more private aeroplanes were being built except by one small firm to fill a diminishing market, because the controls on private flying were now so strict, to prevent collisions with the many air liners, as to make flying less attractive for a hobby. If now at the age of fifty-two my flying days were over, well, I had had a good innings, and flying days were ending for all amateurs. It was no tragedy and there were other things to do, where sudden stabs of pain would not preclude companionship. Yet as I sat there in my bed thinking of all these things the break was a great one, because aeroplanes have been my interest since I was a little boy and were my whole life's work between the two world wars.

I will not say that aeroplanes and flying form the earliest recollections of my childhood, but they come very close. I was born in 1899 in Ealing, a suburb to the west of London, on the edge of the country in those days. So much was it in the country that a very early recollection is of seeing a balloon descend voluntarily about a mile to the south-west of Somerset Road, where I was born. I can remember very clearly seeing the big golden thing drift slowly in the sunset light of a calm summer evening, and watching the envelope grow slowly pear-shaped as the pilot pulled his valve, and the slow, vertical descent below the line of the garden wall. I don't think I can have been more than five or six years old when I saw that, too young to go off on my own to have a look at it, but

I understood what the manoeuvre meant and what was happening. I think the truth must be that aviation was in the air in those early days; probably the highly coloured comic that I spent my weekly penny on was full of the adventures of people in balloons.

My father was a civil servant in the General Post Office, in London. He wrote rather erudite travel books in his spare time; but for a troublesome deafness he would have risen very high in the public service. As it was, he didn't do so badly, for he became head of the Staff Branch about 1907 and we moved to a new, modern, larger house in Ealing and he started going to Royal levées and to Courts with my mother. That house again was on the edge of farming land and lay exactly on the line between Hendon and Brooklands, two of the earliest aerodromes in the London area.

I was eight years old when we went to live there, and my only brother, Fred, was about three years older. Thinking back over the five years that we spent in that house, I am surprised to recollect how much I knew about aeroplanes, bearing in mind my age. Perhaps the Children's Encyclopaedia had something to do with it, then a new publication and a very good one. Certainly before I was thirteen years old I built several model aeroplanes of wood, glue, and paper, with rubber motors, and I knew something about longitudinal stability and negative tail incidence. I remember a non-flying model aeroplane of sheet metal soldered together, which seems to show that I was interested in tools. Fred could not have built it because he was classical and literary, taking after my father, who held that a first-class classical education was the foundation of all knowledge. Fred was an apt Latin and Greek scholar, widely read for his age but not much good with his hands, while I had little or no use for the classics or literature. Students of form in the bestseller world must make what they can of that one.

They may make more of this. From the age of five or six I stammered very badly, and I still do on occasion; it has long ceased to worry me and so, as is the way with stammers, it has become less troublesome. From my experience of many treatments for this thing I don't think it is capable of cure except by increasing self-confidence, and probably that only comes with age. A stammer certainly makes things tough for a little boy at school, and an unsympathetic master can make lessons so intolerable that escape becomes the only possible course. It was for me, so I played truant.

It probably wasn't such a bad school for normal boys, that first preparatory school in Hammersmith. I don't think I was there for longer than a year before I was withdrawn in deep disgrace, at the age of about eleven. My form master was a good one, a young fair-haired New

Zealander called Cox; if he should be still alive and read these words I would like him to know that it was not because of him that I ran away. The other masters weren't so hot, and in my second or third term the place became unbearable.

No thought of telling my parents ever entered my head. I knew that everybody had to go to school and they would never agree to let me stay at home, and I was too inexperienced to realize that perhaps there might be better schools than this one, where all the masters were like Mr Cox. I was a day-boy and used to go to school by the old District Railway from Ealing, a journey of about half an hour. I had a season ticket and on the day of my revolt I travelled backwards and forwards between Hammersmith and Ealing all day with various intermediate stops when I got out and sat upon a foreign platform, watching the trains go by and savouring my great adventure. I went home at the usual time happier than I had been for many a day, and only had to lie a little to explain why I had no homework.

Appetite comes with eating, and a couple of days later I did it again. Before long I discovered that by paying another penny excess fare I could go on to South Kensington. There was the Science Museum, a wonderland of mechanical models in glass cases in amongst examples of the real thing. There was the actual original locomotive, Stephenson's Rocket, and dozens of scale model locomotives in glass cases, some of which would go by compressed air when you pressed a button. There were working models of steam hammers, and looms, and motorcars, and beam engines, and, above all, there were aeroplanes. Sir Hiram Maxim's machine dominated one hall, and Pucher's glider hung suspended beside Stringfellow's model. In the glass cases there were models of everything that had flown up to date, the Wright machine, Mr Henri Farman's aeroplane, the Santos-Dumont Demoiselle, the Antoinette, and best of all, the Blériot XI that had flown the English Channel.

For ten days I browsed in this wonderland with a mounting score of guilt and lies building up that I seemed powerless to do anything about. In the daytime I could forget my crimes in studying the run of the wires from the cloche to the wings that controlled the wing warping on the Blériot, or trying to puzzle out how the engine of the Antoinette managed to run without a carburettor. The evenings at home became the purgatory that school had been, and it was almost a relief when the blow fell and the headmaster wrote to ask what had become of me.

I can't remember very much about the row. My parents were good and kind but they were not mechanical, and it was difficult for them to understand that I was not telling a lot more lies when I told them I had spent most of my time in the Science Museum with the machines. They acted very wisely, because they did not send me back to Hammersmith. Instead, they sent me to live with friends at Oxford to go as a day-boy to the Dragon School, then known simply as Lynams' after the headmaster. So began an association with Oxford which has been, perhaps, one of the happiest and most formative influences of my life.

The masters at Lynams', I found, were all like Mr Cox or even better. True, if you were lazy or unreasonably stupid you got hauled over the desk there and then and spanked with the form master's hard hand till you blubbered, while the rest of the class looked on quaking in their shoes. That didn't seem to matter, because I cannot remember any master in that school who did not inspire in me devotion and affection and respect, though of course ribald stories and nicknames for them were the rule. The headmaster was like nobody that I had ever seen or read about before.

C C Lynam had started the school with his brother in the nineties as a co-educational preparatory day school for the children of university dons. As it grew in popularity boarders became a part of the set-up and the co-educational aspect of it faded; when I was there there were about a hundred and twenty boys, half of whom were boarders, and about ten little girls. The success of the school in scholarship was phenomenal – I remember four Winchester scholarships in one year – partly no doubt owing to the hereditary ability of many of the children. The headmaster was known to everybody as The Skipper because yacht cruising was his passion; he was a big, red-faced, laughing man with white hair that was seldom cut and curled about his ears. His brother would have liked to abandon the co-educational aspect of the school but The Skipper would have none of that, for the simple and elemental reason that he liked little girls. He said that they were a civilizing influence in a boys' school and I think there was some truth in that, because Lynams' was certainly a delightful school for the boys. I do not think that I can pay the school a higher tribute than to say that my stammer hardly mattered there.

The list of the boys who have attained distinction from that school would be endless, and of the little girls who shared my classes I remember best, perhaps, Naomi Haldane, who as Naomi Mitchison turned into a well-known novelist and writer upon social matters, and Norah Joliffe, a soft-spoken, shy, pretty little girl in my form who walked off with every kind of academic distinction and went straight on to become a don at Cambridge, dying before she was fifty. There can be little doubt that The Skipper had good material to work with in his pupils, but I think the main credit for the happiness of the school must go entirely to the headmaster himself.

As I have said, he was a very keen yachtsman. He had a succession of three or four sailing yachts that he called the Blue Dragon, in which he used to cruise around the north of Scotland, the Hebrides, the Orkneys and the Shetlands, during the Easter and the summer holidays. Towards the end of my time at the school he took a term off and sailed his boat across to Norway and up the coast to the North Cape. He was therefore a man accustomed to hardships and to risking his life in a mild way, unlike many schoolmasters. If I have learned one thing in my fifty-four years, it is that it is very good for the character to engage in sports which put your life in danger from time to time. It breeds a saneness in dealing with day-to-day trivialities which probably cannot be got in any other way, and a habit of quick decisions.

I lived with friends, and went as a day-boy to this pleasant school. Mr Sturt was a don at Queen's and my parents had met them on some holiday in Cornwall; they had a house immediately beside the school. The Sturts lived well enough but they were not particularly affluent and I imagine they were glad to have me as a paying guest to go to school with their son Oliver; for me the benefit was great. The Sturts had three children and lived a free and easy life; the summer was one long carnival of swimming or diving or boating, in punts or canoes upon the river Cherwell which runs past the school or in rowing boats or sailing dinghies upon the Upper River, the Thames above the city of Oxford. I mastered all these crafts before I was fourteen, and fished for the first time in my life, for the fat chub that nosed around the boathouse piles and could be seen sniffing at the worm if you kept very still, or for roach in the Thames.

With all these country pleasures I cannot remember any great mechanical interests at Lynams' except the motorbikes of the masters. Motor bicycles at that time, in 1911 and 1912, were novelties, somewhat experimental and entirely fascinating. Most of the masters had a motor bicycle and The Skipper had a little car built up of motor bicycle components, then known as a cyclecar. All these vehicles were continually in trouble and I used to spend hours at the shed door that we were not allowed to enter, watching the masters as they mended punctures or fiddled uncertainly with an engine that refused to start. In Oxford itself there was a fascinating place in Longwall Street, a garage run by a young man called Morris who built light cars made out of bought components in a window of the garage, so that you could see the car actually being made. They said that he was making them at the rate of nearly one a week, fitted with White and Poppe engines. Later on he made them quicker than that.

Those were the amusements of the term time; in comparison my holidays in my suburban home were almost dull. Our summer holiday task at Lynams' was to keep a diary, and the high spot of my diary for the summer of 1911 was the first Air Race round Britain which passed directly over our house on the first lap between Brooklands and Hendon. The little boy who was myself, of course, knew all the aeroplanes by sight and drew them in his diary, the Blériot which won the race, the Morane-Borel, the Deperdussin, and the Valkyrie, names practically forgotten now. I remember particularly the Etrich monoplane, a graceful thing for those days with swept, birdlike wings, that first war over last of all late on a summer evening; it was powered by an immensely powerful motor of 120 horsepower, more than twice the power of most of the other machines, and alone of all the competitors it carried a passenger. Later on, in the early days of the first war, we were to become familiar with a development of this machine as the German *Taube*.

In the year 1912 a great change came into our lives, for my father accepted the job of Secretary to the Post Office in Ireland, which meant that he became King of the Post Office in that country. It was not promotion because the salary was the same as he had been getting in London, and in view of his increasing deafness it may be that he was being shunted into a dead end. He was glad to take the job, however, for a variety of reasons. My mother's health was causing him anxiety; I think he felt that the change to new and more social surroundings from the somewhat humdrum life of a London suburb would help her by creating new interests, and perhaps he felt pleasure himself in the idea of being in complete control of a considerable enterprise, though in a smaller sphere. I should have felt like that myself in his position; life in London has never attracted me very much. To live beside great people and among great affairs is stimulating for a time when you are young. But when you have met a fair selection of the great people, when you have had the great affairs, I think a man of only average ability finds more solid satisfaction in a smaller milieu. For most of us life is fuller and more satisfying when one is a big frog in a little puddle than when one is battling on as a little frog in a big puddle, and perhaps for this reason I have always preferred myself to live in the provinces rather than in London. Thinking back over the years, I rather think that the same motives may have taken my father to his job in Ireland.

It meant great changes for my brother and myself. My father's job in Ireland in those days carried a considerable social position which both he and my mother were well capable of maintaining; my father was a good classical scholar, the author of a number of books, and a very good host with a keen sense of humour. My mother was the daughter of a Major-General in the Indian Army and very well up in all the usages of

9

polite society in those far-off days; there was little that she did not know about precedence, visiting cards, calling, and 'at home' days. Their social position in Ireland required a very different house from the modern villa in a row that we had lived in up till then, and my father leased an old rambling country house at Blackrock ten miles south of Dublin, a house with about thirteen acres of grounds, a large walled garden, good stables, and a long range of glasshouses. In those days of cheap service he had no difficulty in staffing this house with three indoor servants, a gardener, and a gardener's boy without overspending his salary even though my brother and I were at the most expensive stage of education. And here my father and mother blossomed out into the country-house life that in those days was the reward that good and faithful servants of the King expected in their later years and on retirement. For two years until the first war they led a very happy life at South Hill near Blackrock. Though nobody knew it at the time, that sort of country-house life was near its end for the majority of Englishmen, and I am glad my parents had that happiness while it was still there to enjoy.

For Fred and myself, that house opened up new country pleasures we had hardly dreamed of. There was a pony to be ridden or driven in a trap, hay to be made and carted, greenhouses to be walked through in wonder. Fred had not got on very well at Rugby, which at that time was rather a tough school, I think; he had two abdominal operations while he was there and spent more time in the sanatorium than out of it. My father removed him when we went to Ireland and sent him to Trinity College at the early age of sixteen; he lived at home and went to Dublin every day. His room rapidly became filled with books. There was an exciting new poet called John Masefield writing about things that had never found a place in poetry before, so that the critics were saying scornfully that *Dauber* wasn't really a poem at all. There was a terrific man called Algernon Blackwood writing mystical stories with a supernatural tinge, and there were the Pre-Raphaelites to be discovered, with *The Wood Beyond the World* and *The Water of the Wondrous Isles*, and presently there was Swinburne. Life was not all literature for Fred, though, because he acquired a very pretty little .22 seven-chambered revolver with which we both learned to shoot the weathercock with remarkable accuracy. I remember that little gun with pleasure even now, and wish I had it still.

There were other excitements, too. In those two years before the first war our girl cousins from Cornwall came to stay with us more than once. Patty was about Fred's age and was his confidante, and it was from her that I derived what little knowledge I possess about Geraldine Fitzgerald. I only met Geraldine once; she was one of those ravishingly beautiful young Irish girls with dark hair and a perfect complexion, who wanted to go on the stage. There is a Geraldine Fitzgerald in Hollywood who played magnificently opposite Bette Davis in *Dark Victory* years ago, and since has played the lead in many famous movies; if she should be the same she will remember Fred Norway, who at the age of seventeen proposed to her on top of a Dublin tram and was rejected very kindly while she twisted her tram ticket nervously to pieces, and who died of wounds in France two years later. If not, perhaps she will forgive me.

> *Round the next corner and in the next street*
> *Adventure lies in wait for you.*
> *Oh, who can tell what you may meet*
> *Round the next corner and in the next street!*
> *Could life be anything but sweet*
> *When all is hazardous and new?*
> *Round the next corner and in the next Street*
> *Adventure lies in wait for you.*

That isn't mine; I wish it was. It was written by E F A Geach at Oxford a few years after the time of which I am writing, and to me it epitomizes those years before the first war, and my early youth. It may not be good poetry to the critics of such matters, but it has pleased me for nearly thirty-five years.

In the spring of 1913 I left Lynams' and went to Shrewsbury School, into Oldham's house. Shrewsbury at that time was a fine school on the upgrade under a vigorous and imaginative young headmaster, C A Alington, and Oldham's was the newest and one of the best houses in the school. I made many friends there who are close friends still, not least my old housemaster. On form the years that I spent there should have been a very happy time, and when I say that they were not I am saying nothing against Shrewsbury. I had been there little over a year when war broke out, in August 1914, and the remainder of my time at school was mostly spent in preparation for war till finally my own turn came, and I left school, and went to war myself.

In those circumstances I don't think any school could possibly have been a very happy place, resilient though youth may be. I was in uniform already when the war broke out because, like most boys, I belonged to the school Officers' Training Corps and the end of the summer term found me in the annual training camp at Rugeley. That was a tented camp shared with contingents from many other schools under their own masters as officers, where a few regular army officers put us through manoeuvres on a considerable scale based, of course,

11

entirely upon Boer War tactics. Britain mobilized when we had been there only a few days and the regular officers and cooks and orderlies marched off more or less directly to France, and we were sent home, still in our khaki uniforms, all terribly excited.

When I got back to my home in Ireland I found that Fred had already applied for a commission in the army. He failed his medical and had to have a minor operation before going up again; in the meantime my father had had time to think it over and decided that Fred had better go in for a commission in the regular army so that if the war went on for years he would have a profession when it was over. Fred was very much annoyed about this because he reckoned that if he messed around too long he'd miss the war, but my father was adamant and Fred passed into Sandhurst in October 1914. In those days the sausage machine worked quickly, and by April 1915 Fred was commissioned as a second lieutenant in the Duke of Cornwall's Light Infantry, Cornwall being our family county.

We had a motor bicycle between us by that time, a new Rudge Multi. My parents must have been very wise to launch out on this extravagance at a time when my father must have foreseen rising taxation, for the Rudge cost nearly £60, a lot of money in those days. Although completely unmechanical himself, my father saw good sense in Fred's contention that every officer ought to know something about motors, revolutionary though that doctrine seemed. My mother had another angle on it: she foresaw that in the holidays my life would be empty without Fred since we had been so much together, and she thought that if I had a motor bicycle while Fred was away at the war it would ease the loneliness. So in September 1914 when I was fifteen years old I took delivery of the Rudge from the depot in Stephen's Green, Fred being in hospital. I had never ridden a motor bicycle before though I had a very comprehensive theoretical knowledge, and I was too shy to admit my inexperience. The Rudge mechanic gave me a shove off in amongst the trams and for a moment I was out of control while my body accustomed itself to the unfamiliar weight of the machine and the great surge of power that small movements of the throttle produced, for the Rudge was no lightweight but a man-sized, powerful machine. Then I got the hang of it and rode round Stephen's Green a couple of times gingerly manipulating the infinitely variable gear, and finally rode it home in triumph. From time to time in life one gets a moment of sheer ecstasy; I had one of them that day.

Fred had the Rudge at Sandhurst through the winter, and I went back to school, where military training was now to take up much of our free time. In the spring he was commissioned and posted to the depot of the regiment at Falmouth, and in the Easter holidays my father and mother took me there to stay for a fortnight so that we could see something of Fred before he went to France.

I think war was still romantic in those days, early in 1915; certainly nobody yet had any conception of what casualties could do to a nation. Fred was very smart in his new uniform, his Sam Browne belt beautifully polished, his sword impressive, his revolver massive, new, and fragrant with clean gun oil. The only casualty that had touched me till that time was a distant cousin, Captain de Courcy Ireland, who was an officer in the regular army and in the Royal Flying Corps. Enemy action had not yet produced many casualties among flying people because we were still in the stage when if you saw a hostile aeroplane you manoeuvred to get close enough to fire your revolver at it, leaning from your cockpit in the most daring fashion to do so while you flew your own machine with one hand, in itself no small feat in those days. De Courcy was lost flying a Blériot from England to France on Christmas Eve; he took off from some field near Dover and was never seen again. Since then I have flown the Channel many times in my Proctor and I have never done so without a thought for my relation, staggering out across the black December sea in a single-seater powered by an engine of fifty dubious horsepower at the most, cruising at less than sixty miles an hour, incapable of getting higher than about three thousand feet, with no instruments except a rev counter, no radio, no compass, little fuel, battling on to get to France in order that the army might have eyes to see what the Germans were doing on the far side of the hill, and failing to make it.

Fred went to Flanders with a draft, and I rode the Rudge Multi home. It was the first big journey I had made alone in my life, and it took me four days to get from Falmouth to Holyhead. Nearly forty years later it is difficult to see why it should have taken me so long, for I did nothing else but travel. I can remember a vague impression that a hundred miles was an enormous distance and a good day's riding, and I think the fact of the matter must be that roads were generally bad in those days, and motor bicycles much slower than we now recollect. Probably the bad roads, small tyres, and poor springing made a journey very tiring; I can very well remember aching wrists. In adventure and fatigue the journey was probably comparable in these days to a drive from London to Rome or from Boston to Chicago, and that I accomplished it without mishap gave my self-confidence a boost which was rather needed, for I still stammered very badly.

In the middle of the summer term Fred was badly wounded, at a place called l'Epinette near Armentières. In the trench warfare of those days the curious operation of mining was common on both sides. Where the trenches were frequently within a hundred yards of each other you would collect a party of miners, coal miners in civil life, perhaps, and dig a tunnel underground till the end of it was beneath the enemy trench. The enemy was well aware of what was going on, because he could hear the men digging underground, but he was generally powerless to do anything about it. I doubt if such a thing could happen nowadays with the increased firepower of the infantry, but in that war it was a common tactic. The climax, of course, was that you filled the end of the tunnel with high explosive, fired it with a fuse at a suitable moment, and blew up the enemy trench; in the confusion you then assaulted with infantry and gained a few yards. In these days of mobile warfare it seems a great deal of effort for very little advantage, but that is the way things were in 1915.

Fred's bit of trench was mined by the Germans and everyone knew it. The only things that could be done about it were retreat or counter-attack, and the local situation permitted neither. Those last days after the noise of tunnelling had stopped, waiting for the balloon to go up, must have been very trying for Fred; he wrote home a couple of jocular letters about it to my parents. It went up at dawn on June 13th and twenty-four of Fred's platoon were killed or wounded by the explosion; at the same moment the Germans put down an artillery barrage. Fred was unhurt, but his sergeant and several men were buried by the debris. No doubt, having survived the explosion, he had the strengthening feeling that I know so well – 'This can't happen to me' – for he led a party of men out from the remains of the trench to dig out his sergeant. There the shell got him.

In these days of sulfa drugs, blood plasma, and penicillin nobody would die of the wounds Fred got, extensive though they were. He was evacuated down to the base hospital at Wimereux and for ten days or so he made good progress. Then gangrene set in and became uncontrollable, in itself an indication of the march of medical science, because the medical attention that he got was very good. My father and mother crossed to France to be with him, as was common in those days of gentler war, and he died about three weeks after he was wounded with my mother by his side. If Fred had lived we might have had some real books one day, not the sort of stuff that I turn out, for he had more literature in his little finger than I have in my whole body. He was only nineteen when he died, and after nearly forty years it still seems strange to me that I should be older than Fred.

For the remainder of my time at Shrewsbury I don't think I had the slightest interest in a career or any adult life; I was born to one end, which was to go into the army and do the best I could before being killed.

The time at school was a time for contemplation of the realities that were coming and for spiritual preparation for death, and in this atmosphere the masculine, restrained services in the school chapel under Alington played an enormous part. The list of the school casualties grew every day. Older boys that we knew intimately, one who had perhaps been monitor in one's own bedroom, left, appeared once or twice resplendent in new uniforms, and were dead. We remembered them as we had known them less than a year before as we knelt praying for their souls in chapel, knowing as we did so that in a year or so the little boys in our own house would be kneeling for us. Most moving of these casualties, perhaps, were those in the Royal Flying Corps, whose joy in their vocation was so great, whose lives so short. With the love of aircraft that I was developing I envied them so greatly, though it was well known at the time that the average life of a pilot on the Western Front was three weeks. What I did not know until the war was over was that they were being sent to France as fully trained fighter pilots flying Sopwith Pups and Camels with as little as twenty hours' total solo flying experience. And in that war pilots went on till they were killed; there was no relief after a fixed number of missions.

I was writing poetry in the last year that I spent at school, all of it very bad.

In the autumn of 1915 my father took advantage of a break clause in the lease to give up South Hill, the house at Blackrock. I think he was concerned at the rising cost of everything due to the war and the mounting income tax, which was to rise to the unprecedented figure of six shillings in the pound. I think, too, he felt that the house held so many memories of Fred for my mother and myself that it would be better to get rid of it and start again. What he did seems curious now in these days of total war, because for the Christmas holidays he took my mother and myself on a trip to Rome and Naples.

Wars were localized in those days, when the range of aircraft was small and bombing far behind the lines was not a serious menace. The Western Front was ablaze with war from Switzerland to the sea but this war was completely static; there was nothing to prevent the normal express trains full of tourists from running as usual fifty miles behind the lines, and no currency restrictions then impeded foreign travel. One might have thought that the turmoil of war would have prevented my father from leaving his work to take his annual allowance of six weeks' leave, but it didn't. He was a very conscientious man who would never have put his personal interests above the job. I can only conclude that war affected daily life in those days less than it does now; probably civil service staffs were larger, also, for the work they had to do.

Rome was full of officers in magnificent uniforms frequently with sky-blue, flowing cloaks; the Italians in those days believed in getting some fun out of a war. Naples and Capri followed. My parents prolonged their leisurely holiday so that I had to travel back to Shrewsbury alone from Naples, an interesting and stimulating experience for a sixteen-year-old boy who spoke virtually no Italian and only schoolroom French. I think this journey did me a lot of good; although I had to change trains unexpectedly two or three times I had no real difficulties; when I got back to school I found that very few boys had made a journey of that length through wartime Europe. I think my parents showed a good deal of insight and wisdom in pushing me off on it.

The Easter holidays of 1916, in Dublin, gave me experience of another sort. This is not the place to write a history of the Irish rebellion, though to understand my little part in it a few words may be necessary to outline that half-forgotten rising.

For some years Irish nationalism and dislike of British rule had been growing, though the province of Ulster was loyal to Britain. Home Rule for Ireland had been much discussed, but neither the Southern Irish nor the Ulstermen wanted to see the country divided. The Southern Irish were in the majority and wanted complete separation from Britain. The Ulstermen would not agree to any scheme for Home Rule that would place them in the minority, and they armed to prevent forcible incorporation into a United Ireland. The Southern Irish, later to be headed by the Sinn Fein party, armed a volunteer army to resist the Ulstermen and to unite their country in independence from Great Britain.

As the war went on the Germans established contact with the Sinn Fein volunteers by submarine and did everything within their power to stimulate a rising of Sinn Fein against British rule, with the object of making a rebellion in Ireland which would cause the diversion of British troops from the Western Front. In this they were successful, for after a series of preliminary incidents a full-scale armed rebellion broke out in Dublin on Easter Monday of 1916.

The principal street in Dublin is a wide thoroughfare known then as Sackville Street, and now as O'Connell Street. In the middle of this stands the General Post Office, a massive stone building which was, of course, my father's domain and in which he had a fine executive office on the first floor. At that time my father and mother were living at the Royal Hibernian Hotel in Dawson Street, and it was there that I joined them for my Easter holidays.

There had been a tenseness in the city for some days, with much movement of the green-uniformed volunteers in the streets, armed and marching in military formations, occasionally dispersed by the police. On account of the disturbed conditions my father went down to his office on Easter Monday morning, and at about eleven o'clock he was summoned to Dublin Castle, the headquarters of British administration, for a conference.

At noon the thing started, and an armed detachment of the Sinn Fein volunteers entered the Post Office, turned out the staff, and proceeded to barricade the windows to turn the stone building into a fort. At the same time they occupied most of the other strategic buildings in the city, especially those at the street corners and those commanding the length of a street. The British forces in Ireland at that time were small and soldiers in uniform were shot at whenever they showed themselves; for two days or so the rebels had things all their own way. My father was fortunate that he was not in the Post Office when it was occupied or he would certainly have been held as a hostage, and he might well have been killed in the sad atrocities and reprisals that ended the rebellion at the end of the week.

I was in Sackville Street ten minutes after the Post Office was taken, for I had walked down with my mother to bring my father home for lunch. The street was crowded with people, there was a cordon of volunteers around the Post Office, and trigger-happy young men in green uniforms in great excitement were firing off their revolvers from time to time at nothing in particular. I sent my mother home to the hotel and stayed with the crowd myself to try and get along the street to my father's club to see if he was there.

A troop of Lancers on horseback escorting four or five horse-drawn military wagons came into Sackville Street from the north end and came down towards the Post Office on the far side of the road. They seemed to be unaware of what was going on, but they halted before coming opposite the Post Office, perhaps while the officer in charge assessed the situation. Then, in tense silence, they came on down the far side of the wide street. The rebels in the Post Office held their fire till the soldiers were opposite them, and then opened up with a ragged volley. Four of the Lancers fell from their saddles, killed instantly, I think, and one or two horses went down. The crowd scattered in alarm, myself with them, but within two or three minutes we were back again. These were the first men that I had seen killed.

We got a telephone call that night from the Castle to say that my father was safe, and all next day the battle grew. The British forces in Ireland converged upon the city and occupied such strategic buildings as the rebels had left empty, and bursts of rifle and Lewis gunfire down the streets became general, scattering the crowds of interested onlookers from time to time, including me. In this sad but interesting fighting I was far more comfortable and at home than my parents. This was my cup of tea. I was mentally conditioned for war; it was what I had been bred and trained for for two years. I felt that I knew what to do about this.

Next day an ambulance service was organized by the Royal Irish Automobile Club and I joined it as a stretcher-bearer. I had a bowing acquaintance with elementary First Aid since I held a junior St John certificate, and for the rest of the rebellion I cruised around the streets in a motor ambulance picking up casualties and taking them to hospital. I don't think we were ever in any great danger though once or twice we turned a corner with our load of wounded and found ourselves in front of a street barricade and in the middle of a battle, and had to get out of it quick. Once I remember that we left our empty ambulance and sheltered in a doorway for a time, and the vehicles got hit by rifle fire once or twice, by ricochets rather than by direct aim.

In this party I was a callow youth acting as a labourer and a runner for more experienced people; I would not like it to be thought that I was playing a great part. At the conclusion of hostilities we were inspected and thanked by the Commander-in-Chief of the British Army in Ireland, General Sir John Maxwell, and months afterwards the St John Ambulance Society produced a very noble parchment talking about gallant conduct in tending the wounded at great personal risk, which still hangs in my study as a reminder of an adventure that befell the boy of seventeen who was myself.

War was new to England in those days, and you got a great deal for doing very little. For me, however, it was another push along the road to self-confidence, and when I got back to Shrewsbury a few days late for school I found to my own wonder that people were beginning to listen to what I said, or rather, stammered.

At that time, in 1916, no end to the war with Germany was in sight. My father decreed that if with my stammer I could get a commission in the regular army I should do so; I think he may have been influenced a little by the consideration that the training was now considerably longer than that deemed necessary for a temporary officer, for I was now his only child. As I was mechanically inclined he decided that I ought to go for a commission in the Royal Engineers or the Artillery, and to get in to Woolwich meant passing a fairly stiff competitive examination.

I sat for this once, and failed, but I had still time to take it again before the limiting age of eighteen and a half was reached. To make sure of it this time my parents removed me from Shrewsbury at Christmas 1916 and sent me to a cramming establishment in London for six months, a step which was made easier by the fact that my father had been transferred back to London. The appointment of an Englishman had been a sore point when my father had become Secretary to the Post Office in Ireland in the first instance; to assist in the pacification of the country he was moved back to London and an Irishman was appointed in his place. My parents took a large flat in Kensington and furnished a bed-sitting room in it as a study for me, going to great pains over that room. They bought a large roll-top desk for me, second hand, for five pounds; that desk has followed me around for most of my life and most of my books have been written at it.

I passed into Woolwich in the summer of 1918 near the bottom of the list, and somewhat to my own surprise I managed to get through the medical without stammering. I joined the Royal Military Academy soon afterwards, where my officers rapidly discovered that on occasion I still stammered quite a bit. I had elected for the Royal Flying Corps, however, which saved me from being chucked out at an early stage, and I trained as a Gunner for nine months to my own great content till Nemesis overtook me at Easter 1918 shortly before I passed out as a commissioned officer. At that date the Royal Flying Corps ceased to be a part of the army and became a separate entity, the Royal Air Force, so that no more Woolwich cadets were commissioned into the air arm. By that time I was stammering very badly from overwork and general war strain, and at my final medical examination before passing out I failed and was chucked out to become a civilian again.

My parents were still anxious for me to get a commission, and though I knew by that time that the right course for me was to go into the ranks I agreed to try another three months' treatment for the stammer in an attempt to get commissioned into the Royal Air Force. I was depressed and apathetic at that time, and it would have been much wiser if I had enlisted straight away instead of hanging around; for one reason or another I never got into the RAF. In August 1918 my parents accepted the inevitable and I enlisted in the infantry, and was posted to the First Reserve Battalion of the Suffolk Regiment at the Isle of Grain at the mouth of the Thames.

By that time the casualty lists had grown enormously; the bottom of the manpower barrel was being scraped in England and people were being sent into the army and to France who never should have gone at all. Phillip Bainbrigge was typical of these casualties, a brilliant young Sixth Form schoolmaster at Shrewsbury. He was a tall, delicate, weedy man with very thick glasses in his spectacles without which he was as blind as a bat. He had a great sense of humour and enormous academic ability; when the time came for him to go into the army I have no doubt that he went willingly and made a good officer in regard to morale and within the limits of his physical deficiencies. He left as a memorial a sonnet written in the trenches which I have never seen printed, but which seems to me one of the best war poems that I have ever heard.

> *If I should die, be not concerned to know*
> *The manner of my ending, if I fell*
> *Leading a forlorn charge against the foe,*
> *Strangled by gas, or shattered by shell.*
> *Nor seek to see me in this death-in-life*
> *Mid shirks and curses, oaths and blood and sweat,*
> *Cold in the darkness, on the edge of strife,*
> *Bored and afraid, irresolute, and wet.*
>
> *But if you think of me, remember one*
> *Who loved good dinners, curious parody,*
> *Swimming, and lying naked in the sun,*
> *Latin hexameters, and heraldry,*
> *Athenian subtleties of δης and τοις,*
> *Beethoven, Botticelli, beer, and boys.*

Soon after that was written, Phillip Bainbrigge was dead.

At that time it was quite unusual for a boy with an old school tie to go into the ranks as a private soldier; the social barriers were still great in England. It was, of course, very good for me indeed. I will not say that I enjoyed the first fortnight because I didn't; the adjustments to be made were too great. Life in the ranks was much cruder than it is today: the food was coarse, dirty, and badly cooked, and it was difficult to learn to sleep on a straw palliasse on a plank bed. The language of the men was no novelty to me, of course, and I could out-swear most of them, but their attitude to women was shocking to me in my immature state. I remember forming the resolution to do three things each day, believing that if I did these things I should come through the ranks all right and be the same person when I regained my own world: to wash, and clean my teeth, and evacuate. There could be worse good resolutions, I suppose.

I must have been in a hut with quite a decent lot of men, because they left me very much to myself. In a month I had settled down and was enjoying my life. I knew far more about soldiering than the other recruits and my time at Woolwich had hardened me physically, so that the recruit training was child's play to me. Most of the battalion were men who were unfit in various ways, and though if the war had gone on I should certainly have been drafted to France, the stammer was still bad and probably made the medical officer think twice about my value in the front line. For the last three months of the war, therefore, I mounted guard at the mouth of the Thames Estuary against Germans who could hardly have invaded us at that stage of the war, and in that time I recovered the morale that I had lost through my repeated failures to get a commission.

I know of no life so restful as the life of a private soldier. In those days it was assumed that he was quite incapable of any rational thought or responsibility; his corporal shepherded him about and told him where to go and what to do. He never had to think for himself about anything at all. If he didn't turn up on parade it was a valid defence to say he didn't know he had to, and the corporal got blamed for not looking after his men properly. In after years it was considered an eccentricity when T E Lawrence retired to the ranks of the Royal Air Force in time of peace to write *The Seven Pillars of Wisdom*, but it was no eccentricity to me. I know of no mode of life that permits such mental leisure, such time for reflection, except perhaps the monastery or prison. Looking back on it, I think that those months spent in the ranks were better for me ultimately than if I had spent the last months of the war mentally strained by the responsibilities of an officer who takes his job seriously.

I was a cheerful, competent young soldier in the Isle of Grain when to our wonder the war ended, on November 11th, 1918. I had not then acquired a taste for beer but practically everyone else in my hut had, and I had a busy time looking after my friends on that Armistice night. I remember leading one of them outside to micturate and vomit, and the words he used to celebrate the coming of Peace. He said, 'If my wife was to see me now, do you know what she'd say?'

'You're all right,' I told him. 'Anyhow, what *would* she say?'

There was a long pause. Then he pronounced portentously, 'She'd say, "You blackguard!" '

CHAPTER TWO

WITH THE ENDING of the war, considerable mental readjustments were necessary for all young men. For four years of my adolescence I had lived in a world that was growing steadily bleaker and grimmer, and in that four years I had grown to accept the fact that in a very short time I should probably be dead. I cannot remember any particular resentment at this prospect; indeed, in some ways it was even stimulating. It has puzzled many people to imagine how the Japanese produced their Kamikazes, or suicide pilots, in the last war. It has never been much of a puzzle to me, however; in 1918 anybody could have made a Kamikaze pilot out of me.

In the Isle of Grain after the Armistice, therefore, I had to readjust my ideas considerably, and readjust them to the fact that there was a strange stuff called fun to be got out of life. Whatever capricious Fate decides the course of one's life was careful in my case to see that the transition to fun didn't come too suddenly, because my introduction to the merry new world opening before me was by way of a series of funerals. At that time there was a terrible epidemic of influenza ravaging the country, and men and women were dying of it all over England. Deaths in the army became so numerous that my battalion was ordered to provide a permanent funeral party to tour round Kent with a gun carriage and a dozen specially drilled men to conduct military funerals. I was drafted into this party and became proficient in the grand, sweeping motion of reversing arms, and in the moving collapse that follows on the only order in the army that is not given in a tone of command – 'Rest on your arms reversed.' The Dead March still brings back memories to me of pleasant excursions through Kent by train or truck, freed from the pressure of military training and with a new, unknown, and glamorous world opening before me.

At the end of that war demobilization was in order of jobs and not on length of service, and in that unjust system students were the first to be demobilized. My father was anxious that I should go to Oxford and I was willing enough, only stipulating that I should take Engineering, since my mind was firmly upon aeroplanes. My father canvassed opinion amongst his friends on the prospects for Oxford or Cambridge engineers. Somebody who must have been particularly well informed told him that he had never known one of them to fail to succeed in life, but not as an engineer. I think that there may be some truth in that still.

Accordingly two or three weeks after the Armistice I got leave from my funeral party and travelled up to Oxford to be interviewed by the Master of Balliol, A L Smith. My military service totalled just over a year, which excused me from matriculation, 'Divers', or any examination whatsoever till my Finals at the close of my university career, and this talk with A L Smith was the sole criterion for getting me into Balliol and the University, through I suppose some kind of a report from school was added to it. I cannot remember in the least what we talked about, but at the end of half an hour I was accepted and told to come along as soon as I could get out of the army. I bet the Master of Balliol wishes that he could select his undergraduates in that way now! Competitive examinations covering the whole country, as today, may be the fairest way to judge between vast numbers of candidates, but the old system of personal selection at any rate gave the Master the sort of undergraduates he felt that he could teach.

In December 1918 the ranks of the army at home were hurriedly combed for clerks to man the demobilization centres; a student could obviously function as a clerk and the fact that when the centre opened the first man to be demobilized would be me carried no weight with the sergeant. Accordingly I was sent to Shorncliffe Camp near Folkestone for training in the simple clerical routines that were involved. Shorncliffe had been an RAF instructional camp, and there were still one or two aircraft there, derelict in a hangar. I spent hours sitting in the smelly, oily cockpit of a Sopwith Camel, studying the instruments and the controls and making sure that I knew how everything functioned. It was the first aircraft that I had ever had the opportunity to handle and examine intimately, and I made the most of it. I backed it up with a little book by Sayers on the theory of aeroplane construction and by a very comprehensive anonymous book called *Practical Flying*. All told, I did a lot of aviation study in my last days in the Army.

We had a mutiny at Shorncliffe, but nobody was shot for it. We were an undisciplined mob of men drawn from all units, with few officers, discontented with our lot and impatient to go home. One day when the

Orderly Officer came in during dinner and asked, in accordance with the regulations, if there were any complaints, somebody threw half a loaf of bread at him, and then we were all standing up and pelting him with bread; he ran like a rabbit. We then all formed up in a body and marched down to the Town Hall of Folkestone to find the Mayor and complain formally about the quality of the food. We didn't get much change out of the Mayor, but we found the Labour candidate in the forthcoming election, who came out and addressed us and said it was a damned shame, so we all went back to the camp feeling we had struck a blow for freedom. The army dealt with the incident by declaring that our course of instruction was over, and sending us off to our demobilization centres.

Aviation pursued me still, for I was sent to Dover, where the centre was a camp on a saddle of land behind the Castle. And there, railed round and let in to the turf, was the stone silhouette of a little monoplane, because this was where Blériot had landed when he had flown the English Channel only nine years previously. Beside that little stone paving the demobilization centre was set up; I worked there for two days and then walked through it to demobilize myself.

I do not propose to deal with the three and a half years that I spent at Oxford in any detail, because I was a very ordinary, humdrum undergraduate. I excelled at nothing, won one prize only, which I spent upon a set of drawing instruments and a copy of *The Earthly Paradise* by William Morris, rowed in the college second eight, and took third-class honours in Engineering at the end. I left Oxford with a deep affection for Balliol and with a wide circle of friends which still endures, and with the memory of three and a half happy, carefree, and entirely satisfactory years safe in the bag, so that they can never be taken away from me. At the end of them, however, I don't think that I was noticeably different. Perhaps, like others of my generation, I was already mature when I went there.

A number of things happened during my Oxford vacations, however, which were important to me. In recent years the character of university vacations seems to have changed, and it is usual now both in England and in the Commonwealth for an undergraduate to take paid work in the vacations to assist with his expenses. In my day this was most unusual. The concept then was that the vacations were a time for leisure and for private study and reflection upon information that had been gleaned from university dons during the term. Leisure, in that context, meant working at whatever interested one most, whether cruising around the Continent in an old car to study political conditions in post-war Europe, or walking about with a gun and a dog getting to know something about the family estates, or working unpaid in an aeroplane design office, as I did. Paid work was almost unheard of in my day, not, I think, because there was anything socially derogatory about it but because it was seldom possible to get paid for doing the things you wanted to do for a short time, and in those more affluent days most undergraduates had sufficient money to enable them to live modestly in the vacations while they worked upon the things that interested them most.

In that first Long Vacation of 1919 I did no work, but laid the foundations for a recreation that has served me well. My old friend and schoolmate, Oliver Sturt, had come up to Oxford after a short service in the Navy. He found an advertisement in the Personal column of *The Times* by an old Southampton solicitor, Mr Hepherd, who wanted two undergraduates to help him to sail his yacht; we put in for the job and got it.

The *Aeolia* was a heavy, straight, stem yawl of 28 tons Thames measurement, gaff rigged of course, and with a long bowsprit. Her gear was massive and complicated by modern standards, and she had no engine; relatively few yachts had an engine in those days. Hepherd kept her in the Hamble River off Luke's Yard; before the war he had had three paid hands, but now with increasing costs he had only one, a Brixham fisherman. Getting that cumbersome old boat to sea under sail down the narrow river was a nightmare, for there was barely room for her to gather way upon one tack when it was necessary to come about again. Running on the mud and kedging off was normal, and collisions with other boats moored in the river were so frequent that it was the usual practice for the owner to keep a supply of visiting cards handy near the cockpit. When you collided with another yacht and carried away his crosstrees or his forestay you would apologize politely for what was an everyday occurrence and hand your card to the owner or his paid hand requesting him to send you in the bill, and go bumping on your way to sea, while the paid hand on the other boat got busy to replace the broken crosstrees or the forestay. No bad feeling was engendered by these incidents, because they were normal to the sport of yachting in those days.

In the old *Aeolia* I learned a lot of seamanship that summer. We started on a cruise to Cornwall by going aboard at Southampton one afternoon; we sailed a little way down Southampton Water and anchored off Netley for the night. That was the night of the official Peace celebrations and it blew a gale. We dragged our anchor for two miles down Southampton Water in the middle of the night and never knew it, for the bottom is soft mud so that the dragging chain made no noise. We finished up foul of the Hamble Spit buoy with our anchor chain wound round the buoy chain and the big red rusty metal buoy surging up and down alongside us and savaging our topsides. Getting out of a mess like that in bad weather under sail alone is no joke, especially when you don't know which way round to go to unwind the chains; Oliver and I tossed for it, and he lost, and went overboard and dived down in among the seaweed under the buoy to feel for the lie of the chains. I have always admired him for that job, though I suppose I should have done it if it had come to me. In the middle of this mess a ship's lifeboat came drifting down towards us, derelict; we went out in the dinghy and secured it astern of us.

There was, of course, no question of nipping into port to hand over that lifeboat to the Customs and claim salvage; only vessels with engines can indulge in deviations of that sort. We towed that lifeboat with us for a week till we made port at Weymouth, fifty miles or so to the west. *Aeolia* was a fine seaworthy vessel of her type, and with a good turn of speed when she was clean, but she had lain in the Hamble River all the war and Hepherd had not been able to get her slipped for a scrub before we started, owing to paid-hand trouble and the slow demobilization of men from the Navy, so that we started on that cruise with five years' accumulation of wood, barnacles, and sponges on her bottom. That was a calm, hot summer; the climax was reached when it took us three days and four nights to cross the West Bay from Weymouth to Brixham, a distance of about fifty-five miles. We had to row ashore one blazing afternoon to buy bread at Seaton, a row of about six miles in to the beach from where the vessel was becalmed, Oliver and I rowing rather a heavy dinghy with the two girls of the party in the stern, laden with shopping baskets. A little breeze came up while we were on shore, and enabled the vessel to stand in towards the town to shorten our row back.

At Brixham, full of sailing smacks in those days, we laid the ship against the quay at high tide and let her dry out, and cleaned her bottom, and painted one side of her with antifouling composition before the tide stopped work; after that she sailed very well. We put her ashore again upon a beach in the Helford River and let her lie down on her side as the tide fell while we camped on shore, and painted the other side. There was a lot more hard work in yachting in those days than there is now, and that summer I learned a great deal about kedge anchors, warping, and manoeuvring a big boat under sail in narrow channels that has stood me in good stead ever since.

I have given some space to that first cruise westwards from the Solent because although I have made many since, you can only do a thing for the first time once. Since then I have sailed in a number of yachts and owned two cruising boats, and I have cruised the coast from Portsmouth to the Scillies a number of times, but that first cruise in the old *Aeolia* stays in my mind as the best remembered, and perhaps the happiest, of the lot. Hepherd must have been well over seventy years old, I think; he had spent all his holidays upon the sea throughout his life, which was then near its end, and much of what he knew he taught me that summer, and in the following summer when I sailed with him again in a smaller vessel, the *Rothion*, of 11 tons. He went then to spend the winter in Ceylon with a daughter married to a tea planter, and he planned to come home again in May for a summer on his boat, because he knew no other way of life that brought him such content. I would have cruised with him again that summer, but he died on the way home, in the Mediterranean. It was his birthday and he had celebrated it by winning a deck quoits competition, and perhaps with a good dinner. When his cabin steward called him next morning he asked to see the doctor, and ten minutes later he was dead. He was buried at sea in the Mediterranean, a good end for an old man who showed me great kindness, and who enjoyed his life and the sea right up to the last.

The other thing that happened to me in the Oxford vacations was that I commenced work with aircraft. Through the Professor of Engineering and a colleague of his I got a somewhat indirect introduction to Mr C C Walker. Mr Walker was one of the senior officials of The Aircraft Manufacturing Company at Hendon, known as Airco for short. Captain Geoffrey de Havilland was the chief designer of Airco and the company had built large numbers of de Havilland machines throughout the war, from the DH1 to the DH11. By modern standards the factory at Hendon would be small, but in those days it was enormous and far too large to be kept going on the peacetime demand for aircraft.

I wrote to Mr Walker offering him my services without payment in the university vacations, and to my concern he did not answer my letter. Taking my courage in both hands I went to Hendon and walked into this big works and asked to see him. I found him perfectly charming, and glad to have me as an unpaid, very junior assistant in the design office and on wind-tunnel research. And so I learned my first lesson in commercial life – when in doubt about an applicant, wait and see if he's got enough initiative to come after the job; if he does, engage him, and you won't go far wrong. In later years when I was sitting on the other side of the desk I pursued those tactics whenever I could and always engaged the man who took most trouble to get the job, and I was never disappointed.

Airco at that time was near its end as a company manufacturing aeroplanes and de Havilland and Walker were already making plans to start a new company of their own, to be known as the de Havilland Aircraft Company. In the meantime they were allowed to go on working in the empty design offices that had been so busy in the war, with a very small staff most of whom were working out their notice. They had the use of a wind tunnel which was seven feet square in its working section and capable of a wind velocity of about a hundred feet per second, a good equipment for its day, and here they were testing models for the new commercial aeroplanes they hoped to build.

I was fortunate in beginning my association with de Havillands at this time, before the new company was formed, when they had practically no staff at all and were glad of any unpaid help. It is interesting to think back to those beginnings of a great company. When I went back to them for the summer vacation I found that all the paid design staff at Airco had vanished except one apprentice called Mackenzie, but de Havilland and Walker were still working in the echoing, empty offices, and the wind tunnel was still going upon the aerodynamic models of the new designs, and one woodworker was still making the models. Throughout that summer Mackenzie and I worked the wind tunnel and carried on the tests, assisted now and then by Mr Walker when the job demanded three men, plotting the results on many graphs and estimating the performance of the aircraft, doing the hack work for two great designers, listening to their sane, practical experience as they pored over the results upon our drawing boards for hours on end. Some people are born lucky, and I count myself lucky that my aviation career opened in such circumstances as those.

There were still a few aircraft going through the shops, to be examined thoughtfully in the lunch hour. Mostly these were repair and overhaul jobs. The London–Paris service in those early days was run by Aircraft Transport and Travel Ltd. using mostly DH16s; the DH16 was a single-engined aircraft with a Napier Lion engine, based upon the DH9a of the war. It was a biplane with one pilot in an open cockpit just behind the engine and under the centre section of the upper plane, and behind him was a very cramped little cabin for four passengers. There was, of course, no wireless and no toilet or anything like that; the machine cruised at about a hundred miles an hour, so that if there was a beam wind or a headwind the trip to Paris would take over three hours. Engines were not so reliable in those days as they are now and there were no navigational aids at all; judged by modern standards there were many accidents, but the service grew.

It was exciting to be in aviation in those days, because development went at such a pace. Already the new model of passenger transport was in operation, the DH18. That was the first aeroplane that de Havilland designed solely as a transport, without using any of the units in production for military aircraft. It was a full-gap biplane, which means that the fuselage was so deep as to fill the space between the upper and the lower wings, so that the top wings sprouted from the top of the cabin and the bottom wings from the bottom; in those days this was a novelty in a large aeroplane. To us this was a very big machine: it had one Napier Lion engine of about 450 horsepower; it carried eight passengers and one pilot, and it had the very high stalling speed of about fifty-five miles an hour, which caused a great deal of pessimistic head-wagging among the pilots when it was first introduced. An interesting feature of the machine was that the pilot was seated in an open cockpit behind the cabin looking over the top wing, an arrangement which gave the pilot a fairly good view when flying but a very poor view of obstacles ahead of him upon the ground. The cynical pointed out that since the pilot's position was the safest in the aircraft, being nearest the tail, it ensured that the designer would get an intelligent account of the accident.

I did not go to de Havillands for the short Christmas vacation of 1920; my father's retirement from the Post Office was near and he took his six weeks' leave that winter at Bordighera on the Italian Riviera. I went out and joined my father and mother there in winter sunshine, the first of a number of visits I have made to that coast since then. Bordighera was a good centre for ageing people in those days, and probably still is for those who can solve the modern currency difficulties; it was quiet and cheap and Italian, a good place for sitting in the sun and sketching, a good centre for pleasant inland walks on hills covered in pine trees and wild thyme and dotted about with walled hill villages and terraced flower gardens. Places like that upon the Continent were full of old English people escaping from the grey chill of an English winter; it is one of the tragedies of modern England that this simple pleasure is denied for economic reasons till the aged are so ill as to be able to get currency upon a doctor's certificate.

When I went back to work at de Havillands in the Easter vacation of 1921 the new company had been formed, and the move to Stag Lane aerodrome near Edgware had taken place. Stag Lane had been a training aerodrome in the war, a very minor one run by a civilian flying school, and there were still funny little training single-seaters known as the Caudron Louse lying derelict in corners. The new company was in a tiny way of business, and they were still glad to have my unpaid work, for money was very tight. The buildings consisted of one wooden hangar of perhaps ten thousand square feet floor area which accommodated the woodworking machinery, the machinists and the fitters' shop, and the aeroplane erection, and three canvas-covered Bessoneau hangars in rather dilapidated condition which housed the aeroplanes. The head office was a little weatherboard building of three rooms, one of which was shared by Captain de Havilland and Mr Walker, one by Mr St Barbe the business manager and Mr Nixon the secretary, and one by the telephone girl and the typists. The drawing office was an old army hut which in the interval between the end of the war and its occupation by the new company had been a chocolate factory, unsuccessful. In this there were assembled ten or twelve draughtsmen of the old Airco staff, and Mr King who did all stress and performance calculations, and from whom I was to learn my job.

In these surroundings the new company began work, and many of the team in those days are still with the company in these days; I sometimes wish I was. It is no small achievement for a man to have assisted to build up a great enterprise like de Havillands from such small beginnings; a man who has done that can look back on his life and feel that it has been well spent. And in those days the beginnings were small indeed. To run the lathes and milling machines – or should those words be singular? – power was needed, and the cost of bringing electric power to the site was probably prohibitive to the infant company, though there was electric light. Perhaps the cost of an electric motor was the difficulty. At any rate, Mr Hearle and Mr Mitchell, his foreman engineer, got hold of an old German Benz aero-engine from some scrap heap; gas was available on the site, and so they set it up to run on coal gas to drive the machinery, using three of the six cylinders, and that old engine drove the shafting for the machine shop for two or three years.

It was all like that. Apart from aeroplane construction, the earliest venture of the new company was the de Havilland Air Taxi Service, which used a light bomber of the recent war, the DH9, converted to carry the pilot and two passengers. That was a biplane powered by a Siddeley Puma engine. At the conclusion of the war many brand new Puma engines were hit twice with a sledgehammer and sold for scrap metal, and the infant company acquired a considerable number of these engines for a pound or two and proceeded to cannibalize them and rebuild them into engines for the charter fleet.

Most of the test flying at that time was still done by Captain de Havilland himself, but presently the company engaged a second pilot. Hatchett had been a sergeant pilot in the war, and he was a skilled woodworker; when he was not flying he worked on the bench. He was a very steady and reliable pilot. I think the next pilot to join the organization was Alan Cobham, and I remember his arrival very well because he brought an aeroplane with him, by road. He had been joyriding somewhere, and had discovered a complete new DH9 on some aerodrome that had escaped the sledgehammer altogether; perhaps Cobham stood the man a beer. At any rate, he bought it for ninety pounds and towed it behind his car to Stag Lane aerodrome to commence an intricate negotiation with Mr Hearle with the intent that the company should get a cheap aeroplane and Cobham a job. The deal went through. In those early days Cobham was not rated as the best pilot that the company employed, but he had a fantastic capacity for hard work and organization; he could work eighteen hours a day month after month, and he was soon to prove it by a series of pioneering flights about the world that brought him a great reputation, and a knighthood. Hubert Broad emerged from the half dozen pilots of the charter service as the best test pilot and he remained the chief test pilot for a number of years. Charles Barnard was the most ribald. I had the characters of all these men in mind for Philip Stenning, a character in my first published novel, *Marazan*.

Another pilot of the charter service was Ortweiler, a very slight, dark-haired, childish-looking young man of Jewish extraction, who had been an undergraduate at Cambridge after the war. He had been in the RFC as a fighter pilot and had been shot down over Belgium. In captivity he became an enthusiastic escaper. He was incredibly youthful in appearance, and spoke German fairly well. On his first escape he bought a German schoolboy's cap; wearing this and telling a tearful story about having been sent home from school to go to his grandmother's funeral, he travelled as far as the Dutch frontier by train and was only recaptured on a frontier road. He finally escaped to Holland from an island in the Baltic, travelling by train disguised as a commercial traveller and crawling for three days through the marshes at the frontier. He flew with the taxi service for about a year, and was killed in a crash at the aerodrome of Cuatro Vientos, at Madrid. He was a pleasant young man, and we had a lot in common.

The de Havilland Company was in continuous growth throughout my association with it, but in those earliest days, in the summer of 1921, I doubt if it employed more than a hundred people, counting directors, pilots, design staff, and everybody. In so small an organization which at the same time covered practically every branch of aviation, I had a magnificent chance to get a knowledge of all sides of the business, and I think I took advantage of it. Mr King and I worked side by side, the senior performance calculator and the junior assistant, and as the new projects came to life upon our graphs and columns of figures de Havilland and Walker still spent long periods cogitating upon our drawing boards, to my immense benefit.

The policy of the firm at that time was to make its living by designing and selling civil aeroplanes rather than military ones. The greater freedom from Air Ministry interference suited the genius of the directors for one thing, but to a great extent this policy arose from de Havilland's strong antipathy to war and anything to do with it. In the two wars he put the whole of his genius to the design of military aircraft with outstanding success, but this quiet, highly-strung man detested war and everything associated with it. I well remember an incident at my board in that early drawing office at Stag Lane. I had been investigating the weights of aeroplanes of increased size to the same overall characteristics at Walker's command, to try to get an idea whether it would pay to build big. The discussion at my desk ranged beyond technicalities into policy, till Walker said thoughtfully, 'Of course, if a machine can carry a thousand pound bomb, it doesn't follow that a bigger one carrying a two thousand pound bomb will do twice the damage. It might pay to have two of the smaller ones.' De Havilland stood up, said, 'I wish you wouldn't talk like that,' and walked out of the office.

In this small, friendly company the office staff had plenty of opportunities for flying with the pilots, and the company encouraged this for general experience, provided that it cost the company no money. I flew first as a passenger with Hatchett in a DH9 on a routine test flight. I was still writing bad poetry:

> This wood, this metal to the touch
> Stays solid, even though so much
> Is changed, fantastic ...
>
> Only this liquid element
> That beats and clutches. One would float
> Placidly, like a bottle dropped
> From some swift-flying motor boat.
>
> Only the sun, the sky, the air
>   And mossy pincushions of trees
> Upon the hazy picture there.
>   Only the solid wings, and these.

After that I flew whenever I could get into the air, and I flew with most of the firm's pilots. De Havilland at that time had a DH6, a very slow, safe training biplane of the first war, that he kept for a short time for his personal use, and be took me up in that one day to show me what he meant when he talked at my desk about stability. There was something fresh to be learned every day, and in those days the master was still only a jump or two ahead of the pupils, so that the instruction was virile and stimulating.

Thinking back over those years, I think that Oxford was less important to me than my vacation work, which perhaps explains why I did no better than third-class honours in my Finals. It was difficult to pump up any enthusiasm for the theory of concrete dams or electrical machinery when I was so deeply concerned in aviation. I must have felt, instinctively I think, that in my vacation work I was in on something really big, something that would grow and be important to the world. All through my life I have been subject to these hunches, as I suppose many people are. I have felt inarticulately and for no special reason, 'This really is something', or 'This can't possibly be right. There must be something wrong with this one, some disaster coming.' Usually I have found that these instinctive feelings have been justified.

I went down from Oxford in the summer of 1922 and spent a month cruising in the Channel on a chartered six-tonner with two friends. De Havillands had offered me a job as a junior stress and performance calculator at a salary of five pounds a week, but when the autumn came the company was in difficulties and having to economize. They put me off till the New Year. My father retired on pension from the Post Office about that time and intended to spend most of the winter at Bordighera; I joined my parents there in the autumn and spent several months with them, exploring the countryside, learning a little Italian, and probably writing a little. I think I had given up writing poetry by that time, and I had not then started writing unpublishable novels. There is at least one unpublishable short story which dates from that autumn. I suppose most young authors go through the process of development that I went through. First I wrote poetry, probably because a poem is the shortest complete work that is possible, and being entirely emotional it requires little experience of life. Moreover, you don't have to have a typewriter to write a poem. What I didn't realize, of course, is that a piece of writing is like a camera: the smaller it is the more carefully it has to be made. In a novel a few awkward passages can get lost in the crowd, but in a short poem every word must play its part and be exactly right, and the temptation to use the wrong word for the sake of rhyme or rhythm is very great.

Probably the next stage is that the budding author acquires a typewriter. Those who are blessed with a flowing hand may be able to write a short story in longhand though it has to be typed in the end, for no editor will read a manuscript in these days. For myself, I have so cramped and stilted a handwriting that my hand is aching with fatigue after a hundred words, so I wrote nothing longer than that until I got a typewriter and learned to use it, when I found that I could go on as long as my brain would function. I had an old Blick to start with, which was a very elementary form of portable, not easy to use but better than handwriting. I think a good typewriter is as important to an author as brushes and palette to an artist, because when writing on a typewriter it is important to be able to forget the machine. It may not be quite a coincidence that my first publishable novel, *Marazan*, was the first that I wrote on a brand new typewriter bought out of my earnings as an engineer.

I started regular work with de Havillands in January 1923. The firm had already grown considerably, and they now had an order for eleven of a new type of transport for the London–Paris route. The DH34 was still a single-engined biplane powered by one Napier Lion engine, but the trend of development towards the modern aircraft was beginning to appear. Two pilots were seated side by side in an open cockpit behind the engine and in front of the top wing; behind them the full-gap fuselage accommodated a cabin for eight passengers and, I think, a toilet. This was a bigger aeroplane even than the DH18: I forget its fully loaded weight but it was probably about 8,000lbs. It stalled at the incredibly high speed of 61mph, so that its introduction caused something like a strike of the pilots of the operating companies, who held that an aeroplane with so high a landing speed could never be operated safely. Looking back thirty years, there may have been some reason on their side, for the machine had no brakes, wireless of the most elementary nature operating by morse code with a tapping key, no flaps, no blind-flying instruments; in consequence forced landings in fields along the route had to be borne in mind if bad weather should make it impossible to complete a flight. However, the pilots got to like it in the end and the machine served the airlines well for several years, till larger, multi-engined aircraft took its place.

That spring my parents returned from Italy and took a small country house fifty miles south-west of London, at Liss off the Portsmouth Road. In those days nobody knew much about the depreciation of money or realized that a reduced standard of living had come to stay, and my parents started off with two maids in the house and a gardener three days a week. Money worries pursued them though I was virtually off their hands; they kept the situation under control because my mother all her life had kept accounts religiously, so that they knew exactly where they were. Their retirement, however, was not the carefree time it should have been and after some years they gave up the attempt to live in England in the only manner that appealed to them, and took to wandering, spending their winters abroad and their summers in a variety of hotels at home.

The motor bicycle had given place to a two-seater car, a Morgan three-wheeler, while I was at Oxford. I got rooms in Stag Lane just outside the de Havilland aerodrome and settled down to work, going down every weekend by road to stay with my parents. In Petersfield I soon discovered No. 1 The Square, an old half-timbered house run as a second-hand bookshop, art gallery, and custom jewellery shop by a crowd of artists led by Harry Roberts, an East End doctor who had a large, rambling estate of woodland in the hills outside the town, near Steep. I made no other friends in the neighbourhood but they were enough.

In the spring of 1923 I learned to fly. The company by that time had started a flying school as another branch of its activities, and they were training reserve pilots for the Royal Air Force on Renault Avros, a somewhat unusual version of the well-known Avro 504 trainer which was probably dictated by the fact that rotary engines were going out of use and henceforward training had to be upon machines with stationary engines. My flying had to be conducted with the strictest economy, for my parents were selling capital to provide this opportunity for me and flying on the Renault Avro cost five pounds ten an hour, a sum which even in these days of lessened money values would be regarded as prohibitive. Mr Nixon was adamant in refusing to reduce this figure even for an employee, and I had seen sufficient of the economies forced on the company to feel no great resentment at this very economic charge. Indeed, even at the time when I was arguing for a reduction I felt a sneaking admiration for him in his uncompromising stand: the first objective of the company at that time was to stay in business. They had no elbow room for generosity, though individually they went to untold trouble over employees who were sick. It was a pleasant, friendly company, though tough in business, of necessity.

I see from my pilot's log book, kept in the same paper-covered RAF book of the first war for twenty-eight years, that I had nine hours' dual instruction before going solo, about an average time for those days. That first solo flight was an anxiety and a delight; already I had seen a good many minor crashes and some quite serious ones, and the jocular phrase that one was going out to flirt with death was not entirely jocular in 1923. Humour was grim on Stag Lane Aerodrome at times. There was a crash wagon with fire extinguishers on it ready at all times when flying was in progress, as is usual, and this crash wagon was provided with a steel rod about eighteen feet long with a large, sharpened hook at one end; this was for the purpose of hooking the body of the pilot out of the burning wreckage when the flames were too fierce to permit any gentler method of rescue. It was the custom at Stag Lane when any pupil was to do a first solo to get out this hook, to show him that his friends had it ready to assist him in any difficulty that might arise.

The private pilot's licence had not then been introduced, and a pilot was recognized as such when he had passed the tests for the Royal Aero Club certificate, which entailed an ascent to six thousand feet, flying several figure-of-eights at about a thousand feet, and a landing without damage. For some reason that I cannot understand I did not take this test till February 1924, perhaps because of shortage of money. My early flying was certainly very much restricted for this reason: ten minutes was a normal flight for me in 1924, in which time one could get in about two practice landings. After I qualified, however, I handled the controls of a number of large aircraft in the course of test flights for the company, because by 1924 I was flying fairly frequently as test observer when the regular observer was on leave or occupied in other ways.

So the pleasant, busy months passed. I worked on the calculations for a great variety of those early aircraft and flew in most of them as a test observer or just plain ballast. Perhaps the most interesting of all was the tiny DH53 single-seater designed for the Lympne light aeroplane competition of 1924. This was one of the earliest attempts to build an economical small aircraft for the private owner; it was a little monoplane with a Douglas motorcycle engine that delivered about twenty-five horsepower. It proved to be too small for the market, but it flew beautifully, especially when the rather more powerful 750 cc Blackburne engine was fitted. I still have the propeller that I designed for it, a little wooden thing only four feet from tip to tip.

While I was working at Stag Lane I was well placed for writing in the evenings, for my digs were only a few yards from the aerodrome, so that none of my spare time was wasted in travelling to work. I had my desk with me, and I had few distractions except weekends at home; I should say that I probably spent two or three evenings of each week in writing. I think I probably turned fairly quickly to writing novels. There are one or two short stories which were written in that period, but none of them were published and none of them went out to more than one editor. When they came back I was content to put them away and forget about them, realizing their immaturity.

I don't think there is a great deal in the theory that writing ability is dictated by heredity, but I think there is a great deal in environment. My father and my grandmother both wrote a number of books, so that the business was familiar to me before I started. I knew before putting my first finger to the typewriter that what I was about to write would probably be useless and unpublishable through inexperience, because everybody has to learn his trade and the trade of a writer can only be learned by writing. Apart from writing I was getting on well in a good job as an engineer; there was no economic compulsion on me to hawk my stuff around and try to sell it in order to live. In all my early work the correspondence shows that I was quite content to accept a refusal, put the thing on the shelf, and start on something else. At that time, of course, I had no literary agent.

I finished my first novel in 1923, sent it to three publishers, and put it on the shelf, where it will remain because it is a very poor book. I read it the other day after brushing off the dust of nearly thirty years, or rather skimmed it through: I don't think anyone would have the patience to read the whole thing. I doubt whether much, if any, of it was written twice: the evidence of the type is against that, and the timing. I wrote another one in 1924 which was equally bad, and again I was content to put it on the shelf and do something else.

In the autumn of 1924 I left de Havillands, with some regret. It was a delightful company to work for, but it was staffed by seniors who were all young men and all vastly more experienced than I was, so that no promotion could be rapid. In aviation at that time there were opportunities on every side for those who had the wit to take them, and Mr B N Wallis, who was then a designer of rigid airships working for Vickers Ltd., was gathering together a staff for the design of a very large airship to be known as the R100. I joined this staff in the capacity of Chief Calculator, which should not be misinterpreted. I knew nothing of airships at that time and the Airship Guarantee Company, a subsidiary of Vickers Ltd., employed three consultants who were to teach me the fundamentals of my job and carry out research into the methods. Professor Bairstow was our authority on aerodynamics, Professor Pippard on structures, and Mr J E Temple was the most practical and useful of them all because he had been Chief Calculator for Wallis on the design of a former ship, the R80, built by Vickers at the conclusion of the war. My job was to get together a staff of calculators to do the work on R100, translating the theories of the consultants into the forces and stresses in each member of the ship and so providing the draughtsmen with the sizes for each girder and each wire.

This was an important matter, for the previous experience of England in the construction of rigid airships had not been happy. Rigid airships had been built during the war upon the lines of the German airships that had been shot down. Vickers had had a hand in this programme with the construction of R80 and other ships, and R80 at any rate had been properly stressed according to the best aerodynamic data available at the time. Most of the other ships had been designed and built by a staff of government officials attached to the Air Ministry, but the methods of the German designers were not known, of course, and these ships had been built empirically and by copying the sizes of the girders in the German ships. The last of them was R38. On her third flight a structural weakness in the girders was revealed, but was made light of. On her fourth flight she was doing turning trials over the Humber in very perfect weather when she broke in two, the front part catching fire and falling in the river and the rear part coming down on land. Forty-four lives were lost in the accident. At the inquiry into the disaster it came out that the officials responsible had made no calculations whatsoever of the aerodynamic forces acting on the ship in flight; it was not therefore very surprising that she broke when doing turns at full helm and full speed.

On taking up my new job I spent many hours in reading old reports and records to find out what had been done in the field of airship calculations before, and when I came on the report of the R38 accident inquiry I sat stunned, unable to believe the words that I was reading. I had come from the hard commercial school of de Havillands where competence was the key to survival and a disaster might have meant the end of the company and unemployment for everyone concerned with it. It was inexpressibly shocking to me to find that before building the vast and costly structure of R38 the civil servants concerned had made no attempt to calculate the aerodynamic forces acting on the ship, and I remember going to one of my chiefs with the report in my hand to ask him if this could possibly be true. Not only did he confirm it but he pointed out that no one had been sacked over it, nor even suffered any censure. Indeed, he said, the same team of men had been entrusted with the construction of another airship, the R101, which was to be built by the Air Ministry in competition with our own ship, the R100.

The situation in the airship world at that time was curious. It was generally agreed in 1924 that the aeroplane would never be a very suitable vehicle for carrying passengers across the oceans, and that airships would operate all the long distance routes of the future. We were all quite wrong, of course, but at that time it seemed reasonable: no aeroplane had yet succeeded in crossing the Atlantic from east to west, whereas a German airship, the Graf Zeppelin, was already carrying commercial loads of passengers both ways to South America upon a regular schedule. In England Sir Dennis Burney was perhaps the leading airship enthusiast, acting with Vickers Ltd., and in 1923 this group put forward a proposal to the Government that they should build six commercial airships and set up a company to operate them on the Empire routes. This proposal was approved in principle, but before an agreement could be signed and sealed the Conservative Government went out and the first Labour Government came in, and the whole thing was thrown back into the melting pot.

The Government of Mr Ramsay MacDonald appointed a Cabinet Committee to investigate the whole matter and to decide a course of action. There was, of course, a strong inclination towards State enterprise and a disinclination to put the whole airship programme in the hands of private capital; moreover there was a nucleus of civil servants in the Air Ministry who had been associated with the R38, who considered that they alone knew how to build airships. The controversy of capitalism versus State enterprise has been argued, tested, and fought out in many ways in many countries, but surely the airship venture in England stands as the most curious determination of this matter. The Cabinet Committee heard all the evidence, and had difficulty in making up their minds. Finally, in effect, they said, 'The Air Ministry at Cardington shall build an airship of a certain size, load-carrying capacity, and speed, and Vickers Ltd. shall build another one to the same contract specification. By this ingenious device we shall find out which is the better principle, capitalism or State enterprise.' I joined the capitalist team.

However satisfactory the competitive experiment may have been to that Cabinet Committee, it cannot be said that it brought peace to the competing staffs. Each had his own peculiar viewpoint, and the two were quite irreconcilable. The Air Ministry staff at Cardington considered that they were engaged upon a great experiment of national importance, too great to be entrusted to commercial interests. For the sake of appearances it had been necessary to give commercial interests some small share in the experiment, but it was impossible to suppose that any private company could compete with Cardington in this matter, backed as it was by all the finance and research resources of the Government.

The staff of the private company took a different view. In 1916 the principle had been laid down for aeroplanes that all construction should be left in the hands of private enterprise, a decision which had been imposed by bitter experience. In the realm of airships this principle had never been observed, and the bitter experience was not yet at an end. The disaster to the government-designed R38 was still fresh in the memory. These were the people, said the private staff bitterly, these very same men all but one who had killed himself in R38, who were to be entrusted with the construction of another airship when by rights they ought to be in gaol for manslaughter.

Most of those men are now dead, killed in the accident to the airship they designed in competition with us, the R101, and it may be that these acerbities ought not to be revived twenty-five years later. If I revive them for a moment now it is because there are still lessons to be learned from this peculiar experiment of Government and private enterprise working in direct competition on constructions to the same specification, and because the bitterness, almost amounting to direct hostility, between the competing staffs had its effect on history; if there had been more friendly cooperation between the design staffs the disaster to R101 might not have happened.

In the five years that were to elapse before either airship flew neither designer visited the other's works, nor did they meet or correspond upon the common problems that each had to solve. Each trod a parallel road alone, harassed and overworked. Towards the very end of the construction I made contact with my opposite number, Dr Roxbee Cox, and went on a visit to Cardington to see their ship, but his chiefs prevented him from accepting my invitation to visit us at Howden. If the Cabinet Committee wanted competition they had got it with a vengeance, but I would not say that it was healthy.

So the thing started, and each staff began work on the preliminary researches that precede design in a big job like that. It was no fault of the Cardington party that they had the Air Ministry press department always nagging at their elbow for a story to put out in order that the expenditure of public money might be justified, but the effect was a stream of optimistic forecasts in the newspapers from the men who were building the R101 which in the end were to build a ring fence around them from which there was no escape. It was our good fortune, on the Vickers staff, that we had no press department and therefore few published statements to prevent us from changing our plans quickly when we found it necessary to do so, and in that design we were venturing so far into the unknown that we perforce made many changes of plan. In the end, and largely through the press department, I think, the Cardington designers found themselves hemmed in behind a palisade of their own published statements which could not be broken through without some personal and public discredit, till one course only was left open to them, a course they never would have taken had they been free men, a course which was to lead to tragedy and death.

CHAPTER THREE

WORK ON THE design of R100 began in a somewhat humdrum manner. Aviation work up till then had meant for me life on an aerodrome amongst experimental aeroplanes, with pilots to talk to every day, and flying for myself whenever I could afford it. The airship job began with office work in Vickers House in Westminster, followed by more than a year in a derelict office in the depressing industrial suburb of Crayford in Kent. The work was stimulating and even fascinating in its novelty, but the contact with aviation in those first eighteen months was purely theoretical.

There was a great deal to be done before we dared to begin on the working drawings for the airship, and we had little past experience to guide us. Wallis was a veteran designer of the Vickers airships of the war years, but few of the rest of us had ever seen an airship, much less flown in one. From the start it was evident that it would be necessary to depart entirely from the Zeppelin design since this ship was to be more than twice the size of any airship that had flown before, and to attempt to build an airship from first principles alone, guided only by sound theory and calculation, and by the use of the most up-to-date aeroplane practice where that was applicable.

There were an infinite variety of problems to be solved. It seemed necessary to design a special airship engine that would run on kerosene and hydrogen drawn from the gasbags, to maintain the ship in equilibrium; all this had to be thought out and put in hand, and the experimental engine built. Little existed in the way of theory on the air forces acting on an airship or the distribution of the forces in the structure; a great mass of new theory had to be evolved from first principles, tried out, and proved true. The ship was to be built at Howden in Yorkshire, on flat land adjacent to the Humber and roughly equidistant between York and Hull. Howden aerodrome and airship shed, derelict since 1921, had to be reconditioned and made ready for the installation of machinery. Attempts were made to produce improved varieties of gasbag material and improved designs of mooring mast. A new system of gasbag retaining mesh wiring had to be developed from pure theory and tried out on water bag models. New designs of girder had to be evolved, and new machines produced to manufacture the helically wound four-inch duralumin tubes of which the girders were to be built. Girder tests had to be carried out at Birmingham University. Eighteen months were occupied by these and many other matters; it was a time of urgent preparation, strenuous and unpeaceful.

During most of that period I lived in digs in Hatherley Road, Sidcup, a suburb of London not far from the office at Crayford in Kent where I was getting my staff of calculators together. I built a five-valve wireless set for my parents in those months, and I started on a third novel, entitled *Marazan*, which was to be my first book to be published, by Cassell. I had evidently learned from my previous efforts, because I wrote *Marazan* twice through from start to finish and large portions of the book were written a third time; I was evidently resolved to spare no effort. It probably took me about eighteen months of my spare time to write, working on it in the evenings as a relaxation from my airship work.

I must have had a good deal of energy in those days, because on summer mornings I used to get up at about half past five, drive six or seven miles to Chislehurst where there was a livery stables, ride for an hour on Chislehurst Common, and get back in time to bathe, breakfast, and catch my train to Crayford. I think I felt that my surroundings at that time were so drab that it was necessary to regain contact with the country and do something different from all the other daily-breaders; I think the airship calculations benefited from these early-morning rides, and perhaps they benefited from the novel, too. I have always liked to do two jobs at the same time: one helps you to rest from the other and the fact that in the evenings my mind was fully occupied upon the novel gave me a clearer view of the airship problems next morning, I think, than some of my colleagues could achieve.

By the spring of 1926 most of the preliminary work was over and we were ready to commence the design of the actual airship, and at that time we all moved up to Howden. The little town stands in dead flat country unrelieved by hills, and clings desperately to its ancient status of a town among the villages of the district. Modern times have not dealt kindly with the place. It was a centre of learning in pre-Reformation days and a fine avenue of trees still leads beside the ancient fish ponds to the site of the college, but the roof of the great church fell in about the time of the Armada, and ruins surround the portion still in use. In the last century Howden was an export centre for the Yorkshire horse trade, shipping horses to the Continent. There are large houses in the town, the homes of prosperous dealers in the past, now fallen into decay. The presence of the airship station during the first war did something to restore prosperity for that brief time, and it may be that we, too, did something for the town while we were there. I hope we did.

The air station was some three miles from the town, set in the middle of flat farming land. About a thousand acres had been cleared of hedges but not levelled; in the centre of this desolate heath stood one enormous shed surrounded by the ruins of what had been other sheds. This great building was built of corrugated iron on a steel framework; it consisted of two bays internally like two great cathedrals side by side though bigger than any cathedral ever was. Each bay was capable of housing an airship seven hundred and fifty feet long and a hundred and forty feet in diameter; a row of brick annexes which were to be offices and workshops ran along one side of the shed. The floor area of the two bays was seven and a half acres. Already in those early days the building had suffered from neglect; towards the completion of the ship the rain streamed through the roof upon the work with every storm.

In 1925 we sent a little party up from London to put this derelict air station into some sort of order for manufacturing. They found the floor of the great shed littered at one end with the feathers and remains of many hens: a vixen had had her lair for years in the covered concrete trench beneath the floor that housed the hydrogen and water mains. The rough shooting was quite good. Rabbits infested the enormous piles of steel and concrete debris formed by the demolition of the other hangars; partridge, hares, and duck were common on the aerodrome immediately outside the shed, and we got many snipe. This state of affairs continued till the day we left, though the game moved out a few hundred yards from the shed as the work got under way.

Throughout 1925 and 1926 we laboured to make order of the chaos we had found, and to design the airship at the same time. By the end of the latter year there were twenty houses on the aerodrome occupied by the wives and families of the staff. The water supply and sewage plant had been put in order, and a considerable power plant installed to supply the electrical needs of the station. A hydrogen-generating plant had been set up beside the shed, and the site had been cleared of the enormous ruins that disfigured it. Offices and works had been set up and equipped; by the end of 1926 the place was running as a reasonably efficient manufacturing concern.

In the middle of all this absorbing work *Marazan* was published. Perhaps no novelist ever treated the production of his first book more lightly; I expected to make little money out of it, and the expectation was realized. By the time the book went out of print it had just made the advance royalty of £30. It stayed out of print for twenty-six years; when it was finally reissued in a cheap edition it made £432 in royalties in the first six months. I think it is a very good thing that we cannot see into the future. If I had know that a future as an author awaited me I suppose I should have given up engineering at an early stage, and my life would certainly have been the poorer for it.

One or two points about the publication of that early book may interest young authors. Mr Newman Flower of Cassell asked me to come and see him, which I did before we moved to Howden. At that interview he said he liked the book and wanted to publish it, but that there was one obstacle; he said that it concerned a matter with which they frequently had trouble when dealing with young authors. I asked what it was, whereupon he said, 'The House of Cassell does not print the word "bloody".' So we changed them all into 'ruddy'.

He then posted me an agreement for the publication of the book. By that time I had joined the Authors' Society, and had made a study of the terms of a desirable literary agreement. I wrote back to him objecting to practically every clause of the agreement, with the result that he replied that there were so many differences between us that he thought that no business would be possible, and sent me back the book.

The firm of literary agents, A P Watt & Son, had been agents for my father in the past, and for more famous men, including Rudyard Kipling, Conan Doyle, and Edgar Wallace. I had been at Balliol with a young member of the firm, R P Watt, and at this stage I took my troubles to him, remarking, I think, that I had made a fool of myself. He undertook to put the matter right and handle the book for me, with the result that Cassell published it upon the standard agreement used by A P Watt & Son. Since then I have never done any of my own literary business at all, but I have left it all to Watt. I could not have a better agent, or a more loyal friend.

When this book was published, I had to face up to the question of acknowledging the authorship. Writing fiction in the evenings was a relaxation to me at that time, an amusement to which I turned as other people would play patience. I did not take it very seriously, and I don't think it entered my head at the time that it would ever provide me with a serious income. During the daytime I was working in a fairly important position on a very important engineering job, for a very large and famous engineering company. It seemed to me that Vickers would probably take a poor view of an employee who wrote novels on the side: hard-bitten professional engineers might well consider such a man to be not a serious person. Of my two activities the airship work was by far the more important to me in the interest of the work, apart from the fact that it was my livelihood, and I was pretty sure that in my case writing in the evening was no detriment to the engineering.

For these reasons I made up my mind to do what many other authors in a similar case have done in the past, and to write under my Christian names. My full name is Nevil Shute Norway; Nevil Shute was quite a good, euphonious name for a novelist, and Mr Norway could go on untroubled by his other interest and build up a sound reputation as an engineer. So it started, and so it has gone on to this day.

So much for the book, which, as I say, was a matter of small moment to me at that time, for at Howden our difficulties were enormous. The contract for the construction of the ship had been taken at a fixed price, which was usual in those days though in later years the continual losses under fixed-price contracts forced a more equitable form of agreement in the industry for the construction of experimental aircraft. However, there it was; it had become apparent even in those early days that a loss would be incurred upon the building of the ship, and the future did not hold sufficient prospect of continuity to justify a greater capital expenditure than was necessary for this one contract. It has been said that an engineer is a man who can do for ten shillings what any fool can do for a pound; if that be so, we were certainly engineers. Excluding hand tools, there were not more than a dozen machines employed in the construction of R100. Economy was the paramount consideration in the shop equipment. A bitter little tale went round at Cardington, where they had everything they cared to ask for, to the effect that R100 was getting on rather more quickly now that one of us had bought a car and lent the tool kit to the workshops.

At Howden I lived with two of my staff of calculators in the village, in digs with a friendly garage proprietor; it was three miles from the airship shed and we used to walk that every morning and evening, sometimes with our dogs. We all had cars; the Morgan three-wheeler was soon to give place to an ancient Morris Cowley two-seater that served me well for some years. We tried to inject some nightlife into Howden by gathering up the local girls and starting a Badminton club in a disused village hall, but that was a bit of an uphill job because the Howden residents were not nightlife minded. We joined a club in York and used to go there on Saturdays for relaxation and shopping, and on occasion we used to go as far as Leeds to dance at the Palais. We did a good deal of rough shooting, but my own main relaxation quickly became the

Yorkshire Aeroplane Club, at that time in a hangar on Sherburn-in-Elmet aerodrome between York and Leeds.

This was one of the first light aeroplane clubs to be assisted by the Air Ministry; it was started off with the gift of two de Havilland Moths with Cirrus Mark 1 engines, and a subsidy of a thousand pounds a year. That made a flying club financially possible, and the Yorkshire Club quickly attracted a fair cross-section of young Yorkshire men and women, so that a Sunday spent at the Club was a merry Sunday. Later on, I was to meet my wife there for the first time. As a pilot of a sort and as an aeronautical engineer I soon found myself elected to the Committee and charged with the business of looking after the day-to-day running of the enterprise. We had a full-time pilot instructor in charge, and a ground engineer, and I got into the habit of going over to the aerodrome twice a week to help them to sort out their troubles, and to do as much flying myself as I could afford. Quite early on I distinguished myself by hitting a wire fence with the undercarriage of the Moth as I was coming in to land and depositing it upon the aerodrome in an inverted attitude; after that episode it was to be twenty-four years before I damaged an aeroplane again, at Brindisi when I was flying back from Australia.

The Yorkshire Aeroplane Club taught me a good deal about management. Our first pilot was a charming man, a good pilot and a good instructor. He was separated from his wife and lived in the village inn, and as he was a sociable, humorous, and weak character the village inn became the focus of a rowdy party almost every night. Next morning the pilot would be watery-eyed and disinclined to fly, with some reason, and members coming to the aerodrome for a lesson would find that they could not go up because the pilot had a hangover and wasn't feeling well. So in the end he had to go.

Our next pilot was a hard-headed bachelor, again quite a merry customer. He was efficient and good company, and though the rowdy parties continued there was never any difficulty with a hangover. Unfortunately he was involved with a married woman living apart from her husband, who established herself in the village while her divorce matured; so far as I remember, our pilot was the co-respondent. The Wives Trades Union of Yorkshire took the matter up, and members started to complain that their wives were becoming very unpleasant, and would not come to the Club because they would have to meet 'that woman'. In the end the pilot realized the position and got a better job in Canada, where I meet him from time to time and I am always glad to do so.

Our third pilot was the best of the lot. He was a stout, good-humoured man of forty-five, happily married, with three children at school, a little suburban house with a garden which he cherished, and a couple of dogs. He was an unadventurous man who never boasted of the time he flew the aeroplane through the hangar as all the others had done, but he had been a Martlesham test pilot in his day and probably knew more about aeroplanes than any of them; later, in the second war when he must have been nearly sixty years old, he became a test pilot again and flew over seven hundred Lancaster bombers on their first test flights. He was quite content with the instructional routine in our club; if asked he would perform aerobatics on the Moths and Bluebirds, but he never did them voluntarily. Like another of my pilot friends, he had no ambition to be the most famous pilot in the world. He just wanted to be the oldest.

These pilots taught me that the good test pilot is not the daring young bachelor of fiction, with half a dozen girl friends and a big sports car. It may be necessary to employ such men very occasionally for the sake of their physical fitness: if, for example, a machine has to be flown to forty thousand feet unpressurized. But such occasions are very rare indeed, for the obvious reason that production aeroplanes have to be capable of being flown by ordinary people. In the hands of such a man your aeroplane will never be safe. Such a pilot is fundamentally irresponsible because he has no stake in the country, nothing to lose. He will cheerfully risk his life to satisfy his vanity or to improve his skill; his life is a small matter, but the safety of your aeroplane is important. The good test pilot is the happily married man with a wife and young children dependent on him, helpless people that he loves and who will be grievously injured if he loses his life. Such a man is interested in preserving his own life, and your aeroplane; he will engage in no daring adventures outside his instructions, and he will land immediately if anything seems to be wrong with the machine to tell you all about it. In the hands of such a man your experimental aircraft is as safe as it is possible for it to be. The happily married man with a large family is the test pilot for me.

At Howden the ship grew slowly. Her girders were formed of three duralumin tubes rolled up helically from sheet metal and riveted with a helical seam; Wallis finally perfected this method of construction during the summer of 1926. The first girders were built during the autumn, and the first transverse frame, a polygonal ring of girders a hundred and ten feet in diameter, was lifted and hoisted into a vertical position hanging from the roof of the shed by about Christmas of that year. Another frame soon followed it and was joined to the first by the longitudinal girders; one section of the ship was then in place which would eventually house one of the gasbags. There were many delays. We were feeling our way with an entirely new form of construction; in a sense we were experimenting on a gigantic scale. From Hansard we learned that at Cardington an entire section of their ship had been erected for experimental purposes and scrapped, at a cost to the taxpayer of £40,000. The designer of the capitalistic ship could take no such refuge from responsibility.

The scale of the work produced its own peculiar difficulties, for most of us were unaccustomed to working on high places. When we first arrived at Howden I can very well remember venturing up the stairs to the passageways in the roof of the shed a hundred and seventy feet above the concrete floor, petrified with fear and clinging to the handrails with sweating hands at every step. I remember, sick with fright, watching the riggers clambering about on the first frame to be hoisted, carrying out their work a hundred feet from the floor with the girders swaying and waving at each movement that they made. Within a year I, too, was clambering with them on my lawful occasions, studying wires that fouled and joints that would not close, and saying what was to be done about it. By the time that the ship was half built we had lost all sense of height; it seems to be a matter of habit, because in my case the fear of heights has since returned, and is as strong as ever.

An incident in the early days at Howden confirms this. At that time there was some unemployment among ships' riggers at Hull, and a rigger turned up at Howden for a job. Jimmie Watson, our works manager, asked, 'Can you climb?' The man said he could climb anything.

We had a number of fire escapes at Howden to reach up from the ground to the structure of the ship, and one of these was being overhauled that day and stood fully extended in the shed. Jimmie said, 'Well, hop up to the top of that.' Now a big fire escape is a horrible thing to climb when the top is free and not resting against a wall; I hated them till the end of our time at Howden, and never climbed one if I could avoid it. It is about ninety feet long, and by the time you are halfway up the base carriage is behind you so that there is nothing but the concrete floor below, and you feel that every movement that you make will overturn the thing and send you crashing down to death. As you go up, the ladder sways with every movement, so that at the top each step upwards sets it swaying three or four feet in space. With your intellect you know that it is safe, but I know nothing more terrifying in the air or on the ground.

The rigger got up halfway, and stuck; Jimmie called to him to come down. The man came down very crestfallen; he said that he had been out of work some time and needed the job badly. We couldn't take him on unless he could climb, but the men were sorry for him, and Jimmie took him into the canteen and stood him a beer before sending him away. After his beer the rigger asked if he could have another shot at that bloody escape. So they sent him up again, and that time he got three-quarters of the way up before he stuck. So they had him down and gave him another beer, and so strengthened he got right up to the top, and got his job. Within a week of starting work he was perfectly all right and able to climb anything, without the beer.

It was not possible to heat the huge shed at all. Howden stands upon low ground; in winter there is standing water on the aerodrome and in the height of summer water is found two feet below the surface of the earth. In consequence the air is always humid; a more unsuitable locality for airship manufacture would be difficult to find. Very frequently the shed was filled with a wet mist so that every girder became coated in water; mould attacked the fabrics in the store, and the corrosion of duralumin became a serious matter. We became experts in corrosion. Halfway through the construction it became evident that the structure of the ship was being seriously attacked, and Wallis took the bold step of deciding to revarnish every girder of the ship by hand. It took thirty men three months to do and probably added the best part of a ton to the tare weight, but when the ship was finally demolished in 1931 the structure was in a very perfect state. On winter mornings it was not uncommon, after a heavy mist and frost, to find the girders sheathed in ice, stopping all work upon the ship that day on account of the danger in climbing.

The labour difficulty was always grave. We were three miles from the little town of Howden and twenty-five from civilization in the form of Hull. It was difficult to get skilled aircraft hands to work upon the ship however high the wages that were offered; accommodation for workmen of good class was almost non-existent. In Howden fourteen of our men slept in three rooms of a small pub.

We employed a large percentage of our labour in the form of local lads and girls straight off the farms as unskilled labour, training them to do simple riveting and mass-production work. The lads were what one would expect, straight from the plough, but the girls were an eye-opener. They were brutish and uncouth, filthy in appearance and in habits. Things may have changed since then – I hope they have. Perhaps the girls in very isolated rural districts such as that had less opportunity than their brothers for getting in to the market town and making contact with civilization; I can only record the fact that these girls straight off the farms were the lowest types that I have ever seen in England, and incredibly foul-mouthed. We very soon found that we had to employ a welfare worker to look after them because promiscuous intercourse was going on merrily in every dark corner, and we picked a middle-aged local woman thinking that she would know how to deal with problems that we had not contemplated when we started in to build an airship. But the experiment was not a success. I forget how we solved the problem; probably we never did, because as the job approached completion the need for unskilled female labour was reduced and we were able to get rid of the most jungly types.

Still, the ship grew. For three years the work in the shops came hard upon the heels of the design; the progress of the design regulated the speed of the work. Looking back upon that time, I think that an inferiority complex plagued us more than we quite realized. We knew in our hearts that the work that we were doing was good and that we were building a fine ship, but there is no denying that the incessant publicity of the competing staff had its effects upon our spirits. At times it seemed that every newspaper we picked up had a column describing the wonders of R101, ending up with a brief sentence that R100 was also being built at Howden. Our puny efforts at a counterblast could not compete with the Air Ministry press department; moreover we had little energy to waste on matters of that sort. We carried on with our designing and construction, wondering what the end of it all would be.

And there were times when we had much to wonder at. News of the progress of the Air Ministry ship was scanty and hard to come by; by virtue of their official position they knew all about our ship but we knew little about theirs. We gleaned our technical knowledge of R101 from patent specifications, from popular articles in the press, and from hearsay. Early in the design our calculations had disclosed a curious aerodynamic feature in the stability of these huge ships: not only could they both easily be steered by hand without the assistance of a servo motor, but no balance area was required upon the rudders although they were over a thousand square feet in area. At a comparatively late stage in the design we learned on sure authority that R101 not only had balanced rudders but had servo motors fitted at great weight and cost to assist the helmsman in the steering of the ship. Out flared the inferiority complex; we suspended work on the rudders and spent three days in checking through our calculations to find our mistake. At the end of that time we knew that our figures were correct, and we were left dumbly staring at each other. Either these ships could be steered by hand or they could not; it was impossible that we could both be right. There must be something in this that we did not understand.

The engine installation was another one. An airship requires engine power to go astern to check her way as she approaches the mooring mast and in R100 we had arranged for two of our six engines to drive their propellers through a reversing gearbox for this purpose. As R101 approached completion we were astonished to hear that her reversing propellers had proved a failure, and in consequence four of her five engines were arranged to drive ahead and the fifth one would only go astern. The fifth engine apparently was to be carried as a passenger on all her flights solely for the purpose of going astern for a minute or two at the start and finish of each flight, and with its power car it weighed over three tons. Again we were left staring at each other, speechless. It is the greatest mistake to underrate your competitor, and in spite of their past record it was incredible to us that our competitors should perpetrate such childish follies. There *must* be something in this that we did not understand.

As the years went on the same perplexities came to us very frequently on one point or another.

The conditions imposed on the two staffs by their respective organizations provided an interesting comparison. With our capitalistic organization we could go to no great expenditure upon experimental work; we were supposed to know our job and to be able to build an airship as a bridge might have been built. On the other hand we had freedom to change our minds and to make rapid alterations in policy and design if circumstances should require it. As an example, we changed our engine policy three times during the construction of the ship. At first it seemed expedient to design a special engine for R100 running on hydrogen and kerosene. After a year's work it became evident that this engine would not be fully developed before it was required for installation in the ship. The work was stopped, the design and work in progress was sold off in the most economical way, and we decided to fit diesel engines of the type that were being developed by the Air Ministry for R101. That phase lasted for six months; it then became clear that the diesel engines would be grossly overweight and unsuitable in other ways for use in our ship. At this stage we cut clean through our difficulties and decided to use aeroplane engines running upon petrol in the normal manner. Six Rolls-Royce Condor engines were selected, and the engine installation gave us no further trouble.

At Cardington the circumstances were entirely different. A large expenditure upon research and experiment was permitted to them; if they asserted that certain research was desirable before their design could proceed, that research was invariably put in hand. In this way they built an entire experimental section of the ship, and made innumerable experiments on such accessories as gas valves, servo motors, steam heating of the passenger quarters, evaporative cooling of the engines, etc. All these researches were admirable in themselves, but unnecessary for the production of a successful airship; we bought our gas valves for R100 from the Zeppelin company and if airships had gone on we would have made them under licence. On the other hand, it appeared that once they were committed to a definite policy with regard to R101 it was difficult for them to change their minds; if public money had been spent upon an article for the ship, into the ship it had to go. A few months before the first flight of the R101 her designer urged his superiors to fit petrol engines in the ship as we had done in R101, on account of the excessive weight of the diesel engines. The petition was refused by some high civil servant in the Air Ministry whose name is now forgotten, perhaps fortunately; the diesel engines had been developed for R100 and they had to be used. It is interesting to note these relative restrictions imposed on the two staffs: our work was hampered by the paucity of research dictated by the fixed price contract, and theirs by the inflexibility of the official system.

My own work in the calculating office led at times to a satisfaction almost amounting to a religious experience. The stress calculations for each transverse frame, for instance, required a laborious mathematical computation by a pair of calculators that lasted for two or three months before a satisfactory and true solution to the forces could be guaranteed. To explain this for the benefit of engineers, I should say that each transverse frame consisted of a girder in the form of a stiff, sixteen-sided polygon with the flats at top and bottom; this girder was twenty-seven inches deep and up to a hundred and thirty feet in diameter. Sixteen steel cables ran from the centre of the polygon, the axis of the ship, to the corner points, bracing the polygonal girder against deflections. All loads, whether of gas lift, weights carried on the frame, or shear wire reactions, were applied to the corner points of the polygon, and except in the case of the ship turning these loads were symmetrical port and starboard. One half of the transverse frame, therefore, divided by a vertical plane passing through the axis of the ship, consisted of an *encastré* arched rib with ends free to slide towards each other, and this arched rib was braced by eight radial wires, some of which would go slack through the deflection of the arched rib under the applied loads. Normally four or five wires would remain in tension, and for the first approximation the slack wires would be guessed. The forces and bending moments in the members could then be calculated by the solution of a lengthy simultaneous equation containing up to seven unknown quantities; this work usually occupied two calculators about a week, using a Fuller slide rule and working in pairs to check for arithmetical mistakes. In the solution it was usual to find a compression force in one or two of the radial wires; the whole process then had to be begun again using a different selection of wires.

When a likely-looking solution had at last been obtained, deflection diagrams were set out for the movements of the various corners of the polygon under the bending moments and loads found in the various portions of the arched rib, and these yielded the extension of the radial wires under load, which was compared with the calculated loads found in the wires. It was usual to find a discrepancy, perhaps due to an arithmetical mistake by a tired calculator ten days before, and the calculations had to be repeated till this check was satisfied. When the deflections and the calculated loads agreed, it was not uncommon to discover that one of the wires thought to be slack was, in fact, in tension as revealed by the deflection diagrams, which meant that the two calculators had to moisten the lips and start again at the very beginning.

The final check was to take vertical and horizontal components of the forces in every member of the frame to see that they equated to zero, that your pencil diagram was not sliding off the paper into the next room. When all forces were found to be in balance, and when all deflections proved to be in correspondence with the forces elongating the members, then we knew that we had reached the truth.

As I say, it produced a satisfaction almost amounting to a religious experience. After literally months of labour, having filled perhaps fifty foolscap sheets with closely pencilled figures, after many disappointments and heartaches, the truth stood revealed, real, and perfect, and unquestionable: the very truth. It did one good: one was the better for the experience. It struck me at the time that those who built the great arches of the English cathedrals in mediaeval times must have known something of our mathematics, and perhaps passed through the same experience, and I have wondered if Freemasonry has anything to do with this.

While all this was going on, I was writing my second published novel in the evenings, *So Disdained*. Again I seem to have taken considerable pains over it: it took me two years to write and all of it was written through twice over, some of it three times. I used to find that the story became fixed in the first writing; I do not think that I ever altered a scene or the essentials of a piece of dialogue in a subsequent writing. A rewriting increased the length by about ten per cent; awkward phrases and sentences were eliminated, and the general style of the writing was improved. Since the first writing probably took a year, one came to the chapter fresh in the re-writing a year older, with a year past in which one had forgotten much of the detail; this undoubtedly helped in putting the thing into a better style. This great amount of rewriting does not seem to be necessary to me now: with increasing experience I find that I can say pretty well what I want to say the first time. Perhaps thirty per cent of my later books have been rewritten; I rewrite the first chapter always as a matter of principle since it is seldom in tune with the rest of the book. I do not seem to get into my stride till the first chapter is over.

We built R100 hanging from the roof of the shed without the use of any trestles or staging; each transverse frame was built horizontally upon the floor, lifted up with a pyramid of wires to the corners, slung by the sides to the roof railways, and the centre was then lowered till the frame hung vertically. It was then slid along into position and the longitudinal girders were put in to attach it to the next frame. The ship remained hanging from the roof of the shed until she was inflated with gas; the slings were only removed a few days before she was ready for flight. This method of erection gave us a clear floor and other advantages, but it brought its own responsibilities. Howden shed was getting old and the roof had been neglected for years; it stood in an exposed position and in heavy gales it was clear that parts of the seven and a half acres of corrugated iron were not too secure. The roof never blew off but with every gale we thought that it was going to, and in bad weather we had to keep a standing watch of riggers ready for the first sign of trouble.

By the early summer of 1929 the ship was getting on towards completion, and the time had come to inflate her gasbags with hydrogen. Her volume was a little over five million cubic feet, giving her a gross lift of about a hundred and fifty-six tons; her tare weight was about a hundred and two tons, so that she had about fifty-four tons available for fuel and oil, ballast, crew, and passengers.

The gas plant was just outside the shed and here the hydrogen was made, not without some danger. The gas was conveyed in a gas main which ran beneath the ground to points immediately beneath the ship; to these points each gasbag in turn was connected for inflation. Each empty gasbag hung like a curtain from the axial girder that ran through the centre of the ship; as the gas was filled into it the top of the bag bellied out and rose slowly till it reached the upper netting, and spread down the sides till it filled the whole section of the ship. There were fourteen gasbags in R100.

To guide the gasbags accurately into place was no mean task. We had no foremen who were experienced in this sort of work, and the financial responsibility was very large indeed. The bags were made of light fabric lined with gold-beater's skin, easily torn by careless handling; the largest of them weighed half a ton and cost about six thousand pounds. If the bag were wrongly positioned at the first inflation it was necessary to let the gas out again till it could be shifted. The cost of the gas to fill the largest bag was about eight hundred pounds, so that mistakes cost a good deal of money.

Because of this responsibility the gasbags were inflated and hung in position by the design staff. I took one squad of riggers on to the girders of the ship – we had lost all fear of heights by then – and the chief draughtsman took another squad; the operation was directed by B N Wallis talking to us through a megaphone. This unconventional teamwork answered admirably and was much admired by a representative of the Zeppelin company who happened to be with us at the time, and to whom an office worker was an office worker, and a foreman a foreman. He had never seen anything like that in Germany. Neither had we in England, but it worked. All fourteen gasbags were positioned in the ship after a fortnight's sweat and toil with only one small tear.

Through the summer of 1929 the gasbags were inflated, the manufacture of the gas itself taking a considerable time. Finally came the day when the ship floated in the shed; the roof suspensions became slack and the ship swung from trays of balance weights upon the ground. The completion of the outer cover now that the gasbags were in place took some time, and there was an immense amount of final detail work to be carried out before the ship could fly. Perhaps the most important feature was the engine trials.

These trials were a very grave responsibility. R100 had three power cars slung outside the contour of the hull, each housing two Rolls-Royce Condor engines developing between them 1400 horsepower, and one six-cylinder motorcar engine driving a dynamo. Each power car had to pass a test of running for two hours ahead at cruising power and half an hour astern; these tests had to be carried out in the shed before the ship could fly. I have been connected with a great number of first flights of aeroplanes as well as all the flights that R100 made, but I have never seen a test more dangerous or terrifying than these power car trials. The clearance of the great wooden propellers from the concrete floor was no more than fifteen inches, and whatever precautions we took it was impossible to keep the hull of the ship from surging up and down in the fierce air currents generated by the thrust of the propellers in the shed. The noise of these engines running with open exhausts within the corrugated-iron shed made ear defenders necessary and it was impossible to communicate except by writing. Wallis or I stood by the car throughout each trial watching the pointers that we had arranged to indicate the ship's movement and the propeller clearance; we had a system of signalling to stop all engines if the surging of the ship grew dangerously large. All my life I shall remember the sight of those engine cars leaping and straining at their cable drag wires with terrific force, suspended from a hull that was completely full of hydrogen, each car with smiling men gesticulating with thumbs up out of the window in the deafening clamour, myself gesticulating back thumbs up to them and with a cheerfulness I could not feel. If a propeller had hit the floor or if a suspension cable had parted under that test the issue could only have been sheer disaster and the loss of many lives. We had made no mistakes, however, and nothing happened, and at last these engine trials came to an end; but it is my firm conviction, looking back upon those days, that if it is possible to compare dangers R100 was never in so great danger as she was three months before she flew. I do not think that anything the ship did in her flights was so dangerous to her as those engine trials. We were restricted in this matter by the Airworthiness authorities, which meant, in practice, by our competitors at Cardington; if we had had our way we should have done things differently.

That summer *So Disdained* was published in England and Watt succeeded in negotiating an American publication for it under a title that I disliked very much but had to accept, *The Mysterious Aviator*. This was the start of title troubles which have pursued me throughout my writing career; I seldom seem to see eye to eye with my publishers on what constitutes a good title for one of my books. I have now reached the stage when I can generally get my own way by putting on a display of bad temper, but young authors can't play it that way, and I had to take *The Mysterious Aviator* or give up publication in the United States. I took it, needless to say, and tried to forget about it on the principle of taking the cash and letting the credit go; I had, moreover, many more important things to think about that summer.

R101 flew before we did, making her first flight on October the 14th, 1929; from that point we started to learn details about her, mostly from the newspapers. It was quite true that she was carrying an engine as a passenger for astern running only; it was quite true that she had servo motors to work her rudders. Details of her weights gradually leaked out to us: she had a gross lift of only 148 tons and a tare weight of 113 tons, so that she had only 35 tons useful load as compared with our 54 tons. The Air Ministry press department, of course, was in full blast telling the world what a marvellous ship she was; in our offices at Howden a faint sense of impending disaster was stirring in us, I think, even in those early days. An airship is safe in proportion to its useful lift, in proportion to the weights that it can jettison in an emergency, and by that standard R101 was definitely dangerous. In our view, also, she was considerably underpowered.

By this time the crew of R100 were at Howden. The captain and first officer, Squadron Leader Booth and Captain Meager, proved to be most helpful in the later stages of the construction and soon became great friends; we had our troubles with R100 but they were obviously pleased right from the start that they had not been allocated to the other ship. The other members of the crew were as mixed a crowd as it would be possible to find. About one third of them were old, experienced airship hands, mostly of naval origin. Another section of them were premium apprentices from Rolls-Royce, young men from good public schools and with influential connexions. The remainder were fitters and riggers from our own workshops, recruited on account of their competence and intimate knowledge of the ship. There was no discipline among this airship crew in the normally accepted sense. Each man had been carefully picked, and taken as a whole they were a very good crew indeed. About twenty-five men constituted a full crew for the ship, excluding officers, wireless operators, and stewards, but we had over forty men as crew members, I think for training; when we flew to Canada we sent a spare crew over to meet us in Montreal.

In the air their work was above reproach; each man was capable of thinking for himself and taking intelligent action on his own initiative in an emergency. It was possible to go to any man in the ship and get a reasoned and coherent statement of what he had observed, and every man knew every part of the ship intimately. Without exception they were cool and fearless men, and I saw no sign of quarrelling or any trouble in their mess. In times when there was no flying they did not present so good a picture. They had no incentive to perform routine work, and they needed a lot of keeping up to the collar.

This was the chief defect of the airship flying organization. The officers and men were neither members of the Royal Air Force nor civilians; they were not subject to service discipline, nor were they subject to the discipline of the workshops. There was, in fact, no discipline at all other than that imposed by the good sense of the men themselves. As time went on the discipline upon the ground deteriorated badly.

In these last months my own position in the Airship Guarantee Company underwent a change. During the construction of the ship I had gravitated towards the top of the organization. My chief was B N Wallis, whose title was Chief Engineer. To my mind Wallis was the greatest engineer in England at that time and for twenty years afterwards. It was an education and a privilege to work under him, and I count myself lucky to have done so. Sir Dennis Burney, our Managing Director, was equally outstanding; he had the keenest engineering imagination of anyone that I have ever met, coupled with a great commercial sense. He had the ability to stand back and take a bird's-eye view of an entire industry and say – '*This* is the commercial problem. We

want to devise a means of doing *this*. My idea is that we could do *this*.'
And here he would put forward some entirely novel scheme such as
nobody had ever thought of before, grandiose perhaps, but based upon
the soundest engineering principles.

These two men were complementary and the success of R100 was due
to their combined abilities; my own part in it was small. It was
deplorable that they could not agree better, but temperamentally they
were poles apart. Perhaps two geniuses in one company would always
find it difficult to work together. In those years I conceived the greatest
affection and respect for both of them which endures to the present day,
and I mention their differences as shortly as possible and only because
they affected my own position to a great extent.

Perhaps Wallis was more interested in the straight problems of design
than in the flying of the airship, and by the beginning of 1929 the
straight design of R100 was over. Certainly in that year he began
working at Howden upon the geodetic wing design of aeroplanes which
later was to reach its full perfection in the design of the Wellington
bomber, and his absences at the Vickers aircraft works at Weybridge
became frequent. My own abilities were essentially practical; although I
was the mathematician in charge of the calculations I was the only man
in the party with any personal experience of flying an aeroplane, and as
the mathematics eased and the practical problems of finishing the ship
and getting her into the air became paramount I found that people
turned to me more and more, and that I could give quick decisions on
most subjects if Wallis was away, reporting to him or to Burney as
opportunity offered. By the autumn of 1929 the Works Manager was
coming to me so frequently that I was virtually in charge of the whole
outfit. This position was finally regularized by making me Deputy Chief
Engineer under Wallis, and when he finally left the company after the
first flight of the airship I carried on in technical charge and saw the ship
through her trials. 'In the country of the blind the one-eyed man is
King', and that was me. My promotion brought me a comfortable salary
for a bachelor with no very extravagant tastes; I moved to York, where I
lived in the St Leonards Club, motoring twenty miles to Howden every
day, and began to take part in a few modest social activities. Although
nominally I was in charge of the whole staff at Howden it was
understood that if we should get another airship to build Wallis would
come back, and I should have welcomed that; I had no illusions about
my abilities as a designer, while he was magnificent.

In November 1929 the ship was finished. It seemed almost incredible
to us who had worked on her for five years that there should really be
nothing more to do to her before she flew, but the day came when we

ballasted her up in the shed for her lift and trim trials, determining accurately for the first time the loads that she would carry. It was a simple procedure: we mobilized a hundred men to hold her by the power cars and the control car so that she neither floated up into the roof nor sank onto the floor. After each readjustment of the weights the men let go of her together on the blast of a whistle; we watched to see if she would rise or fall. After a few trials she hung motionless for a minute on end, poised in the air above the floor of the shed. Readings of barometric pressure and temperature completed the process; she was then ready to be handed over to the crew for flight.

CHAPTER FOUR

THE CONTRACT FLIGHT trials of R100 were carried out by her Air Ministry crew working under the directions of the constructors. This curious arrangement was due to the scarcity of trained personnel: it was impossible for the constructing company to provide a crew of officers and men capable of handling the ship on trials other than by employing the crew who were to man her when she had been handed over to the Cardington authorities on completion. It will be seen that this position was likely to raise difficulties. The crew of R100 during flight trials were acting on behalf of the constructing company, but they were employed by the men at Cardington who were both our judges and our competitors. Under such a system difficulties were inevitable, and it is a tribute to the captain of the ship that these difficulties at no time became really serious.

A delay of nearly a month elapsed between the completion of R100 and her first flight. A flat calm, such as occurs in anticyclones, is required for handling an airship safely in or out of her shed. There was only one mooring mast suitable for these two ships in the British Isles, at Cardington, and R101 was hanging on it waiting till weather conditions were suitable for her to be taken into her shed. For three weeks R101 occupied the mast before she could be put into her shed; in the December weather a further week elapsed before conditions became suitable to take R100 out of the very narrow shed at Howden.

R100 was as big as an Atlantic liner: she was 709 feet long and 130 feet in diameter, which is to say that she was fifty feet shorter than the old *Mauretania* but half again as wide in the beam. When loaded for flight she was, of course, as light as a feather and so capable of being swayed by the least puff of wind. So far as I can remember the Howden shed provided no more than two feet clearance each side of the ship as she was manhandled out of the door; she fitted the shed like a cork in a bottle so that we needed a dead calm to get her out. If the airship programme had continued it would have been necessary to devise a mechanical means of controlling the ship to take her in and out of the shed, and we spent many months in 1930 working on such matters, but at that time we were dependent upon manpower and calm weather.

The forecast for December the 16th was satisfactory, a dead calm being predicted for dawn. A party of officials came from Cardington on the previous evening to take part in the first flight, including Major Scott who was in charge of all flying operations of the two ships. I got to the shed at about 3am; the country roads were choked with motor coaches bringing the handling party of five hundred soldiers to the shed. It was a wonderful, moonlit night, clear and frosty, without a cloud or a breath of wind. We opened the doors of the great shed for the last time, slunk into dark corners to keep clear of the reporters, and stayed waiting for the dawn. In the shed the crew were running their engines slowly to warm up.

The first light of dawn came at last, and at 7.15 we got on board through the control car in the growing light, and the ship was finally ballasted up. Then the order was given to walk the ship aft. A centre line had been painted on the floor and extended out onto the aerodrome and plumb bobs were suspended from the bow and stern; keeping her straight in this way the handling party walked her out. It was all over very quickly. Inside the ship we could not see when she was clear of the shed, but a great cheer from the crowd told us when the bow had passed out onto the aerodrome.

There was very little to be done. Major Scott had her walked out to a safe distance from the shed, swung her round to point her away from it, and checked the ballasting again. I am told that her enormous silvery bulk was very beautiful in that misty blue December dawn. Scott completed his ballasting arrangements and climbed on board.

The take-off was simple. From the control car Booth emptied a half-ton bag of water ballast from the bow and another one from the stern and, leaning from one of the windows of the car, he shouted, 'Let her go.' Inside the ship we heard the cheers and saw the ground receding, and set about our job of finding out our mistakes.

She floated up slowly; at five hundred feet Booth rang the power car telegraphs for two of our six engines to go slow ahead. As the ship gathered way the elevator coxswain nosed her upwards to about a thousand feet and we made a few slow circles over Howden to try out the controls. This was my prime anxiety, of course; the figures had shown that she could easily be steered by hand with these enormous unbalanced rudders, and now was the moment of proof. But I had nothing to worry about; the first turn showed that she was behaving exactly in accordance with the calculations. She was steered by a wheel like a ship's wheel four feet in diameter. When on a straight course at cruising speed it was impossible to put on more than about three degrees of helm, but that reduction in the effective fin area made her stable on a circle of wide radius and she commenced to turn; as she took up the turn the airflow at the tail was altered and it became possible to put on more helm, so that it took half a minute or more to get her into the condition of turning with full helm upon her minimum turning circle. With this method of control it was impossible to strain the ship by putting on full helm while she was in straight flight because the coxswain was not strong enough, and it proved to be simple and satisfactory.

After a short time we left the vicinity of Howden and flew slowly to York; by the time we got there it was apparent that there was nothing wrong with the ship and we could confidently fly her down to Cardington near Bedford. We circled York Minster and the city, and then, with minds comparatively at ease, we set course for Cardington and went to breakfast.

Breakfast that morning was bacon and eggs cooked on board, the first of many pleasant meals upon that ship. We were all a little elated, and the matter of the parachutes did not appreciably damp our spirits. We had fifty parachutes slung up in various parts of the ship ready for instant use, but there were fifty-four of us on board. We made grim little jokes about the game of musical chairs; after the first few flights the parachutes were removed.

At the same time, throughout the flights of R100 the action to be taken in the event of disaster was always in the background of my mind, and in view of the eventual disaster to R101 it is interesting to recall a precaution that I took for my personal safety. In an airship, unlike an aeroplane, there is no great danger of death from violent impact with the ground. Although both ships were filled with hydrogen there was no great danger of fire in the air, for any gas escaping would go upwards and out of the top of the ship, remote from any likely source of ignition. The chief danger, I thought, was of fire after hitting the ground, when broken electrical cables could make sparks in the presence of large masses of escaping hydrogen or petrol; in that case the fire would spread instantly. This, in fact, is what happened to R101. It seemed to me that in such a case the only chance for survival would be to jump on to the inside of the outer cover and cut one's way out, and drop down to the ground, and one would have not more than five seconds to do it in. For this reason before the first flight of R100 I bought a very large clasp knife and sharpened it to a fine point and a razor edge, and I carried this knife unostentatiously in my pocket throughout the flights that the ship made.

We made a quick trip to Cardington by the standards of those days, cruising at about fifty-five miles an hour on four engines only. We made good about seventy miles an hour over the ground with the assistance of a following wind, and reached Cardington in two hours' flight from York. Here a surprise awaited us: we had assumed that there would be little difficulty in landing the ship onto the Air Ministry mooring mast. So many articles had appeared in the press about the wonders of this new method of handling airships that it came as a surprise to us to find that the experts on this matter were inexpert in the use of their rather complicated apparatus. On this first flight it took three hours to land R100 to the mast; three times we had to leave the aerodrome and fly a circuit and come in again, and make a fresh attempt to establish the connexion between the steel cable dropped from the nose of the ship and the cable from the masthead laid out upon the aerodrome. The mooring system was essentially sound and at the conclusion of the R100 flights sufficient experience had been gained in the handling of the ship and in the use of the mast equipment to enable a landing to be made to the mast in about forty minutes, but this result was not achieved without the experience of numerous mistakes. And here we touched the fringe of one of the chief dangers of the airship programme: too many experiments were being made at the same time.

We landed at about three in the afternoon. That evening we held a conference and decided to fly again next day, taking advantage of the calm, frosty weather. There were several minor defects to be made good upon the ship during the night. One engine had a leaky cylinder and another was suspected of having run a big end; air was eddying in violently at cruising speed through one of the big outer cover ventilators and blowing the gasbags about; this had to be sealed up. A dynamo engine could not be turned over with the starting handle. We held our gloomy inquest on it in the middle of the night, only to discover after two hours' work that the starting handle itself was seized solid in its bearings and the engine was in perfect order. These were the inevitable teething troubles of any very large aircraft, but they meant much work.

I got back to ship that night at about nine o'clock. It was a cloudless, moonlit night, and freezing hard. The ship lay at the mast a hundred feet above the ground, brilliant silver in the beams of the floodlights. There was a crew on board her in accordance with the routine procedure at the mast; I found them at supper in their mess, content and settling in to their new quarters. There was no heating in the ship when the dynamo engines were stopped, and it was very cold. In the control car I found Booth, dead tired, wearing a Sidcot suit and huddled in a small armchair beside the shore telephone, nursing the ship's black kitten as he kept his watch in the brilliance of the floodlights. I went on aft to the power cars, and worked till midnight with the engineers.

We flew again next day with the intention of doing speed trials. The speed of R100 at that time was a sore point at Cardington: with all politeness the officials there professed themselves unable to believe our ship to be at least ten miles an hour faster than their own. R100 was, in fact, the fastest airship that had ever flown at that time, or to this day, for all I know; her full speed was eighty-one miles an hour. We did not reach full speed upon that flight, however. Prowling through the ship in search of trouble somewhere over Kettering I heard a little flapping noise of fabric in the region of the lower rudder, and discovered that a sealing strip across the rudder hinge was coming unstuck. This was not serious, but we did not care to take the ship up to full speed till it had received attention in the shed; we cruised around for a few hours and landed to the mast again in the middle of the afternoon.

The landing on this occasion was a demonstration of the special qualities of the airship. A thin, frosty mist hung over everything; from seven or eight hundred feet it was just possible to distinguish the ground immediately below. In these days every modern aid would be required on such an afternoon to guide an aeroplane onto the runway; in those days flying would have been most hazardous. In the airship everything was peaceful and secure. We had radio-telephone communication with the mast, and coming up to the aerodrome we slowed to a mere crawl, running on one engine at about ten miles an hour with two other engines ticking over slow astern ready to check her way if anything loomed up ahead of us. In the control car there was time for a little conference between the officers over each movement of the controls, as, 'Putting her nose down a bit, isn't she?' 'Think so? We could afford to be fifty feet lower.' 'Starting to show on the fore and aft level, sir – about two degrees nose down.' 'All right. Coxswain, five degrees elevator up.' And so on. During all the flights that R100 made I do not think that it was ever necessary to make a quick decision in the way that the pilot of an aeroplane has to; there was always time to talk the matter over if it seemed desirable and decide what action should be taken next. It is impossible to describe what a sense of security this freedom from quick decisions gave to one who was accustomed to fly aeroplanes; rightly or wrongly I felt as safe through all the flights that R100 made as on a large ship.

We put the ship into the shed that evening, 'put her back in the box' as somebody irreverently described the operation. Here she stayed over Christmas while we sorted out her teething troubles, berthed in her shed beside R101. Some of us had seen R101 before she flew; we now had a good opportunity to examine her in her completed state. We found her an amazing piece of work. The finish and the workmanship struck us as extraordinarily good, far better than that of our own ship. The design seemed to us almost unbelievably complicated; she seemed to be a ship in which imagination had run riot regardless of the virtue of simplicity and utterly regardless of expense. The servo motors were there large as life and every bit as heavy. The gas valves were of a novel design and reported to be very sensitive; being located on the side of the bags a small degree of rolling would cause them to open and lose gas. Airships, however, don't roll very much. The feature of the design that perturbed me most of all was the method of taking the thrust of the engines in the power cars to the hull. The engine in each car drove a pusher propeller. A large thrust bearing was mounted in the boss of this propeller, from which a heavy steel cable ran straight aft to a point on the hull fifty feet back. It was fairly common practice in the airship world to take the thrust through the propeller in that way and in fact it gave no trouble, but it seemed to me most dangerous and quite unnecessary. A competent engineer should be able to do better than that.

It was then a few days before Christmas. I had been working at high pressure for some time and enjoying it; now the first part of the flight trials had been completed and we had nothing much to worry about. I arranged the programme of work that was to be done on the ship, rang up Burney to get leave, rang up someone to inquire a good place to go to in Switzerland, and was skiing at Murren before Christmas. I think in many ways that was the best holiday I have ever had in my life because I came to it with a sense of achievement, of a difficult job well done; moreover for the first time in my life I had plenty of money at my disposal. I don't think it lasted longer than a fortnight because I had to get back to my job, and wanted to, but that fortnight was a good one.

Back at Howden the big shed seemed very empty without the ship. Practically all the men in the shops had been laid off, of course, but Burney had fixed up a design contract for a future airship from the Air Ministry with which to keep the experienced design staff in being till the flight trials were completed and the future programme for airships could be decided by Parliament. By that time, in January 1930, the depression in the United States was in full swing and its impact was becoming felt in England. It was becoming clear that two competing airship design staffs would not be kept in being through the hard times that were in sight; if more airships were ordered either Cardington would build them or we would. The decision which staff would be chosen to carry on largely depended on the performance of the two airships; the designers of the less successful ship would very soon find themselves looking for another job. This was an important factor in the later flight trials of the two ships, and in the ultimate tragedy. Urged by the instinct for survival both parties forced the flight trials ahead quicker than they should have gone, intent on proving that their own ship was the better. It was my good fortune that we had the better ship.

The work on R100 was finished about January 10th, 1930; she was then ready for further flight trials and we stayed waiting for a calm to bring her out of the shed.

Not much notice can be given of a dead calm, and so it was not particularly discourteous that I received a telephone call from Cardington at four o'clock in the afternoon on January 17th to tell me that the ship would be brought out at dawn next day and would fly immediately. Cardington is about a hundred and fifty miles from Howden and that day was my birthday; I had arranged a small party of friends from the flying club at a hotel in Leeds. Remarking that there was time, Master Drake, to finish our game of bowls, I arranged with the calculator who was coming down with me for the flight that he should meet me in Leeds at eleven o'clock and we would drive down to Cardington through the night.

One does those things when one is young. I had reckoned without a freezing fog all down the Great North Road. I had a pretty little Singer coupé at that time, an advanced car for its day, but like others at that date it had no fog lights and no heating. Even parking lights reflected from the fog and made driving impossible, but with no lights at all we could see the sides of the road and could keep up about twenty miles an hour. Very soon the windscreen iced up, but it was designed to open, and we drove along like that. Ice formed on everything. It was nearly an inch thick on the inside of the roof above our heads; it coated our overcoats and formed in a great mass on the steering wheel between my hands: it was a tough drive. We got out every hour or so and stamped about to get the circulation back, and once or twice we found a coffee stall, in Stamford or in Grantham. By five o'clock in the morning we were within thirty miles of Cardington and we could still use no lights, and now we began to meet cyclists on the road, farm hands perhaps, going to milk the cows. We very nearly hit one a couple of times, and each time suffered a hair-raising skid upon the icy road as I braked heavily. I gave up then and parked by the roadside: better to miss the ship than to stand trial for manslaughter. An hour later the dawn came and we could see a little better, and got going again. We drove into the air station at eight o'clock and to my delight the ship was only just leaving the shed; the same fog had prevented the RAF handling party from getting to the aerodrome at the appointed time. We scrambled on board, and had breakfast as the ship rose up in to the air.

All that day we flew above the fog and clouds, in bright sunshine. We suspended a variety of airspeed indicators on cables below the ship and worked her up to her full speed, which as I have said was eighty-one miles an hour. We had several of the Cardington officials on board during this flight, who took this result with long faces. We all tried to get them to disclose what the full speed of R101 was but they turned stuffy and wouldn't tell us; the subject was evidently an awkward one and we had to abandon it.

The value of a full power trial lies in the effect it has in disclosing weaknesses in the outer cover of the ship. In the case of R100 the outer cover took up a curious wavelike formation when the ship was at full speed, which was not evident at cruising speed. These harmonic deflections ran longitudinally down the ship from bow to stern; they did not move at all. I climbed all over the ship with the riggers between the gasbags and the outer cover while the ship was at full speed to examine the attachments of the cover to its wiring system but I could find no place where the attachments were unduly stressed. Finally we came to the conclusion that the matter was of no importance, and was probably due to large-scale eddies of the air that passed over the hull.

The outer cover was a weakness in both R100 and R101. In each ship the policy had been adopted of building with relatively few longitudinal girders compared with previous ships in order that the forces in the girders might be calculated more accurately, and this decision was undoubtedly influenced by the disaster to R38. A ship with few longitudinals, however, must of necessity have larger unsupported panels of outer cover fabric than a ship with many. In both ships the outer cover was the main weakness. Extended flight trials were to prove that our outer cover on R100 was just good enough for the service demanded of it, but only just.

R100 made another flight about January 22nd to investigate the curious deformations of the outer cover at full speed; we flew to Farnborough, where an aircraft from the experimental station came up and flew alongside us to photograph the cover while I was crawling about inside the hull with the riggers. At cruising speed, about seventy miles an hour, the cover was quite normal. The officials at Cardington grumbled a bit about it, inferring that we were selling them a bad airship, but they had no leg to stand on technically and it was decided to let the matter go. So far as I remember, Burney clinched the matter by pointing out that our contract only called for a top speed of seventy miles an hour; if they wished we would put a stop on the throttles of the engines to prevent the ship from going faster than that, which would make the cover quite all right.

The contract for R100 called for a final acceptance trial of 48 hours' duration, and a demonstration flight to India. This latter flight was changed to a demonstration flight to Canada when the decision was taken to equip R100 with petrol engines, because it was thought that a flight to the tropics with petrol on board would be too hazardous. It is curious after over twenty years to recall how afraid everyone was of petrol in those days, because since then aeroplanes with petrol engines have done innumerable hours of flying in the tropics, and they don't burst into flames on every flight. I think the truth is that everyone was diesel-minded in those days; it seemed as if the diesel engine for aeroplanes was only just around the corner, with the promise of great fuel economy. It was decided amicably, therefore, that R101 would make the flight to India since she had diesel engines, and we would fly to Canada instead.

The final acceptance trial of R100 lasted for fifty-four hours; it was an easy and effortless performance bearing out the old saying of the RNAS that the only way to get a rest in the airship business is to take the thing into the air and fly it. We left Cardington on the morning of January the 27th with twenty-two tons of fuel on board to burn before coming down, and we landed again on the afternoon of the 29th having lived very comfortably in the meantime. The weather from the start was vile. At Cardington it was misty with a moderate wind and signs of rain; we came down to seven hundred feet over Oxford but saw nothing of the ground. We never flew lower than about seven hundred feet in R100 and seldom so low as that; our normal flying height was between fifteen hundred and two thousand feet. We passed on to Bristol in very bad weather, cruising at fifty-five miles an hour on three engines.

By the middle of the afternoon we were on the south coast of Cornwall in a wind of over fifty miles an hour; we put on a fourth engine to bring the speed up to sixty-five, being unwilling to increase speed more until we saw how the ship behaved in the rough weather. She answered her controls well, but in this wind she took a long, slow pitching motion of about five degrees each way. This very slow pitching was the only motion that she ever took in bad weather except once in the vicinity of Quebec when she rolled a little in a patch of violently disturbed air. Nobody could ever have been sick in that ship.

By dusk we were at the Channel Islands and heading up Channel to spend the night out over the North Sea. The ship had quite comfortable little two-berth cabins for fifty passengers, and we who had no routine duties went to bed at a normal time. At two o'clock in the morning I woke up, and becoming aware of my responsibilities I went down to the control car. I found them changing watch. On inquiring where we were, I was told that we were passing over Lowestoft. I asked what we had come there for, and was told that since the wife of Steff, third officer, came from Lowestoft we had come as a graceful compliment to empty our sewage tank over the town. Steff was killed in R101; I do not think that he would mind if I recall our ribaldry that night. The ship was then thrown into a turmoil because somebody had drunk the captain's cocoa; I'm not sure it wasn't me. Seeing that she was in good hands and not falling to bits, I went back to bed.

I was up again at dawn, to find us crossing the coast at Cromer on our way to London in increasing fog. As we got near the city the normal white fog changed to thick, black, greasy stuff that left great streaks of oily soot upon the outer cover; it wreathed apart once and disclosed the Tower Bridge immediately below us; then it closed down thick and black. We saw nothing more till that evening after tea, when we picked up the lights of a fishing fleet in Tor Bay.

At about eight o'clock, in the darkness, we went out to the Eddystone and using the lighthouse as a centre we did comprehensive turning trials on port and starboard helm for nearly an hour, calculating the radius of the turns by timing ourselves on a complete circuit and getting the circumference of the circle from the air speed. I have often wondered what the lighthouse keepers thought to see the lights of an apparently demented airship going round and round their lonely rock in the dark night.

All night we cruised the Channel. We went up as far as Portland, and out into the Atlantic to the Scillies. At dawn when I came down to the control car we were cruising over Cornwall; in the rising sun the valleys were all filled with mist as if it had been poured out of a bottle, and this mist was white and gold and pink in the clear light, very beautiful. That morning we went up the Bristol Channel at an easy speed; near Bristol we ran into cloud and rain again. We landed to the mast at Cardington in the middle of the afternoon, with the ship very wet but none the worse for her long flight.

I think it was during this flight that I went outside on top of the ship for the first time. R100 had a little cockpit on top at the extreme bow, forward of the first gasbag and reached by a ladder in the bow compartment; this was for taking navigational sights with a sextant. From this cockpit a walking way ran aft on top of the ship along one of the girders; this was a plywood plank a foot in width with the outer cover stretched over it. To give courage to the inexperienced it had a rope lashed down along it every two feet or so, to serve as a handhold. This walking way ran the whole length of the ship to the rear of the fins, where another hatch was provided behind the last gasbag. The slope of the hull at the bow cockpit was about forty-five degrees, which made the first part a little tricky to climb, and personally I always went from bow to stern because the rush of air pushed you up the first climb and you didn't have to look down. When the ship was cruising at about sixty miles an hour, as soon as you got to the top, or horizontal, part of the hull you were in calm air crawling on your hands and knees; if you knelt up you felt a breeze on your head and shoulders. If you stood up the wind was strong. It was pleasant up there sitting by the fins on a fine sunny day and whenever I went up there I would usually find two or three men sitting by the fins and gossiping. We kept a watch up there in daylight hours to keep an eye on the outer cover, and the riggers got so used to it that they would walk upright along this little catwalk with their hands in their pockets, leaning against the wind and stepping over my recumbent body as I crawled on hands and knees. Burney lost his wristwatch up there one evening; it lay on top of the ship all night and was found by one of the riggers at dawn next day, and returned to him.

This was one of the features of an airship which distinguished it from an aeroplane. You could climb all over every part of it in flight and carry out any repairs or maintenance that might be necessary. If the wind hampered the work you reduced speed. We did not care to run R100 slower than about twenty miles an hour because some elevator control was necessary to keep the ship at a given height without continually valving gas or jettisoning ballast, but that speed was sufficiently low to permit the most extensive repairs, as we were to find later.

After this flight the ship was put back into her shed for a considerable time. We formally handed her over to the Air Ministry, which means that we gave her to our competitors at Cardington, her English trials being satisfactorily concluded. They proceeded to make a number of modifications to her in preparation for the Atlantic flight. She did not fly again till some time in May, when we made a flight of twenty-four hours' duration in her, cruising over Lancashire and Yorkshire. In this flight the light tail-fairing of the hull, the last ten feet, well aft of the gasbags and the fins, suffered damage due to a high aerodynamic pressure. Wind-tunnel tests on the model had shown suction forces over most of the hull aft of Frame 3 at all angles of inclination, but at the extreme tail of the model a pressure had been shown. By the time this was appreciated the tests were over, the model had been dismantled and the wind tunnel was working upon other matters; we discussed this one isolated point of high pressure with the aerodynamic specialists. Nobody, with the knowledge we possessed at that time, could explain theoretically why there should be pressure there, so we assumed it was a false reading due to some experimental error. But it wasn't, and this little empty framework of light girders collapsed. The Cardington designers, who were now in charge of R100, solved the problem by cutting off the offending pointed tail and modifying her stern to a bluff, rounded shape not unlike the cruiser of a ship. This had the advantage of shortening the ship by fifteen feet without much detrimental effect, but it cannot be said that it improved her looks.

This modification kept R100 in her shed for a month or so, and in the meantime R101 came out to the mooring mast for further trials. It had been realized before Christmas that the small disposable load of R101 would make a flight to India impossible because she couldn't carry enough fuel, and a programme had been put in hand to try to put her right. All unnecessary equipment, including the useless servo motors, was taken out of her, her gasbag wiring was let out to increase her gas volume, and – last resort of desperate engineers – she was to be parted in the middle and an extra parallel portion inserted in her length, containing an extra gasbag. These alterations finally brought her disposable load up to 49.3 tons, still five tons less than that of R100. In fairness, however, it must be realized that her diesel engines used less fuel than ours, so that in the end there might not have been much to choose between the ships in regard to range and load-carrying capacity.

It was impossible to insert the extra bay in R101 at once, and when she came out to the mast for further trials in June the ship had been gutted of all superfluous equipment and the gasbags had been let out. Immediately she was put onto the mast, in a very light wind, the outer cover split longitudinally, making a tear a hundred and forty feet long. The wind was rising so she could not be put back in the shed, and the riggers mended it at the mast. A second, shorter split occurred next day, and was mended. They reinforced the cover with tapes stuck on inside with dope, and made a short test flight. They then made two more flights in daylight on consecutive days, each lasting for about twelve hours; these were less for technical reasons than to show the ship at the rehearsal for the RAF display at Hendon, and at the display itself. Publicity was important to them. They did no full power trial, probably because they were afraid of the outer cover.

During these two flights R101 grew steadily heavier, due to loss of gas; from the addition of the water ballast dropped and the fuel consumed she seemed to be losing lift at the rate of nearly a ton an hour. At the time it was thought by the captain of the ship that this was due to the over-sensitive gas valves chattering on their seatings, but more probably it was due to the chafing of the gasbags against the girders of the ship since the wiring had been let out to increase the volume, which had resulted in many holes.

Some correspondence, revealed at the accident inquiry, took place in the Air Ministry about these gas leaks. The inspector of the Aircraft Inspection Department, whose duty was to ensure the airworthiness of the ship so far as her construction was concerned, put in a written report upon these leaks, finishing up, 'Until this matter is seriously taken in hand and remedied I cannot recommend to you the extension of the present "Permit to fly" or the issue of any further permit or certificate.' Nobody at the Air Ministry knew much about airships, and this criticism was forwarded to Cardington for comment. The designers of the ship were thus being asked to adjudicate upon the soundness of their own work, being asked to decide if their ship was safe or not. Their credit, in comparison with ourselves, was at stake now. The palisade was hard around them, forcing them along a road that they never would have taken had they been free men. To put it in another way, if R100 had had gas leaks of that magnitude they would have declared her unairworthy at once, and rightly so.

They replied, in effect, that gasbags in airships always had touched the girders, and that a little padding of the girders was an effective cure. They probably indicated unofficially that they thought the inspector was an old woman making a mountain out of a molehill. The tone of the official correspondence supports that view.

So R101 was put back in to her shed. She was parted in the middle and the new bay was inserted; she was fitted with two new engines capable of reversing by an adjustment to the camshaft, the many points where the gasbags were bearing heavily against the girders were padded, and most of her outer cover was renewed.

It was stipulated in the contract for R100 that the ship must demonstrate her ability to carry out intercontinental flights by a flight to Canada. I do not think that this requirement was exactly a contractual liability, because to the best of my recollection our expenditure upon the ship ceased when she was handed over to the Air Ministry at the conclusion of the English trials. But the requirement had been written into the contract six years before, in 1924, and up till June 1930 it had never been questioned. R100 was to go to Canada and R101 to India, as soon as the English trials were over.

The Cardington engineers, after the June trials of R101, began to put forward tentative and unofficial proposals for a postponement of these long flights to the following year. They said that the two airships were in an early stage of development and that neither ship was fit to make a long flight at that stage. A disaster might set back the whole cause of airships in England, and it would be a pity to run any risk for the sake of getting on quickly; development would go better if we did not hurry it. They suggested, through unofficial intermediaries, that both staffs should take that line, and jointly ask for a postponement of these long flights.

Perhaps if we had realized at the time how very, very bad their ship was, how real the danger of complete disaster if they started for India, we might have taken a different attitude to this approach. Their own secrecies concealed the real facts from us: we guessed that their ship was a bad airship, but we did not know the whole story. We brushed aside this approach, perhaps roughly. We said that our ship was perfectly capable of flying to Canada; the Canadian flight was a part of our contract and it was necessary for us to do it. Again, the bitter competition between the staffs loomed large. A heavy loss had been made upon the construction of R100. If this was to be recouped from future airship contracts, ours must be the organization to carry on the work and they must give up. We would complete our contract and prove the efficiency of R100 by flying to Canada; they could please themselves whether they flew to India or not. With that perhaps we drove the final stake into the palisade around them, blocking their one way out.

It must have been about this time that a very distinguished scientist visited Cardington to see R101. He was of course, completely ignorant of airships and R101 was very big and very well finished, altogether a magnificent-looking piece of engineering. He was shown over the ship by her chief designer, who later was to lose his life in her, and at the conclusion of the visit the scientist was full of praise for what he considered to be a wonderful achievement. He said that the designer must be a very proud man.

The chief designer answered, 'I suppose it ought to be a great satisfaction, but somehow I feel too tired.'

CHAPTER FIVE

FROM THAT TIME on the atmosphere at Cardington became very bad, certainly so far as we were concerned. Arrangements were being made for the flight of R100 to Canada with very bad grace. For some technical reason I had to go to Cardington about the middle of July; I flew down in a club Moth piloting myself, and landed it just outside the airship hangars. This method of travelling in summer weather saved several hours of driving time and much fatigue, but it might have been better if I had gone down by car because any suggestion that we knew more about the air than they did probably rasped sore nerves, and none of them could fly an aeroplane. My technical business involved a conference with the chief members of their organization, all but one of whom were later to lose their lives; they were quite polite, but nobody invited me to lunch in their mess room although our business was to extend into the afternoon, and I would have gone without lunch altogether if the captain of R100, distressed by this incivility, had not taken me to his home. When our conference was over the officers and crew of R100 came to help me start my little aeroplane and see me safely off the premises, but nobody else came. Perhaps they were all watching from their office windows, hoping I would crash.

Towards the end of July R100 was brought out to the mast again and we made another flight in her of twenty-four hours' duration. Technically this flight was completely uneventful. One incident perhaps deserves a record. In the dark night, out somewhere over the Atlantic near the Scilly Isles, we asked for our position by wireless. Perhaps the two direction-finding stations were nearly in a line with us, making a bad cut, perhaps they were merely sleepy. They replied with creditable promptitude that our position was two miles south-west of Guildford.

Major Scott made a signal in reply: 'Many thanks for position; sea very rough at Guildford.' Politeness invariably pays.

This was the seventh flight that R100 made, and the last before she crossed the Atlantic. There were no troubles to be rectified, and little to be done before we started off except to put more fuel on board. We returned from this flight on Saturday. On the following Tuesday morning we set off for Montreal.

Looking back upon those days, I have sometimes wondered if we were very rash in taking the Atlantic flight so early in the ship's career. On the whole I do not think we were. R100 had made only seven flights before we started for Canada, but in those flights she had flown over a hundred and fifty hours and had covered seven or eight thousand miles. She had repeatedly been flown at full speed, and she had flown for long periods in very bad weather. We had no reason to anticipate any trouble with the engines, as these were of a well-proved aeroplane type.

At the same time, there is no doubt that our Atlantic crossing was dictated by political motives alone, as in the case of the Indian flight of R101. It is doubtful if any responsible technician would assert that a large and totally experimental aircraft is fit to cross the Atlantic on its eighth flight; the most that he could say would be, as I said, that he knew of nothing that would prevent it doing so in safety. This guarded approval of the project was all that could fairly be given at that stage. In that respect our position was precisely similar to that of the designers of the R101, except that we had more flight experience behind us, and a better ship. Considered purely from the technical aspect, it was not very prudent for either airship to attempt a long flight at that stage of development. We did it, and got away with it.

Whenever I make a lengthy or an interesting journey I usually keep a diary, and my diary tells me that I spent the Sunday on the ship with the crew, making a very comprehensive inspection. One of our many petrol tanks was leaking a little, and we changed it for a new one. I went to London about midday on Monday, buying an overall and rubber shoes on the way, and reported to Burney that we were ready to start. That evening, at my club in Pall Mall, telephone calls confirmed the start for 3.30 the next morning. So I stood myself a very good and expensive dinner, followed by a glass of brandy and a cigar, read a novel by A P Herbert for a couple of hours to my great content, went to Burney's house with my linen kitbag, and drove with him to Cardington in the middle of the night. On this flight Sir Dennis Burney and I represented the constructors, and a Lieut-Cdr Prentice represented the Admiralty; three members of the Cardington party travelled with us, and a representative of the Aircraft Inspection Department.

The diary, written during the flight, may tell most of the story from now onwards. For July 29th, 1930:

We slipped at 3.50am, summer time. We have 34.5 tons of petrol on board, which should be ample. At the last moment the ship was light, and we delayed some time in filling up two emergency water bags ($^1/_2$ ton) forward. We slipped with practically full emergency ballast, dropping one bag aft to get the tail up.

It was just light enough to see the fields. The preparations were better done than I have ever seen them: nobody but the officers and the coxswains in the control car, and everything smart and efficient in the dim light. We slipped, and a great cheer from the tower told us that we were clear. Booth rang on all engines and put her nose up, and we forced her up to about 1,000 feet in the half-darkness. Our course will take us over Liverpool. There is a small depression NW of Ireland; by passing north of this we should get a favouring wind this afternoon. We hope to make good time.

We had a very expert meteorologist on board, who later was to lose his life in R101, and every six hours we took a radio signal consisting of a great number of code groups sent out specially by the Air Ministry for us; from this we made up a fresh isobaric weather plot. An airship is so slow that one never butts into a headwind if it can possibly be avoided, and we altered course repeatedly to go the right way round the depressions and find a favouring wind. That morning we went north-west till we were off the west coast of Scotland and north of Ireland; we then turned westwards and found a beam wind, as forecast. I slept till about 8am, and then breakfasted. Petrol was pumped manually to the gravity tanks above the power cars in R100, and we all assisted the crew in this monotonous chore; for the rest, I roamed the ship as usual, looking for trouble.

1.25pm. A good lunch – soup, stewed beef, peas, potatoes; greengages and custard; beer, cheese, coffee. We are butting along in low cloud at about 1,300 feet on 4 engines at 50 knots. The wind is northerly and strong; we are off the NW corner of Ireland making good about 40 knots on 270° mag. Everyone a little comatose after lunch, and the crew are playing their gramophone – 'Can't help loving that man of mine'. Probably we shall head a little south soon and get south of a high pressure area down there, and so find a favouring wind. Sea about Force 5 and very desolate; it beats us all how anyone should have the courage to attempt the Atlantic in an aeroplane.

In R100 the passenger coach was within the hull about one third of the ship's length from the bow; large windows in the outer cover permitted quite a good view from the passengers' promenade decks. The control car was immediately beneath the passenger coach, outside the contour of the hull. All three power cars were aft of that, the nearest being about 120 feet aft. The passenger coach and the control car were therefore practically noiseless, and the gramophone was heard as clearly as in a house on land. The walls dividing the cabins were of fabric, so that a man snoring in the next cabin could be a real nuisance at night, so quiet was the ship.

Wednesday, July 30th, 8.40am zone time (GMT-2). Position is about 54°20'N and 35°W. We altered course a little in the night to steer rather more northwards, heading for Belle Isle at the north of Newfoundland and the entrance to the St Lawrence. This because the meteorological chart made up at 1am disclosed a shallow depression east of Newfoundland. By going round the top of this we shall get a following wind, and this we have now actually got and have had for a couple of hours. We are cruising at 50 knots on four engines, but are making good 74 knots over the ground, on practically a due westerly course. This is fine, and we hope to pick up Belle Isle about 900 miles from here this evening. We are running in thick fog.

Gasbag 7 appears to be leaking as it was when we started and has risen a good bit; the others are holding well.

I slept splendidly in pyjamas, sheets, sleeping bag, and blanket from 11pm to 7.30am. There has been no motion of the ship whatever on this flight. Pumped petrol before turning in and again before breakfast this morning. The comfort of this flight is almost staggering. Sleep all night in bed, get up, shave in hot water, dress and eat a normal breakfast served in a Christian way. If this water collector can be developed, as I think it can, we may be able to have baths in future ships.

11.0am zone time (GMT-3). We had a sweepstake on the day's run, noon to noon GMT. Eldridge won it with 1,095 sea miles; we are doing much better now.

Everything in the ship is satisfactory. In the fins this morning I came on Deverell repairing a little chafed hole in the cover about the size of a penny; the crew are continually on the look out for incipient damage of this sort and take it before it has time to get very far. They did a little sewing and doping on the top elastic hinge strip of the port elevator yesterday in anticipation of damage that bad not yet happened. A good, keen crew.

We have just stopped the aft engine in the aft car and put on one of the wing car engines to replace it, still running on four engines. A flexible water-pipe to the radiator is chafing on the car structure and something has to be done about it. This is the first time we have had to stop an engine for adjustment or repair; the job will take about an hour.

4.30pm zone time (GMT-4). The fair wind has gone and we have a 20 knot wind against us, very nearly dead ahead; this is in accordance with our prediction from the depression centred about Hudson Bay. We have put on power and are now running on six engines, the forward ones at 1,500rpm and the aft ones at 1,600rpm. This gives us about 58 knots (or 66mph) and we are making good about 42 knots over the ground. Belle Isle is just about 100 sea miles ahead.

It has turned cold and grey; visibility is moderate between frequent rain showers. At this speed pumping petrol is serious work; in a larger ship it will be necessary to put in mechanical pumps.

Thursday July 31st 2.30am zone time. We are well inside Newfoundland running up the St Lawrence River; had asked to be called to help pump petrol. We are still running on 6 engines at 58 knots, but have a headwind and are only making good about 36 knots over the ground. Johnston is asleep in a chair in the saloon, in Teddy and uniform cap. He is a splendid navigator and works like a horse; I believe he had only two hours' sleep last night.

A Teddy was a combination flying suit used only in airships; it was made of Teddy Bear fleece inside and out. Airships were normally unheated and were difficult to heat technically, though we had an elementary electrical heating system in R100. I had a Teddy issued to me for the flight; I never had occasion to wear it, but it was a very warm and comforting garment for those who had to stand motionless on watch. Squadron Leader E L Johnston was probably the most experienced navigator in the Royal Air Force at that time. He was killed in R101.

12.45pm zone time. We have been troubled with leaks in Gasbags 7 and 8 since we started, and 7 has risen to about 3ft below E longitudinal. So the crew set out to find them, and Hobbs succeeded in getting to and mending 3 holes in Bag 7 and 2 holes in Bag 8. They were all 3 inch slits along E radial wire. To help him reach the holes we rose to 3,000 feet, to bring the bag to him. A good show on his part; those holes would fully account for the loss of gas.

These holes were on the flat surface of the gasbags, as it might be on the flat end of a cylindrical cheese. If they had been on the sides of the bag it would have been easy to find and repair them. To reach these holes meant a somewhat hazardous climb along the radial wires between the bags, with some danger of being gassed by the hydrogen issuing from the holes. Hydrogen is fairly easily detected, however: it has a peculiar warning of its presence, more of a savour than a smell. I do not think it is toxic: a man gassed by hydrogen recovers quite quickly in clean air. The danger in this case lay in falling, for it was impossible to provide the rigger with any form of safety line.

(Written at) 10.20pm zone time. *Dies irae, dies illa.* At about 3pm, off Courdes Island, 50 miles from Quebec, we got into a wind which headed us from off some high hills on the north shore.

I should explain that this was a northerly wind. The north shore of the St Lawrence at this point is mountainous with ranges up to 5,000ft high; this cold north wind was cascading down over these hills into the hot air of the valley, producing a region of considerable turbulence.

This was very bumpy, and gave us the worst motion that the ship has yet had. In pitch she oscillated rapidly over about 10°, coupled with a good deal of yawing and rolling. We were cruising at 58 knots and had just increased to about 60 knots a minute or two before. To ease the motion we headed over to the south side away from the hills and soon got out of the disturbed air. Our height was about 1,200 feet and she hunted over about 300 feet.

Immediately afterwards the starboard and aft cars rang for assistance and pointed out tears in the fins.

The fins of R100 were not visible from the control car, but could be seen from the engine cars.

I went aft with Meager and Wann; speed was reduced. In the lower fin two tapes had torn away making 3ft slits. I left Wann to watch these and went on after Meager to the starboard fin. Here there was a large hole on the backbone girder, lower surface, near 14. Meager went down to get help, and I went out along 14 finpost in to the backbone and managed to pull the loose, beating fabric inboard and stop the spread till riggers came with Meager and relieved me.

Captain G F Meager was the first officer of the ship, and a great friend.

Meager asked me to go and have look at the port fin while he went to the top fin. I went by way of Frame 15, and found a hole large enough to drive a bus through, in the lower surface, centred on 13a. It extended from the radius to the backbone, and about fifteen feet long. The tapes were sound but the fabric was hanging in rags, and the whole was beating badly.

The fins were formed on girders which stuck through the ship in a cruciform manner. The outer ends of these girders were connected with a backbone girder, which formed the outer longitudinal edge of the fin. On this structure a system of wires was stretched. The fabric cover was then laid on the fin and tightened down to this wiring system by means of cord lashings.

Throughout the ship the panels of the outer cover were reinforced with T tapes sewn to the fabric, the tapes running in lines three feet apart. These tapes carried eyelets every foot of their length, by which the cover was lashed to the wiring system. What had happened now was that the outer cover fabric had blown off the tapes. The radius referred to was where the fin cover joined the hull cover at the base of the fin. The hole measured about 15ft by 12ft.

Went down to the keel and found Meager and Moncrieff; top fin was OK. As soon as the starboard and lower fins were sewn and sealed the full staff of riggers came to the port fin, with several engineers. At one time we had fifteen men up there.

The hole was in the lower surface of the fin, which was about four feet thick on the average, tapering to less thickness at the outer edge by the backbone girder. The job therefore required the riggers to climb about on wires like tightrope walkers, with nothing but the waters of the St Lawrence a thousand feet below. They wore safely belts, with which they could sometimes hitch themselves onto a wire.

We made good all round (the hole) first; laced upper and lower hull covers to the apex boom of longitudinals D and E, and laced the top and bottom fin covers up to finpost 14 to make a leading edge if the whole of 13a went. Then, by climbing out, managed to 'furl' the rags of fabric on the tapes and reduce fluttering. Then passed a rope or two out at the most forward split and in at the aft split, and bowsed inwards, and so tautened the tapes. Finally passed a sheet of cotton, nearly large enough to fill the hole, out at forward slit and managed to tie it to the tapes and so make good the majority of the hole. When finished it didn't flap much at 45 knots. After 2 hours standing still just stemming the wind we were able to get ahead a bit, and make good about 20 knots over ground.

The sheet of cotton fabric was carried on board for just such an emergency; it was already provided with tapes and eyelets round the edge and all over it. It was, in fact, a sort of collision mat. I think we had two of them on board; we had a lot more when we started home for England! I cannot remember why it was of cotton, for the rest of the hull fabric was linen. I think we were cruising at about 20mph while all this was going on.

Quebec was reached at about 6pm. A smaller town than I should have thought; they were massed on all the promenades and in the parks to see us, and a tremendous hooting and sirens. Luckily our relatively sound fin was towards the town!

Headed for Montreal; it was nearly dark by 7.30. Had a sherry with Burney, Booth, and Scott. They had wirelessed us that a thunderstorm was coming to us, not a very large one. While we were drinking our sherry the first pitch was felt, and Booth and Scott went down into the control car. Height about 1,200ft, speed 40 knots. Burney and I went out into the promenade. The ship then hit a vertical gust and began to rise rapidly. Elevators were put hard down to keep her down, till she reached an angle of about 20° nose down. In that position she rose rapidly to 4,500ft, the last 1,000ft being covered in 15 seconds according to Giblett. She then steadied and was brought under control in heavy rain. In this rise the ship swung eight points from her course.

Supper was laid on the centre table of the saloon and shot off, downstairs, up the corridor, till some of it reached Frame 2.

I think the ship must have been at least 35° nose down for a bit of cold meat or a slice of bread to get as far up the nose curvature of the ship as this.

> Two twelve foot tears were made in the lower fabric of the starboard fin, which were repaired later. The lights went out and put the ship into complete darkness for ten minutes, adding to the difficulties. It rained so hard that .3 ton of water came into the collector in ten minutes.
>
> This was quite a small, normal thunderstorm – so far as we know at present. A rate of rise 4,000ft/min on the ship when driven nose down was achieved, according to good evidence. This would seem to indicate air currents of higher velocity than this.
>
> Since then we have dodged three others, and are now heading for Montreal and hope to moor at dawn. Further comment on these experiences may be deferred till we are all less tired.

I remember the look of that storm very well. It stretched across our path as a bank of clouds apparently about fifteen miles long, slightly bronze in colour and raining underneath. At that time little was known about the violent air currents in and around line squalls; a great deal has been learned since then by brave men soaring in sailplanes. Major Scott was in charge of flying operations, over the captain of the ship. I was in the control car with him before we went up for the sherry, and heard him make the decision to go through it rather than fly round it; we had ample fuel and there was no occasion to take the ship, already damaged, through this storm. In my view, even with the lesser knowledge of those days, Scott should have known better and this decision was a reckless one.

Major Scott was in charge of the last flight of R101, and was killed in her. That flight started in poor weather, and two hours after the start of the flight, six hours before the airship crashed, a very bad forecast was issued to the ship by radio which might well have caused him to decide to turn back to Cardington and start again when the weather had moderated. If I say that I think he showed bad judgement on this previous occasion it is not to blacken the character of a brave and a likeable man, but because after twenty-five years it should be possible to write candidly about human frailties in the interests of history. Aircraft do not crash of themselves. They come to grief because men are foolish, or vain, or lazy, or irresolute, or reckless. One crash in a thousand may be unavoidable because God wills it so – not more than that. After twenty-five years it should be possible to write truthfully about the other ones.

As at all grave times, there was a lighter side. When the ship plunged nose down a relay of the lighting system jumped out extinguishing all lights, and the same motion upset a five-gallon drum of red dope which had been left open in the crew's quarters immediately above the control car, having been used for the fin repairs. There was an emergency lighting system in the control car of small orange bulbs over the essential instruments, and this kept going. The situation in the control car therefore was that the ship was so far nose down that it was necessary to hold on, apparently plunging straight into the ground, in thick cloud and rain, with the altimeter going madly the wrong way, completely out of control. At that moment, in the faint orange light, a torrent of sticky red fluid resembling blood poured down into the control car. Grand Guignol could not have done better.

None of us slept that night: we were all busy comparing notes and sorting out exactly what had happened to us, and writing it down while it was fresh in the memory in order that we could provide for future airships being designed to withstand these violent storms which we had met in Canada but not in England. The fin repairs required attention, too, but these were straightforward, being long slits only.

In the middle of the night, at about two in the morning, the myriad lights of a city showed up ahead of us where Montreal should have been, but in the black sky above these lights, suspended in the night, we saw an enormous fiery cross. I stared at it in consternation till somebody voiced my secret thoughts, and said: 'That's not Montreal. That's the New Jerusalem. This is it, boys.'

We discovered later that Montreal, being a Roman Catholic city, has a great cross made of steel girders erected on the top of Mount Royal; this is picked out in electric lights. That night it brought a healthy laugh among a lot of very tired men.

We moored to the mast at St Hubert airport at dawn, 78 hours out from Cardington; we had five tons of fuel left. The great circle distance is about 3,300 land miles, so we had averaged about 42mph. It must be remembered that at that time only one aeroplane had made a direct flight across the Atlantic from East to West against the prevailing wind, starting from Ireland and crashing on an island off the coast of Newfoundland at the very limit of its fuel, so that our performance, being twice the speed of ship and train from London to Montreal, gave some commercial promise.

The Canadians gave the ship a tremendous welcome. Over a hundred thousand people visited the airport to see the ship each day for several consecutive days; the city was placarded with welcoming notices, and they even wrote a song about us with a picture of Booth on the cover of the sheet music. There were innumerable functions in the fortnight that we stayed there, but my own time was largely occupied with making good the fins and other defects in the ship. In this we were greatly helped by the aircraft department of Canadian Vickers; needless to say, I saw to it that we had plenty of spare fabric sheets prepared for our journey home.

We stayed in Montreal for twelve days. The defects in the ship were all repaired in two or three days, and the ship then made a local flight to Ottawa, Toronto, and Niagara Falls that lasted for twenty-four hours. I stood down from this flight to permit the maximum number of Canadian passengers to be taken; this was the only flight that the ship ever made when I was not in her. Accordingly I saw her flying for the first time over Montreal; she looked quite a good job.

As they were coming in to land the reduction gear of the starboard forward engine failed, and apparently shook the propeller so that a part of the metal sheathing flew off and penetrated the ship, touching a boom. I must go and investigate this tomorrow. In addition, when landing they did in the ship's main rope as on the second flight, but they have a spare out here.

I understand that though they have spare engines out here they did not ship out the slinging derricks for changing an engine, and accordingly it is very difficult to change the damaged engine. A pretty position to be in! For this reason they have decided not to change this engine, but to go home on five.

Next day I prescribed the necessary patch for the boom of the girder which had been damaged. The decision to go home on five engines was a reasonable one in the circumstances, since the prevailing wind across the North Atlantic is from the west and we could expect a quick and easy trip. We had spent some time and ingenuity in designing the slinging derricks, which were a sort of detachable crane that could be fitted to an engine car to lower an engine down to the ground when the ship was at the mast, and to hoist up another one. It was irritating that an organizational failure at Cardington prevented this equipment from being on hand when it was needed.

This trip to Canada was my first visit to the American continent. I had two good friends from my Oxford days living in Montreal, and in my short leisure time there I saw something of the way of life in the Dominion and in the countryside around Lake Magog, where one of my friends, Percy Corbett, was buying a small farm. For the first time in my life I saw how people live in an English-speaking country outside England, and in view of my decision twenty years later to go and live in Australia it is interesting to read the last words that I wrote in that diary about Canada.

> I would never have believed that after a fortnight's stay I should be so sorry to leave a country. I like this place: I like the way they go about things, and their vitality. The tremendous physical health of everyone. I am going home, and sorry to go; though I am leaving this country for a little time I cannot believe that I am leaving it for good. I have never been in a place that has got hold of me so much as this has done. We are going home, and there will be a great welcome waiting for us at Cardington, but it will not be like the welcome that they gave us here.

The homeward journey to Cardington was uneventful. We left Montreal in the evening in order to have the calmer conditions of night flying over the continental land mass; we had eleven Canadians on board as passengers, mostly journalists.

> August 13th 10.10pm. Slipped at 9.28 Montreal Summer Time and got away well, with 9,600 gallons of fuel. Headed south and proceeded on a wide circle westwards to cross over Montreal from west to east. We are now heading down the St Lawrence with a moderate following wind. Cruising on 3 engines at 1,600rpm, making about 47 knots with a following wind of 10 knots, say 57 knots over the ground. Height about 1,000 feet, moonlight on the river, very pretty. We have just passed Sorrel.

An uneventful journey is a good journey for the technician.

> We have had a sweepstake on the day's run, which I have won with 1,250 nautical miles, gathering in $6.75 … We are cruising normally at 52 knots on four engines. It is very damp and warm. Everything is streaming water, and the whole ship is very wet … . Yesterday afternoon after lunch everyone went to bed. This afternoon it will be the same, and I shall follow suit. This is an ancient maritime custom, and should not be neglected.

So we came back to England:

Saturday August 16th 8.20am. We have had breakfast and passed Avonmouth and Bristol; two aeroplanes came up from Filton and flew beside us for a little time. We are now sliding on over Gloucestershire on a direct course for Cardington.

This has not been a bad trip. We have done what we set out to do when we left England more or less at the time scheduled, and at this stage of airship development I think that constitutes a good performance. It is a pity that the fin went on the way over, but one has to gain experience.

10.0am GMT. Over Bedford; we have about 3,200 gallons of petrol left. $56^1/2$ hours from the time we left Montreal. We can see the aerodrome; there are not more than fifty cars in all to see us arrive. We slink in unhonoured and unsung in the English style, rather different to the welcome that we had in Montreal.

11.0am. Locked home (to the mast). There are now about 200 cars in all. Time of passage, $57^1/2$ hours.

So ended the Canadian flight of R100, and the last flight she ever made: the ship never flew again. She was put back into her shed at Cardington, and the whole effort of that station was devoted to the R101 in preparation for her flight to India which ended in disaster. After that disaster the airship programme in England was abandoned, perhaps rightly in view of the increasing efficiency of the aeroplane. R100 was broken up and sold for scrap; only a few pieces of her structure now survive as museum curiosities and as memorials to our endeavour.

The success of our Canadian flight undoubtedly was instrumental in bringing about the disaster to R101. Up to that point it was still possible for the Cardington officials to declare that neither ship was fit for a long flight. But when we came back relatively safe and sound from Canada that last way of escape was closed to them; now they had to fly R101 to India or admit defeat, accepting discredit and the loss of their jobs. They chose to fly.

CHAPTER SIX

I MADE MY last visit to Cardington, in a technical capacity, some time in September 1930. It was quite shortly before the last trial of R101, so I suppose it would have been about the middle of the month. I cannot remember what I went for, but at that time I was drawing up a programme of modifications to R100 as a result of the experience of our Canadian flight, and I imagine that I went to discuss this with Squadron Leader Booth, the captain, and Captain Meager, the first officer of the ship. Probably the Aircraft Inspection Department inspector came into it, too, because I would have wanted to have a personal talk with him before finalizing the modifications.

On that visit, I found a terrible atmosphere at Cardington. I write that with some diffidence, because I made no notes and kept no diary, and I cannot remember now what it was that impressed me so badly except one thing: that the crews of both airships appeared to be completely out of hand. A long period of inactivity was evidently ahead of R100 and the crew were working largely upon R101; they seemed to have become uninterested and idle. The officers of R100 had been put very much on one side by the Cardington officials and were being allowed no part in the preparations of R101, and the men did not seem to be obeying any orders unless it suited them to do so, which was seldom. There was an atmosphere of cynical disillusionment about the place, very depressing.

I found Booth and Meager virtually doing nothing in a little office in the shed that housed R100. They were pleased to see me, but I think they had been warned not to talk to me too much; members of our organization were quite unwelcome at Cardington at that time. They gave me a cup of tea and then, thawing, they shut the door, looked out of the window into the shed to see that no one was about, and pulled out from under a desk a couple of square yards of outer cover fabric. Booth said, 'What do you think of that?'

It was ordinary outer cover, linen fabric, silver doped on a red oxide base. On the inner surface two-inch tapes had been stuck on with some adhesive, evidently for strengthening. I didn't know what I was expected to say, and turned it about in my hands, and suddenly my hand went through it. In parts it was friable, like scorched brown paper, so that if you crumpled it in your hand it broke up into flakes. I stared at it in horror, thinking of R100. 'Good God,' I said. 'Where did this come from?'

'All right,' said Booth. 'That's not off our ship. That's off R101.'

I asked, 'But what's happened to it? What made it go like this?'

They told me that the new outer cover for R101 had been doped in place upon the ship. When it was finished, it was considered that it ought to be strengthened in certain places by a system of tapes stuck on the inside, and for the adhesive they had used rubber solution. The rubber solution had reacted chemically with the dope, and had produced this terrible effect.

There was nothing that he or I could do about it. I said, 'I hope they've got all this stuff off the ship.'

He smiled cynically. 'They *say* they have.'

Two points in this incident deserve some notice. Firstly, Cardington was a department of the Air Ministry and had immediate access to the whole of the government research organization. There was undoubtedly somebody at Farnborough who could have told them at once that rubber solution and dope did not agree; undoubtedly the dope manufacturers could have told them. I think that at that stage, three weeks before the R101 disaster, they were floundering, making hurried and incompetent technical decisions, excluding people from their conferences who could have helped them.

The second point is this. R101 made one short test flight on October the 1st in very perfect weather; during this flight she made no full-speed trials because the oil cooler of one engine failed. She started for India on October the 4th, and met some very bad weather over France. She crashed at Beauvais, and the initial cause of the disaster was almost certainly a large failure of the outer cover on top of the ship near the bow. It seems to me very probable that some of this rotted fabric had been left in place, but nobody will ever know that for certain.

With that my personal association with R101, such as it was, came to an end and anything further that I know was derived from hearsay at the time and from the report of the inquiry into the accident. If I go on now to round off the story and to draw conclusions it is for a definite purpose, and that purpose is this.

In many fields of technical development security is now paramount, and there is a growing tendency for government officials concerned with a particular technique to say that no security is possible unless the development is carried out by government officials. That may or may not be true. The one thing that has been proved abundantly in aviation is that government officials are totally ineffective in engineering development. If the security of new weapons demands that only government officials shall be charged with the duty of developing them, then the weapons will be bad weapons, and this goes for atom bombs, guided missiles, radar, and everything else.

The airship programme constitutes one of the few occasions when a government department has been placed in direct competition with private enterprise. Twenty-five years should be sufficient to soften the acerbities of the time, and no security plea can be brought forward to mask a close analysis of the reasons for the failure of the Government's airship. These reasons were fundamental to the incursion of a government department into industry and are the same today, whether the product be airships or guided missiles. It seems useful, therefore, to pursue the airship matter to its end.

In this account I have done my best to avoid mentioning the names of the five men who held positions of prime responsibility at Cardington, four of whom were killed in the disaster to the airship. The disaster was the product of the system rather than of the men themselves. The worst that can be said of them is that they were not very good engineers. They may have been a little vain in undertaking work beyond their capacity especially in view of the disaster to R38. If this be a fault it is a fault that most adventurous engineers would yield to, if they were allowed. Industry, however, is ruled by Boards of Directors whose function is to prevent the engineers that they employ from taking on work that is beyond their powers and so producing a disaster. They do this by virtue of their own long industrial experience, which enables them to assess the difficulties of the job and to engage staff suitable to do it. The men at Cardington had no comparable restraint: the civil servants and the politicians above them in the Air Ministry were quite unfit to exercise that type of control.

The Secretary of State for Air, Lord Thomson of Cardington, must however be mentioned by name in spite of the fact that he also died in the airship, since he was primarily responsible for the organization which produced the disaster. Christopher Birdwood Thomson was a professional soldier, born of a military family on both sides. He was a gracious and cultured man who entered the army as a sapper in 1894 and made fairly rapid progress, becoming a member of the Supreme War Council in 1918. By 1920 he had developed strong Labour interests and had attained the rank of Brigadier-General; he then resigned from the army as a protest against Allied intervention in Russia. He did one or two odd jobs for the Labour Party as a military expert and stood twice, unsuccessfully, for Parliament in the Labour interest, in 1922 and 1923. In 1924 Mr Ramsay MacDonald appointed him Air Minister in the first Labour Government with a seat in the Cabinet, and since he was unable to secure election to Parliament in the normal way he was created a Baron and made a member of the House of Lords. It was largely through his influence that the original plan of Vickers Ltd. to build six airships and operate them was scrapped and the competitive plan instituted that resulted in the production of R100 and R101, and as if to indicate where his preference lay, he chose Cardington for his title. The Labour Government that put him in this position lasted only nine months; when the Conservative Government under Stanley Baldwin succeeded it with a huge majority it stayed in power for five years with Sir Samuel Hoare as Secretary of State for Air, till both airships were practically complete. The second Labour Government came into power then and Lord Thomson again became Secretary of State for Air five months before R101 made her first flight. The first Baron Thomson of Cardington was therefore responsible for giving the job of building R101 to the men at Cardington in the first place, and for the conduct of the Air Ministry throughout the period covering the flight trials of both airships.

A wholly apocryphal story is told of a shareholders' meeting of a great London store at a time when it was not doing so well. An infuriated shareholder, who was no gentleman, got up to castigate the distinguished Board of Directors. 'When our country is in peril on the sea,' he announced in measured tones, ' 'oo better to turn to than Admiral Sir Duncan Frobisher? When our country is in peril on the land, 'oo better to turn to than Major-General Lord Banklington? But what the bloody 'ell do they know about 'ams?' Upon Brigadier-General Lord Thomson must rest the responsibility for the decision that the staff at Cardington were suitable persons to build another airship, but it is difficult to see what experience in his previous career qualified him to make such a decision.

Still, there it was, and Lord Thomson became the patron of the airship staff at Cardington. During his five years out of office the position was, no doubt, reviewed from time to time by his successor, Sir Samuel Hoare, and some of the things said by Sir Dennis Burney probably made high civil servants and members of the Air Council wonder if all was well in the Government's airship department. There seemed to be no occasion to upset the programme, however; no question of any danger could arise until the airships were ready for flight. The Air Council might possibly have initiated an investigation, but it must be remembered that the Air Council was composed of officers who had attained their experience with aeroplanes, and who disclaimed all knowledge of airships. The whole of the airship experience in government service was concentrated at Cardington; if these men had been judged incompetent there were no other airship experts in the country to put into their place. An unfavourable report would have been tantamount to a recommendation that the attempt of the Government to build airships should be abandoned because an Air Vice-Marshal who had no experience of airships had cold feet. It is hardly surprising that no member of the Air Council felt impelled to take such action.

Under this ménage practically every principle of safety in the air was abandoned, perhaps unconsciously. The first principle of safety in the design of aircraft is that there should be a second check on the design, conducted by an entirely independent body of experts, usually in government employment. This principle was applied in the case of R100: every detail of the design had to be submitted to the Air Ministry as the design progressed and was sent by them to Cardington for comment; as construction progressed towards completion the officer in charge of flying and the captain designated for the ship made frequent visits to Howden and put in reports at length to their chiefs at Cardington. In cases where the government inspector had any doubts about what was good practice on R100 he applied to Cardington for guidance. Throughout the construction of R100, therefore, the men at Cardington were both our judges and our competitors. It must be recorded to their great credit that no serious friction arose from this peculiar organization; they exercised their powers with restraint and interfered with the design and the construction of R100 very little. For myself, I was glad that someone else was criticizing our designs although I would have preferred it not to be a competitor; everyone makes mistakes from time to time, and in aviation any second check is better than no second check.

No such second check was ever imposed on the design of R101, except in the case of the strength of the main structure and the aerodynamic design. As with R100, two university professors of wide experience in these fields were engaged to report on R101, and these men did their work conscientiously and well. The aerodynamics of R101 were all right, and so was her structural strength. Wide though these fields are, however, they cover only a small part of the safety problem of an airship. Questions of fire hazard, outer cover defects, gasbag and gas valve leakage, servo motors, structural overweight, astern power, and engine defects were never referred to these two professors, who had no knowledge or experience that would have enabled them to express an opinion on such matters. The only people in the country who could have given useful guidance on a number of such points were ourselves, at Howden, the competing staff. No limited company in the aircraft manufacturing industry, however, has ever served as an airworthiness authority, and none of the troubles of R101 were ever referred to us for an opinion. No second check was ever made upon such points. When the inspector on the ship put in a very strongly worded report to his chief at the Air Ministry dealing with the number of gasbag leaks on R101, the report was forwarded to Cardington for comment and the soothing assurances of the designers were accepted. These men were their own judges. Looming over them like Destiny by that time was Lord Thomson of Cardington, who had taken his title from his confidence in them, who had made them and had power to unmake them. It was impossible for them to admit mistakes without incurring discredit far exceeding their deserts, for everybody makes mistakes from time to time. Surely no engineers were ever placed in so unhappy a position.

They suffered, too, from having no contract to fulfil. For R100 it was stipulated in contractual form that the airship must attain a speed of seventy miles an hour and that her tare weight should not exceed ninety tons, that her gas volume should be five million cubic feet, giving her a disposable load of sixty-two tons; she was to do English trials according to a definite schedule, ending up with a forty-eight-hour endurance flight. When these conditions had been complied with the contract would be finished and the ship would be accepted, and our expenditure on her would be at an end. There was therefore a strong financial incentive urging us to meet the conditions. In fact they were met substantially. R100 was about 3% larger than the contract called for and she was a good deal overweight, so that she only carried fifty-four tons; on the other hand she was eleven miles an hour faster than the terms of the contract required, so that we could probably have brought her to the contract weights by taking out two of her engines and appurtenances and still have fulfilled the contract in regard to speed. She passed through all her English contract trials with very little trouble.

No such contract incentive was there to help the Cardington designers with a target for performance. They were given the same specification as R100 as a basis for design, but no penalties of any kind attached to a departure from it or a failure to fulfil it. It was difficult for them, therefore, to stick to the main aim of producing a good airship. The diesel engines were a case in point. It was thought very desirable to develop a diesel engine for use in airships in the tropics, but as the engines finally arrived for installation in the ship they were nearly twice as heavy as the first estimate of the weight. There was no penalty, however, if the ship as a whole came out overweight; no shareholders would lose any money. The diesel experiment was a desirable one, so into the ship the engines went – and by reason of the increased weights the airship as a whole had too little reserve of lifting power and had to have an extra bay put into her, with all the consequential changes that that entailed. Not only the diesel engines were responsible, of course; most of the components of the ship shared in this process leading to a bad and a heavy airship unchecked by any penalty on overweight.

The last and saddest defect of this organization showed in the flight trials of the R101. No contractual programme had to be fulfilled and so the trials were liable to be modified by any publicity or political whim, and they were so modified. The last two flight trials of the R101 before she was cut in two for the insertion of the extra bay were not conducted on a programme that gave overriding importance to technical matters, as they should have been if the production of a good airship had been the main objective. Instead, she was flown to Hendon to take part in the rehearsal for the RAF display and the flight next day was to take part in the display itself; during that flight she was put into a dive over the display area that was packed with crowds and pulled up steeply at five hundred feet, a manoeuvre that resulted in a small structural breakage. It is difficult for a technician to condone the recklessness of a manoeuvre such as this carried out by an airship on its flight trials, over a crowd of a hundred thousand people.

She did not fly again until the extra bay had been inserted, when she was taken out of the shed for the last time on October 1st, 1930.

The unhappy ship now became the plaything of a politician. A programme of flight trials for R101 had been drawn up by her captain which finished up with 'a flight of 48 hours' duration under adverse weather conditions to windward of base. Ship to be flown for at least 6 hours at continuous full speed through bumpy conditions, and the rest of the flight at cruising speed'. It was agreed by everyone that when R101 had completed that trial satisfactorily the flight to India could be undertaken with no more than a reasonable degree of risk.

What nobody had foreseen, however, was that the first Baron Thomson of Cardington would insist on flying to India in her, and that his political engagements would make it necessary for the ship to start for India before a specific date. The reasons behind this extraordinary conduct of the Secretary of State for Air have never been divulged publicly; he certainly was not in the habit of going for test flights in experimental aircraft and there had been no suggestion that he should fly to Canada in R100. Perhaps he felt that his personal credit was involved in the success of the Cardington ship. He was a Labour politician and clearly believed heart and soul in the efficiency of State enterprise, to a degree that blinded him to all the technical evidence of the shortcomings of R101. It was rumoured at the time that he was designated to be the next Viceroy of India and that he wished to visit his new empire in the new vehicle of Imperial communications that he had had a hand in producing, arriving from the skies in a manner unknown to any previous Viceroy. If that be true it might provide a motive for his conduct, which resulted in the loss of the ship and the death of forty-eight persons, some of them my own close friends.

It may be, too, that our flight to Canada had given a groundless confidence to people who were wholly ignorant of technical matters; perhaps they thought that because one airship had battled through storms, repaired its damage, and flown in tolerable safety to Canada and back another airship of different design could obviously fly equally well to India and back. It must be remembered that every year the non-technical public grows better informed in technical matters, and that such reasoning, which may seem ludicrous now, was by no means uncommon among politicians and civil servants in 1930.

At that time an Imperial Conference, to be attended by representatives of all the Dominions, had been summoned to meet in London. In these days of air travel such conferences seem to happen every few months, but in those days it was unreasonable to expect the Prime Minister of Australia or New Zealand to attend such a conference except at long intervals of years, since his travelling time would occupy two months or more. It was desired to interest the Dominions in airship travel at that conference in order that they might set up bases for the airship services that were envisaged. In the opinion of the Secretary of State for Air the flight of R100 to Canada was not enough. It was necessary, in his view, for R101 to fly to India and back with himself on board before the conference discussed air matters, in order that he might step into the conference room fresh from his rapid trip to India and blazing with publicity, and so carry the Dominion premiers along with him upon a programme of expenditure that would place airship services within the British Commonwealth on a firm basis.

The conference was to assemble in the middle of September 1930 and many other subjects beside airships were to be discussed. Investigating the agenda Lord Thomson decided as early as November 1929 that a suitable time for R101 to fly to India and back would be the end of September 1930, and this date was announced to everyone concerned, with an indication that this date was unalterable because the first Baron Thomson was making his political arrangements on that basis.

Experimental work, however, is not susceptible to such pressures; if a gasbag chafes and leaks or an outer cover splits, no vapourings of a Secretary of State will put it right. To rectify such troubles a designer must be given time to think and to experiment; it does not help for an impatient politician to bedevil the designer by pointing out that the delay is inconveniencing the politician, the great man himself. It is doubtful if such considerations ever entered Lord Thomson's head, for in July 1930 he was minuting:

> So long as R101 is ready to go to India by the last week in September this further delay in getting her altered may pass.
>
> I must insist on the programme for the Indian flight being adhered to, as I have made my plans accordingly.

Perhaps the words of the designer may be recalled again, because it was about that time that he said:

> I suppose it ought to be a great satisfaction, but somehow I feel too tired.

The end of the story was not very far away now. R101 was parted and the new bay was inserted in her middle, with all the huge complications to her various controls and services that such an operation entailed. At the same time two reversing engines were fitted, and the staff at Cardington did all that could be done within the time to rectify the chafing gasbags, the leaking gas valves, and the dubious outer cover. It proved quite impossible to complete the work in time for the ship to fly in September, and it appears that Lord Thomson arranged for the air matters which the Imperial Conference were to discuss to be postponed till October the 20th. A schedule was laid down by Lord Thomson at the end of August by which the ship was to leave for India on October 4th, arrive in Karachi on October 9th, leave Karachi on October 13th, and arrive back in England on October 18th in order that Lord Thomson could step into the conference room as fresh as a daisy on October 20th. All this was to be done in a totally experimental airship that had never flown at full power, was suffering from grave gasbag and cover defects, and had done no trial of any sort in her lengthened form. To the politician it appeared to be a perfectly reasonable proposal. To us, watching helplessly upon the sidelines, and perhaps also to the unfortunate hard-driven men at Cardington, it appeared to be sheer midsummer madness.

By superhuman efforts they got the ship out of the shed and onto the mooring mast on October the 1st. They made a trial flight of sixteen hours on that day and the next; immediately they left the mast the oil cooler of one engine failed so that it was not possible to do a full-power trial. No record of that flight exists, because there was no time to write one; the only reference to it is to be found in one or two personal diaries. Flying conditions were dead calm and so perfect that it was hardly a trial at all, and in these circumstances nothing in the ship gave trouble but the oil cooler.

A final conference was held by Lord Thomson at the Air Ministry on the evening of October 2nd. He wanted to start for India on the following evening but the staff protested that it was necessary for the crew to have some rest. He agreed, and suggested that they start on the next morning. They argued him off that on the grounds that it would entail landing to the mast in Egypt to refuel in the heat of the day, which would be undesirable. An agreement was finally reached to start for India on the evening of Saturday October the 4th. Perhaps the catastrophic nature of his autocracy began to occur to Lord Thomson towards the end of this conference, because he said, 'You must not allow my natural impatience or anxiety to start to influence you in any way. You must use your considered judgement.' Fine words for the record, but finer if they had been said a year before and had been backed by sympathetic understanding of the difficulties of his staff.

Before the conference broke up a member of the Air Council, diffident no doubt because of his inexperience with airships, pointed out that the ship had never done a full-power trial. This interesting point was discussed a little, and it was resolved that the ship ought perhaps to do a full-power trial near home, after leaving Cardington for India. Nothing of the sort was ever done, quite rightly, for there is a time and a place for everything. The time and place for the first full-power trial of R101 was not in bad weather in the middle of the night.

Before an aircraft may fly over foreign territory it must have been granted a certificate of airworthiness by its country of origin. The two university professors had been engaged again to report upon the R101 as lengthened by the addition of the extra bay, and the Air Council had stated that they would be guided by that report in the decision whether or not R101 should be granted a certificate of airworthiness. That report was never received; the two professors were engaged in writing it when they received news of the disaster. So far as they had written, it was dubious in content: they called attention to large changes in the forces in the structure of the ship as compared with previous calculations submitted to them, and complained of the paucity of information on the final condition of the ship. If they had ever finished their report, however, they would probably have approved the issue of a certificate, but before doing so they would probably have demanded further information which might well have spun the matter out for another three months. There is no indication that there was anything very disastrously wrong with the ship within the limited fields that they had been commissioned to examine.

When every safety precaution, including the 48-hour flight trial with its six hours at full power in bumpy weather, had been abandoned, a scrap of paper could not be allowed to hold up the Indian flight. The international agreement on the safety of aircraft, however, had to be complied with, so a certificate of airworthiness was written out in the Air Ministry and handed to the captain of R101 just before the start of the last flight, as soon as the inspectors were satisfied with the physical condition of the ship. It stands to the credit of the French Government that after the disaster on French soil they did not make an issue of this matter; between friends some things are better forgotten.

R101 started from Cardington on her last flight at 6.30 on the evening of Saturday October 4th, 1930, carrying six passengers including Lord Thomson and his valet, and six officials from the Royal Airship Works, four of whom held positions of prime responsibility in the design of the ship.

At the time of the start, the weather forecast was not good, though it was not so bad as to prevent departure. It covered a period to 1am on the following morning, and showed deteriorating conditions with westerly winds of 20 to 30mph over Northern France and better conditions farther south. In view of a falling barometer Scott, who was in charge of flying operations, did what he could to expedite departure, though his anxiety was not so great as to prevent him from wasting twenty minutes in circling over Bedford before setting course for London.

In those days the art of weather forecasting was not so well advanced as it is now, and bad weather was developing more quickly than had been anticipated. At 8.08pm a revised weather forecast was wirelessed to R101, which was then over London. It forecast a wind over Northern France of 40 to 50mph drawing more southerly, that is, becoming more of a head-wind, with much low cloud and rain.

At that time it would have been quite possible for Major Scott to have abandoned the flight and to have returned to the mooring mast at

Cardington to wait for better weather conditions. Bearing in mind that he was in charge of an airship that had never flown in bad weather and which had done virtually no trials at all since the major operation of lengthening her to increase her lift, it now appears reckless that be should have pressed on, in view of this forecast. It is, however, very easy to be wise after the event, and especially twenty-four years after. In those years, standards of safety in the air have undergone great changes. A pilot who turns back and lands because he considers it dangerous to go on is likely to receive praise and advancement in his profession nowadays, but that was by no means the mental atmosphere in 1930. In those days a pilot was expected to be brave and resolute, a daredevil who was not afraid to take risks. Moreover, the Secretary of State for Air, Lord Thomson of Cardington himself, was on board, and to turn back would destroy the whole of his political programme. One imagines that this weather forecast must have been discussed quietly in a corner, with long faces, but the ship went on.

With the increasing component of head wind, R101 crossed the Channel slowly, somewhat hampered by the fact that one engine went out of action for a couple of hours and was not got going again till shortly before she reached the coast of France at about 11pm. To battle against the wind, she then cruised on all five engines at a speed of 54 knots, 62mph, which was about her maximum cruising speed. It is doubtful if the ship had ever before been flown at so high a speed as that, because initially she had carried one engine for astern use only, and on her one trial flight before she left for India one engine had gone out of action soon after the start. She was, in fact, doing her full-power trial in exceptionally bad weather with low cloud and driving rain, in pitch darkness in the middle of the night, over a foreign country.

By two o'clock in the morning, after flying for about seven and a half hours, she had got no farther than Beauvais, about 220 miles from Cardington. Nothing untoward had happened up till then. In the bad weather she was rolling and pitching a good deal and she was making slow progress, but watch was changed normally at two o'clock, which would not have happened if there had been any sense of emergency. She was then flying about a thousand feet above the ground.

At about ten minutes past two the ship got into a long and rather steep dive, which was sufficiently steep to throw the engineers attending to the engines off their balance. She was brought out of this dive on to an even keel for a few moments, but then dived again and hit the ground, not very hard. Immediately she burst into flames and was totally consumed in a few seconds. The cause of the fire was probably due to the ignition of a mixture of air and of the gas escaping from the damaged gasbags by a spark from a broken electrical circuit.

Of the fifty-four persons on board her, only six survived, four of whom were engineers in the power cars. All the officers of the ship, and all the officials, and all the passengers perished in the fire, including Lord Thomson.

A public inquiry was held to ascertain the cause of the disaster. Nobody from our organization was invited to give evidence or to make any suggestion out of our experience: the bitterness of competition lasted after death. It is doubtful, however, if we could have added very much. The conclusions reached were almost certainly correct, though of necessity they were based on surmise to a large extent. If a technical opinion had been taken from us it could hardly have helped being an unkind one, for we had said derogatory things about the competence of the government staff and we could hardly have gone back on those opinions at the inquiry. I think the decision to take no evidence from us was right.

The conclusion reached was that the disaster had been caused by a large rent suddenly occurring in one of the most forward gasbags of the ship. A plot of the ship's course assuming that such a thing had happened coincided very closely with the reported dives of the ship just before the accident. As to what had caused the gasbag failure, the Court suggested that a large outer cover failure had occurred on top of the ship in a forward region, thus exposing the gasbags to the violence of the airflow at 54 knots. Small rents were probably already present in these gasbags due to chafing, and these may well have joined up rapidly to an enormous tear. To my mind this is certainly the truth of it.

CHAPTER SEVEN

A MAN'S OWN experiences determine his opinions, of necessity. I was thirty-one years old at the time of the R101 disaster, and my first close contact with senior civil servants and politicians at work was in the field of airships, where I watched them produce disaster. That experience still colours much of my thinking. I am very willing to recognize the good in many men of these two classes, but a politician or a civil servant is still to me an arrogant fool till he is proved otherwise.

I had little to do with civil servants of high rank in the years following the R101 disaster, and I had little leisure for some years to think back and analyse the causes of that tragedy. I considered at the time that the disaster was caused by the actions of the men at Cardington; I do not think that now. The men at Cardington were honest, hardworking men doing their best in a job that was rather too big for them. The first-class brains in the Air Ministry, the high executive civil servants at the top, should have been able to assess the position correctly and take action that would have avoided the disaster. They had plenty of evidence, extending over several years.

Either these men at the Air Ministry were extraordinarily stupid, which I do not believe, or they appreciated that quite abnormal and unjustifiable risks were being taken with R101. If the latter be true, then they failed to speak up against Lord Thomson because they were afraid. If just one of them had stood up at the conference table when the issue of the certificate of airworthiness was under discussion, and had said – 'This thing is wrong, and I will be no party to it. I'm sorry, gentlemen, but if you do this, I'm resigning' – if that had been said then or on any one of a dozen previous opportunities, the disaster would almost certainly have been averted. It was not said, because the men in question put their jobs before their duty.

Perhaps it is easy for an engineer to write like this, for he can get another job without much difficulty in some other branch of engineering; perhaps it is even easier for an author. That should not blind us to the facts, however, that in this case a number of high civil servants shirked their duty to preserve their jobs. It may be that under modern conditions of life in England it is unfair to expect a man who has spent his life in government service and is unfitted for any other occupation to place his duty to the State before his job. But if that be so, it should be clearly realized that in certain circumstances these high civil servants will not do their duty, though all the honours in the book be showered on them by the Crown.

Ten years after these events when I was in the Navy I was drafted to a technical department of the Admiralty which was staffed by over a hundred temporary officers of the Royal Naval Volunteer Reserve. As civilians in uniform we found the Admiralty system to be better adapted to conserving money in peacetime than to getting quick production in time of war. We found in many instances that the only way to get things done quickly was to short-circuit the system, getting verbal authority by telephone conversations with the various departments affected and letting the paperwork tag along three weeks later. These methods required senior officers of the regular navy to give verbal decisions which might involve expenditures of thousands of pounds without any paper cover, and naturally made us very unpopular. These naval officers were as brave as lions, and would have risked their lives in a destroyer torpedo attack without any second thought, but to be asked to risk their jobs on a verbal decision involving public money often seemed to them unfair.

Now and again, we would find some cheerful young commander or captain who was not affected by these scruples, who was as brave in the office as he was at sea. Commenting on such a regular officer and on his way of doing business we would say, 'He's a good one. I bet he's got private means.' Invariably investigation proved that we were right. The officers who were brave in the Admiralty were the officers who had an independent income, who could afford to resign from the Navy if necessary without bringing financial disaster to their wives and children. It started as a joke with us to say that a brave officer in the office probably had private means, and then it got beyond a joke and turned into an axiom. These were the men who could afford to shoulder personal responsibility in the Admiralty, who could afford to do their duty to the Navy in the highest sense.

Such men invariably gravitate towards the top of any government service that they happen to be in because of their carefree acceptance of

101

responsibility. They serve as a leaven and as an example to their less fortunate fellows; they set the tone of the whole office by their high standards of duty. I think this is an aspect of inherited incomes which deserves greater attention than it has had up till now. If the effect of excessive taxation and death duties in a country is to make all high officials dependent on their pay and pensions, then the standard of administration will decline and that country will get into greater difficulties than ever. Conversely, in a wealthy country with relatively low taxation and much inherited income a proportion of the high officials will be independent of their job, and the standard of administration will probably be high.

I do not know the financial condition of the high officials in the Air Ministry at the time of the R101 disaster. I suspect, however, that an investigation would reveal that it was England's bad luck that at that time none of them had any substantial private means. At rock bottom, that to me is probably the fundamental cause of the tragedy.

The disaster to R101 marked the end of all airship endeavour in England. At the time it seemed a cowardly decision to abandon airships altogether because of one disaster, even though the Secretary of State for Air himself had perished in it. Looking back over the years, the decision to abandon airship development was right, though whether it was taken for the right reasons I rather doubt.

At the end of 1930 the full impact of the depression in the United States was beginning to be felt in England, and a reduction in government expenditure was becoming essential. I think this was the main reason for abandoning the programme; it was one of the frills of government expenditure which so far had not turned out too well, and which it was reasonable to prune.

In fact, the decision was a right one because the performance of the aeroplane was to increase so greatly in the next few years. At the time it did not seem possible that the cruising speed of an airship could ever much exceed eighty miles an hour, for various technical reasons. Developments of the aeroplane were to make this speed seem trivial, but I doubt if these developments were in sight at the end of 1930. It was not till 1933 that the Douglas DC1 astonished the aeronautical world with its revolutionary design based on the new controllable propeller, the retractable undercarriage, and the new conception of the use of flaps. I doubt if any serious technician forecast the commercial use of aeroplanes to cross the Atlantic till that machine appeared, and in fact it was not till about 1945 that fare-paying passengers were flown in aeroplanes across the Atlantic on a scheduled service. We could have made a start with airships by about 1934, but it would have been a dead-end venture, for the aeroplane would have put us out of business in a few years.

At the end of 1930, therefore, the airship staff at Howden was dispersed and we all got the sack. I made an attempt to sell ourselves as a design unit of a dozen men to a well known American concern, without success: airship experience was at a discount in those days. It was a troublesome time for me to be out of a job, because I had got myself engaged to be married during the summer while I was somewhat tied up with other occupations of less importance. Frances Heaton was a young doctor at that time on the staff of the York Hospital, and I must say she took the loss of my job remarkably well, as she has taken all the succeeding crises in our lives.

A senior technician in an industry that suddenly evaporates to nothing finds himself in an unusual position. Although I was still a young man I had become a big frog in a little puddle, too big a frog to be easily absorbed back into the aeroplane industry as it was in those days. After the responsibilities that I had been carrying I should not have relished the return to a drawing office on half the salary I had been earning; I had grown too accustomed to making quick decisions and seeing them carried out. Moreover, I had very definite ideas about the design of aeroplanes. My piloting experience was meagre in hours of flying time for it had all been carried out at my own expense, but it included the experience of flying practically every type of small personal aircraft in use in England at that date; no new type ever came to Sherburn-in-Elmet aerodrome but I had a go on it if it was humanly possible to do so.

In these circumstances I decided that before seeking another job I would try my hand at starting a small aeroplane manufacturing company of my own. I was well placed to do this, in some ways. When Wallis went to Vickers Aviation to work on the design of geodetic aeroplanes we had attracted a very senior designer from de Havillands, Mr Hessell Tiltman, to take charge of the drawing-office and act as chief designer. He knew little of airships when he came to us early in 1930 but he was a great artist on the drawing board; the aeroplanes produced to his designs were both beautiful and efficient. I went into conference with Tiltman and found that he was game to try it with me. We had a nucleus of drawing office staff and foremen with good aeroplane experience who had confidence in us and who wanted to go on working with us; as a technical unit to build aeroplanes we had a good deal on our side. The thing we hadn't got was any money.

In those days the capital required to start an aeroplane manufacturing company was not large, judged by modern standards. In 1930 the demand for small two- and three-seater aeroplanes for personal and club flying was brisk all over the world. These units were small in value, and since wooden construction was still the rule no very great numbers had to be produced to manufacture at a profit; the cost of jigs and tools for a given design was small by modern standards. A capital of thirty thousand pounds would have been reasonable for such a business in those days and would have justified a start with a good prospect of success, while fifty thousand pounds might well have made the venture fairly safe, given good management and technical competence. As the swift years went by the capital required for profitable operation doubled and redoubled every year as aeroplanes grew larger and as wooden aircraft ceased to sell and had to be replaced by metal construction, but in 1930 forty thousand pounds seemed reasonable capital for such an enterprise.

Our first job, therefore, was to consider the design of a small two- or three-seater aeroplane that would represent an advance on anything then flying or that we had heard projected. With Tiltman's design genius and my own knowledge we were well fitted to draw up a good specification and to produce an attractive drawing; the design that we produced was never built, though if it had been I would say that it would be flying still. It was a very attractive little high-wing monoplane with a de Havilland Gipsy motor, seating the pilot in front of a two-seater side-by-side cockpit for passengers, a novel arrangement that permitted a most versatile range of uses for the machine. That drawing, and our own reputation, were the basis upon which we had to seek forty thousand pounds of risk capital.

Much has been written in recent years about the provision of risk capital for industry, but few of the authors who pronounce so learnedly upon this subject have ever had the job of looking for the stuff. Men who start businesses upon a shoestring and battle through to success are frequently reluctant to recall and publicize their early disappointments and rebuffs, or if they had the will they may not have the knack of writing. There seems to be a tendency in England nowadays to consider that risk capital for new companies can be conjured up by civil servants and economists waving a sort of magic wand over the bankers. In my experience nothing could be farther from the truth. Risk capital is gambling money such as might be staked upon a horse race, and if I tell the story now of how we started Airspeed Ltd. it is in the hope that other young men starting other businesses may benefit from our perplexities and heartbreaks.

At that time, in the autumn of 1930, I was living permanently in the St Leonards Club in York, a pleasant little club opposite the theatre which was frequented by the leading business and professional men in the city. One of the leading members was a Mr A E Hewitt. Hewitt was a very able commercial solicitor with a great sense of humour, a wise counsellor and a firm friend in every adversity. He would have moved to London to a wider sphere of action if a troublesome ailment had not forced him to restrict his activities; as it was, he was a director of a number of local companies where his knowledge of commercial law and his sane judgement made his advice of value.

Somewhat diffidently, I took my idea for a new company to Hewitt and found, rather to my own surprise, that he took the proposition quite seriously. It must be remembered that in those days aviation was booming, but up till that time there had not been very many investment opportunities in it. R100 had been built within twenty miles of York and was generally considered to have been a great success, so that we started off with a good local reputation. The depression in America had not affected England very much at the time of our first talks and we were not to know how difficult it would become to find capital for a new enterprise in the succeeding months and years. At that time, in Hewitt's view, it seemed a fairly easy matter to find forty thousand pounds of risk capital for such a venture as the one that we proposed.

Hewitt had a brother-in-law in the Royal Air Force who was the youngest Group Captain in the service and who was to rise to high command in the second war. He sent me down to Wittering, where this young man was in command of the Central Flying School, and he sent me there for two reasons. In the first place, no doubt, he wanted an assurance from his knowledgeable relative that we were people of good repute in the aircraft industry and that our proposals were technically sound. In the second place, he knew that the young Group Captain was still uncertain of his future in the Royal Air Force, and he thought shrewdly that his relative might well appreciate the chance of an investment at the inception of a new aircraft company with a view to a seat upon the Board on his retirement from the service. From our point of view, of course, no director could have been more welcome than this young senior officer with such exceptional knowledge of the requirements of the Royal Air Force.

At Wittering I succeeded in satisfying this very keen critic that our proposals were sound and that we were capable of doing what we set out to do. It was agreed that if the company came into being Hewitt would have a seat upon the Board and would hold it for his relative until he had decided whether he wanted to retire from the Royal Air Force or not.

This all seemed very satisfactory, for in view of our ignorance of company affairs Hewitt would add great strength to the venture.

In the meantime Tiltman had made contact with Sir Alan Cobham. We were both known to Cobham, but he knew Tiltman better and had, quite rightly, the highest opinion of his design ability. Sir Alan was at a transition point of his career in 1930. His energy and his adventurous spirit had enabled him to carry out a number of pioneering flights about the world during the years after the war, which had brought him a great reputation and a knighthood but not much else. Unwilling to remain merely a pilot all his life, he was at that time considering various business ventures, one of which was to engage the greater part of his attention in the next few years. That was his very successful aerial circus, National Aviation Day Ltd., which was to have considerable impact upon our affairs. A toe in the manufacturing side of the industry was not an unwelcome idea to Cobham, and after a meeting with Hewitt he accepted the idea of an investment and a seat upon the Board of the infant company.

The next step was to produce the first of a series of draft prospectuses, and in this I was, of course, coached by Hewitt. A prospectus is a full statement of the affairs of the proposed company, with details of the previous careers of the directors, details of the auditors, the bankers, and solicitors, an account of why the company is being formed, what it proposes to do, and what profits it can reasonably expect to make. It ends up with an invitation to the public to subscribe for whatever class of shares is being offered, and discloses any share dealings or offers to other persons, especially to the directors. It is issued in the name of the directors, who certify that it is a full and complete statement of the company's affairs.

The important point about a prospectus is that it has to be an honest document. The directors of a private or public limited company have little to fear if the enterprise fails, provided they have been honest and truthful and have done their best; their personal liability in such a case, I think, is limited to about ten pounds. If there has been dishonesty or deceit, then the managing director, or the whole Board if it can be shown that they have been involved, may well go to prison for a considerable number of years. I shall have occasion to return to this point later on.

With Cobham and Hewitt energetically behind us, the venture was now beginning to achieve some momentum. It is necessary for those who wish to start a new company to have *some* money of their own, if only to pay the preliminary expenses; I had about a thousand pounds and Tiltman had rather less. Greatly daring, we now took an office at a rent of fifteen shillings a week in a building near the market in York, and here Tiltman set up a drawing board and a desk and commenced the design of the small monoplane. A name had to be given to the new company, of course; we considered a dozen alternatives and finally decided upon Airspeed Ltd. as being short, euphonious, and indicative of what we wanted to do.

One of the first men that I approached to take an investment interest in Airspeed Ltd. was Lord Grimthorpe. I could not have approached a better man. At that time Lord Grimthorpe was a relatively young man and a large landowner in the East Riding of Yorkshire; he was Master of the local hounds and hunted twice a week in season; he was a keen performer on the Cresta Run, a pilot and the owner of a private aeroplane, and chairman of a large firm of motorcar agents in London. It is fashionable today to disparage the part that the titled aristocracy can play in industry; I can only say that my experience is otherwise. Lord Grimthorpe became the first chairman of Airspeed Ltd. and supported the company throughout its early financial difficulties to an extent which would have been a heavy burden to the wealthiest of men. Without his support initially I do not think the company could have started; without his continuous financial support in the years that followed it would certainly have come to grief.

Years later I was told by one of his close friends why he did this. At a time about a year after the company began operations when he was becoming very deeply involved, his friend asked him why he did not cut his loss and get out of so unprofitable a speculation. His reply was that the business interested him and he thought it would do well in the end. As regards the money side of it, he said that he realized the likelihood that he might lose the whole of his investment. The money was, however, being wholly spent in wages in his district of Yorkshire, where there was then a great deal of unemployment. In times of depression he felt it to be his duty to hazard his money in an effort to create employment in his part of the country; if finally the money was lost he would take satisfaction from the fact that through his agency nearly a hundred working men had had employment through the years of the depression.

From what I have heard of the preliminary struggles of small businesses during the early years of the present century I do not think that Lord Grimthorpe was exceptional in the altruistic view he took of his investment in our company. I think his conduct could be paralleled in many other little companies with many other wealthy chairmen. I have no doubt that the inheritance of great fortunes has led in the past to much money being spent frivolously and foolishly and in a way which irritates less fortunate men, but it has also led to much money being spent generously and wisely for the benefit of the same men. If Lord Grimthorpe was one of a long line of wealthy men who helped pre-war British industry to come into being he was also one of the last, because death duties and high taxation have now so reduced the resources of these people that they can no longer function as they used to.

When a small company is initiated and commences operations on risk capital, capital which may well all be lost if the venture proves unsuccessful, very special qualities are demanded of the chairman. He must be one with the investors, which means that he himself must hold a considerable block of shares in the company. This money he must personally be prepared to lose if things go badly, which means that he must himself be of a speculative turn of mind. He must be bold and adventurous and capable of quick decisions in matters of policy, because at that stage a policy of caution may be fatal. I can imagine no worse chairman for a company in its difficult early days than a banker.

The qualities that I have outlined are precisely those which are developed by leisured people in the hunting field and on the Cresta Run, who in between these activities breed racehorses and bet on them. Other sports, such as amateur yacht racing, produce the same qualities no doubt, but all of them demand a fairly leisured life. I do not know of any working career that produces these qualities: they are not found developed to the same extent in politicians or in civil servants or in those who work on salary for any boss. I think that by excessive taxation in the higher brackets the British people have destroyed a class of chairmen for small companies without whom much industry in Britain could hardly have come into being, and without whom fresh industry in England is unlikely to be initiated again. A man's views, I say again, are coloured by his own experience. I shall have something to say about the source of risk capital a little later on, but here and now I say that if the risk capital were available it would be difficult in modern conditions in England to find chairmen with the qualities needed to administer it to the best advantage.

The Board of Directors of Airspeed Ltd. was now taking shape: in the draft prospectus of this time the tentative board consisted of Lord Grimthorpe, Sir Alan Cobham, Hewitt, Tiltman, and myself. In Yorkshire circles that was a strong team, and in ordinary times there would have been little difficulty in finding money to back it. Times were not ordinary, however. The depression in America had been going for well over a year and its repercussions in England were serious:

unemployment was mounting daily, trade was falling, and everywhere investors were reducing their commitments, pulling in their horns.

I now learned that there is only one way in which to find risk capital, and that is to go round asking people to invest. There is no royal road to risk capital, no tap that can be turned on by any bank, no agent who will serve a useful purpose. The man who believes in the company and wants to see it started must take the draft prospectus in his hand and go around to people that he thinks have money, generally total strangers and tough guys in business matters, and try to talk them into putting money into the new company. In 1931 one had to talk quite hard.

I had a friend in York whose unhappy business was to try to sell Rolls-Royce motor cars in that time of depression; I think he had a worse job than I had, but not much. The rebuffs that we both got were of much the same quality. My own routine was to go as inexpensively as possible to some city in the north of England, say Newcastle or Leeds, and go into conference with a local stockbroker, who would give me names and details of wealthy people in the district who would be likely to invest in such a company as ours. The depression was hardly realized in England at that time even by the stockbrokers; it was something new that had developed after eighty years of industrial prosperity and free investment. It was regarded as something very temporary that would quickly pass; if things were difficult today, in three months' time investment would be flowing easily again.

Sometimes the stockbroker would make an appointment for me to see the client; at other times he would say cautiously that perhaps I had better approach him myself. This meant an uphill telephone conversation with a worried, short-tempered man to try to induce him to see me in order that I might sell him something that he didn't want to buy. There was nobody to teach me this part of the job, and I soon learned by experience to write off prospects of this sort. It was very soon apparent that if Airspeed Ltd. got started at all it would start with tenuous capital, which meant that the risk of the investment would be much increased. Unless the investors could afford to lose their money if the venture failed, unless they were in the mood to risk their money on the chance of big profits if the venture should succeed, it would be better not to get them into it even though this should mean that Airspeed Ltd. would never start. Even in those days I sensed the intolerable situation that would be created for the management if shareholders were induced to subscribe on any pretence that the venture was a safe one. What we wanted was a crowd of cheerful gamblers as our shareholders.

I found a considerable number of people of this type in Yorkshire and the north of England. These men would give me an attentive and a sympathetic hearing: they would show evident interest, take a copy of my draft prospectus to read in detail, and ask for a copy of the final prospectus and invitation to subscribe when the time came. I do not think that one of them ever took up shares. They would have been subscribers, no doubt, in times of normal prosperity; no doubt they were in secret difficulties themselves due to the depression, which was novel to them and which they hardly comprehended. They probably anticipated, as we all did, that in a month or two things would improve; in that case they would have been glad to take up shares in the new venture. However, the improvement didn't come.

This trying, unremunerative work went on for two or three months during the winter of 1930-31, a period of travelling to bleak, grey cities, of waiting for telephone calls in very cheap hotels, of frustrations and disappointments. I was lucky in having the hobby of writing to turn to in the evenings, to take my mind off the troubles of the day. I was living, as I have said, in the St Leonards Club in York, and in that club there were one or two restless men whose minds were turned back to the glamour of the war, such as are found in many men's clubs all the world over. The novel that I began to write was *Lonely Road*.

At the conclusion of this difficult time we arrived at the position when we had a number of potential subscribers for shares in the new company, and we had covered the area within a hundred miles of York as well as we were able. We had firm promises from members of the Board totalling about four thousand pounds. This situation could not be described as rosy, but having got so far there seemed nothing to be done but to issue the final prospectus and invitations to subscribe, and see what happened.

An unpleasant and illuminating little incident marred the final drafting of the document. We had discussed the company with the manager of one of the banks known as the Big Five, and had received his consent to the use of his bank's name as the company's bankers. We now received a letter from the bank asking for a fee of a hundred guineas for the use of their name on the prospectus. Hewitt was furious, for a hundred guineas looked like being quite an appreciable percentage of the capital that we were likely to raise. The manager said he had no option – 'it was always done'. Hewitt approached another bank of the Big Five, who waived all claim to a prospectus fee, and we transferred the account. We hadn't enough money to permit the rats to get at it like that. That was over twenty years ago, but still whenever I read an urbane statement by a banker about the assistance that banks give to industry it raises a wry smile.

Accordingly we issued the final and formal prospectus for subscription. I forget how many days our potential shareholders were given in which to subscribe their money; as they didn't do it the point is only of an academic importance. Probably it was a fortnight, in which we were all working like beavers; I myself was engaged in an abortive negotiation with the city of Hull to set up our industry upon their aerodrome if a reasonable subscription of capital were to be forthcoming from their district. As the days went on it became apparent that our issue was to be a failure, and the only bright spot in a grey scene was the arrival of Tom Laing.

Tom Laing was a man of about forty-five, a burly cheerful individual who limped heavily upon a stick, the result of an aircraft crash. He was the son of a Sunderland shipbuilder. In his youth he had been to Oxford, had served a three years' apprenticeship with Metropolitan Vickers in an engineering shop, and had inherited ten thousand pounds. He told me once that such an inheritance was the worst thing in the world for any young man, for the income was sufficient in those days to relieve a bachelor from the necessity of working though insufficient for a married man. In the First World War he served in the Army Service Corps and in the Royal Flying Corps, where he rose to the rank of captain, flying Bristol Fighters. After that war he went to Canada with his brother, fruit farmed for a time, and finally started up a passenger service of Chris Craft speedboats running from end to end of Lake Okanagan. That finished his money.

When a wealthy man comes to the end of his patrimony he shows the world what he is made of. Tom Laing 'jumped the border' into the United States riding the buffers of a freight train, and set out to look for work. He was a powerful and self-reliant man, and he became the chargehand of a platelaying gang on the Santa Fe railroad. He held the job of strawboss for two years, became a signalman for a short time, refused promotion into the railroad office, and left to go back to aviation barnstorming as the pilot of a joyride Curtiss JN4. When winter brought that to an end he got a job as a chargehand in the Ford Aircraft factory at Detroit, installing the wing engines into Ford Trimotors. He left that next year to go back to flying, this time as an instructor. He was crashed by a woman pupil in a Fleet trainer and suffered a crushed foot, so that he walked heavily upon a stick for the remainder of his life. When he came out of hospital he went home to his mother in Scotland, and when he heard about Airspeed Ltd. he came to see us. His proposal was that his mother would invest a thousand pounds in the company and he would work for us as works manager on a salary of three hundred a year, about the wage of a skilled woodworker or fitter in those days.

His proposal raised an important point of principle. Most industrialists would agree that it is thoroughly bad practice to sell jobs for capital. My experience has led me to believe, however, that this purist doctrine may need a good deal of qualification in the case of a hazardous, new venture. A small, struggling company cannot engage a first-class staff in any case; it cannot pay first-class salaries and good men will not leave good jobs to come to a company which may be in liquidation in six months. Tom Laing had no experience of works management but he had all the basic qualifications for a good works manager; at the salary that we could afford to pay he was probably as good a man as we could hope to get. He was enthusiastic over the qualities of our design and for the general prospects of the venture. We took him on as our first employee, and he served the company loyally and well till his death in its service seventeen years later. Without the untiring energy and smiling confidence of this man the company could hardly have got through its early production difficulties. Without the financial assistance given by his mother as the years went on from her quite slender resources, in shares, debentures, bank guarantees, and second debentures, the company might well have failed to battle through to maturity.

As time went on we were to depart from the purist principle quite widely. In those years of depression there were a number of young men with some experience of aeroplanes and with some capital at their disposal who were prepared to invest in the company and come and work for us upon a very low salary or, in one case, on no salary at all. There were so many of them that we could afford to pick and choose, and I can remember rejecting at least two applicants with substantial capital to invest because they would be obviously incompetent and useless to us. In the end there were to be no less than nine shareholders working whole time in the company, all in it financially up to the neck, many of us individually facing ruin if the venture failed. In its first three years, in fact, the company was principally financed by Lord Grimthorpe and by shareholders working whole time in the company on salaries that were frequently less than those of the men working on the bench.

The company held its first board meeting at the end of April 1931. There were practically no subscribers for shares to report; the issue of the prospectus had been a complete fiasco. Apart from those of us who were intimately concerned with the venture, I do not think that five hundred shares were applied for. I think we had stated in the prospectus that we would not proceed unless we had applications for fifteen thousand pounds' worth of share capital; on that prospectus we could not proceed. The issue was a total failure.

This ought to have produced a state of gloom at our first board meeting. I can only remember a buoyant and a cheerful atmosphere. We had firm promises amongst ourselves for about five thousand pounds, and we set about considering what we could do with that.

I hope I did not talk my co-directors into going on; I do not think I did. So far as I remember, it was Sir Alan Cobham who declared that this venture was too good a thing to let drop, who proclaimed his faith in us in a most tangible manner. At that time he was commencing a series of flying displays touring all the towns and cities of the British Isles, an organization which went by the name of National Aviation Day Ltd.; those who have read my novel *Round the Bend* will have found a description of this venture in the first pages of the book. Sir Alan told the Board that be would need two large, ten-passenger aircraft for National Aviation Day specially designed for flying out of fields with a very short take-off run. If the Board decided to proceed with Airspeed Ltd. he was prepared to order those two aircraft from us. Five thousand pounds would be about the price of each aircraft and our five thousand pounds of capital would be insufficient to set up a works and manufacture them. Nevertheless, he was prepared to place that order with us; he was confident that we could find more capital as soon as we had something to show.

This was a bold and generous proposal. I think everybody felt that if Sir Alan Cobham was prepared to speculate on us to that extent it would be cowardly to draw back, and it must be remembered that the money promised was essentially gambling money. It was a laughing, cheerful roomful of punters in that solicitor's office in York who went on to consider the next move.

Clearly, five thousand pounds wasn't going to last us very long. It might well all be gone within a year, perhaps within six months – in any case long before Sir Alan's aircraft could be built and delivered. Moreover, Sir Alan wanted two or three months to arrange his finances before he could order the machines formally or pay any deposit on them. Yet quick action to produce something that would fly was imperative, because until the new company got an aircraft of some sort into the air there was little basis upon which to seek more capital.

At that time the sport of soaring in motorless gliders or sailplanes was attracting a good deal of attention in England. The German exploits in this field under the restrictions of the Treaty of Versailles had shown that quite long flights could be made without a motor by pilots with sufficient skill, and a number of gliding clubs had been formed in England in the last year to try to emulate the German achievements. No British manufacturer, however, had yet marketed a high performance sailplane. It seemed to us that a sailplane would be something that we could get into the air quickly and cheaply while Sir Alan's order was maturing. It would give Tiltman the opportunity to engage a nucleus of two or three draughtsmen for the design work so that he would have laid the foundations of a drawing office before the design work for Sir Alan's aircraft came along. It would give us an opportunity to organize the workshop in a tiny way before Sir Alan's machines had to be built. It would give us a machine which we could get into the air within three months or so before our capital ran out. We could reasonably hope to capture all the British gliding records that we cared to go for with the sailplane, and with that minute achievement we could probably get in more capital. Moreover, it seemed reasonable to hope that we might sell a few of the sailplanes to the gliding clubs.

Accordingly at that first board meeting we amended the prospectus to say that we would proceed upon a minimum subscription of five thousand pounds, and sent out letters to our few applicants for shares to ask if they would play upon that basis. I must have had this proposal all cut and dried before the board meeting, because at the same meeting we resolved to rent one half of an empty bus garage in Piccadilly, near the centre of the city of York. This building had a floor area of about six thousand square feet, and was to be the works of the company for the first two years. The first board meeting then dispersed, having laughingly refused to accept defeat, and Airspeed Ltd. started operations upon a capital of £5,195 and a tentative order for £10,000 worth of aircraft. Tiltman and I were appointed joint managing directors, and Laing's appointment as works manager was confirmed.

There was no time to be lost, for our days were numbered till the capital ran out. We rented a larger office for a drawing office and Tiltman got in one or two draughtsmen. It was to be a month or so before we could get possession of the bus garage, so we started one woodworker on components of the sailplane in a local joiner's shop. Within ten days we had rented a small sales room on a weekly basis and set up woodworkers' benches in it, and in these tiny premises the parts for a batch of three sailplanes went into production. In that time of depression it was not very difficult to get aircraft woodworkers and by the time we moved into the bus garage we had six or seven men working on the bench. These woodworkers, accustomed as they were to man-sized factories, regarded Airspeed Ltd. as a joke. As a class, however, woodworkers are good-tempered and tolerant men in any factory, no doubt because of the quality of the material they work with. Metal workers are normally more nervy and difficult, and panel beaters are apt to be bad-tempered and hostile to the management, because the incessant clamour of their work and the unsympathetic material that they handle all day fray the nerves. Our woodworkers became infected with a little of our enthusiasm and, as time went on and they found that their employment continued, the company, though still a joke to them, became a good joke.

We typed all our own letters, of course, on our own machines, for we had no money for a typist. When we moved into the bus garage we built a little office about eight feet square and a store of about the same size next to it, and in the office Laing and I had our desks while Tiltman worked in his drawing office half a mile away. Construction of the first glider was well advanced by the middle of July, and about that time Cobham gave us his firm order for the two joyriding aeroplanes.

These were to be quite large aircraft for that time. They were to carry a pilot and ten passengers in and out of small fields. Speed was immaterial and the endurance in the air could be two or three hours only, but economy in operation was important and it was essential that each passenger should have a good view. Tiltman produced a biplane design for this machine, which we christened the Ferry, with three de Havilland Gipsy engines, which fulfilled all the requirements. The Ferry had a wingspan of 55 feet and an all-up weight of about 6,000lbs; it had a cruising speed of about 85mph. It had a remarkably short run to take off. It had, in fact, all the performance characteristics of the Gipsy Moth aircraft of the time, but it carried ten passengers. In those days there seemed to be a definite market for a slow, cheaply operated aircraft carrying a big payload because in many parts of the world the aeroplane competes with very slow land transport, with ships or even with pack horses. Not all aircraft need to be fast; cheapness in operation may be more important. With the introduction of metal construction, however, aeroplanes became so much more costly that speed became more important again, in order that the machine might earn its depreciation by running more journeys in a given time.

I think the first sailplane must have flown in August 1931. We had built a trailer to convey it in, in the dismantled state, and we had bought a very old Buick car for £25 to tow this trailer. We took the machine from York to Sherburn-in-Elmet aerodrome for its initial trials, and there we towed it up with the car and a long length of steel cable, myself at the controls. I got about a minute's flight out of it on each of two launches after casting off the tow; it seemed to handle like any other aeroplane upon the glide, bearing in mind the large wingspan, which was 50 feet. It was stable, and the sinking speed seemed to be about three feet a second.

It was essential to get publicity and results with this machine, because our capital was fast running out. I had myself no experience of soaring flight nor had Laing; we therefore had to go outside the company for a pilot. There was a young German glider pilot in England at that time, called Magersuppe, who had come over to demonstrate soaring flight at the expense of one or two clubs. I got in touch with him, and he came up to Yorkshire with a German friend, Haak, that he called his secretary.

Magersuppe, I suppose, was about twenty-one years old and Haak about eighteen, but they were both experienced soaring pilots. I am ashamed to record how little I paid them, and the financial straits that they ultimately got into. My wife and I used to put them up in our flat sometimes and they had a keen nose for Youth Hostels, where they stayed whenever possible. Their angle on the business was a simple one: they wanted to emigrate from Germany, where there was much unemployment at that time. They were good, clean, hardworking lads who spoke excellent English, ready to turn their hand to any manual labour. There was, however, still prejudice against Germans after the First World War and most countries at that time had their own unemployment problem. They had attempted to emigrate to practically every country in the world, and had met rebuffs and frustration in each case. Their forlorn hope now was that they could stay in England and become British citizens by virtue of their skill in soaring flight. When finally I could employ them no longer even on the pittance that I paid they ran out of money and got into debt, and finally they were picked up by the police and deported back to Germany to join the other six million unemployed in their own country. Years afterwards, when I was listening to the bombers overhead during the London blitz, I used to wonder which of them was Magersuppe, and I would wish him luck and think it served us bloody well right. He might have been flying for us.

Magersuppe liked the Tern, as we now called the sailplane. He had his own method of checking the structural strength of the machine, which was new to us in 1931; he got a couple of men to waggle the wing tips up and down and timed the natural frequency with a stopwatch. In the air he was a careful and a knowledgeable pilot. We had some difficulty at first in finding a suitable soaring site, the requirements being for a steep slope facing to the west to give good upcurrents in the prevailing wind. We tried Sutton Bank on the edge of the moors about twenty miles north of York but found it difficult. Then we found a site at a place called Ingleby Greenhow in the Cleveland Hills, and here, soaring above the heather-covered moors, Magersuppe had no difficulty in capturing the British gliding records for altitude and distance. It made no difference to these records that the pilot was a German.

I forget what these records were; they were very modest and were soon to be broken as the sport of soaring flight developed in England. I think the altitude record was gained by a flight about two thousand feet above the launching point as measured on a recording barograph carried in the machine, and the distance record I think was gained by landing about twelve miles from the launching point.

That finished our trials with the Tern, and we did no more with sailplanes. The machine had served its purpose and had proved that we could build something quickly that would fly well. I do not think that any of us expected to make much money out of building sailplanes; in fact the three machines were a dead loss. We assembled and sold the first two and ultimately we sold off the components of the third. Gliding clubs in those days were mostly composed of people with very little money, and the market for an advanced machine that necessarily cost about £250 was trivial. I do not think it was until fifteen years later, after the last war, that sailplanes in this price class began to sell in any numbers.

The result of the Tern flights, however, was that shareholders started to appear. A trickle of outside applications for a few shares each began to come in and were eagerly grabbed, and one of a number of internal shareholders appeared with a proposal to take up a substantial number of shares with a job in the company. I am not going to detail the names of these gentlemen, who formed a very loyal and, on the whole, a very competent team; Tom Laing was the first, and he may stand for all of them.

We worked very fast in the autumn of 1931. I had finished writing *Lonely Road* in the early summer and had packed it off to Watt, who secured American publication for the book with William Morrow Inc., who have been my friends and publishers ever since. Thereafter I gave up writing novels and wrote nothing more for five years. Work was too strenuous in Airspeed Ltd.; I had encouraged shareholders to trust their money to us and it was up to me to see that their money was not lost. It did not seem fair to them to be doing another job in the evenings; if the venture were to fail it must not be said that it failed for any lack of effort on my part. Another compulsion was to grow as the swift months went by. In 1932 and 1933 there was a great deal of unemployment in England, but our working hands grew steadily in number. There was a balcony above the stores where we stored lumber, and sometimes when things were very bad financially and I could see no avenue to raise the next week's wages, I used to go up there and look down at the fifty or sixty men working on the floor below me, and reflect that if I failed to pull the rabbit out of the hat within the next few days all those men would be without a job and on the dole. I cannot recollect that I was worried about myself; Frances was a doctor and I could always get a job

117

of some sort, so we were all right, whatever happened. The men worried me a great deal more than the shareholders in those years.

Quick as we worked, our debts piled up more quickly. At that time I was meticulous in paying the month's trade invoices promptly in order to build up a good name; we swung all our debt on to the bank. The bank, however, was quite capable of looking after itself. In Lord Grimthorpe they had a man of means to guarantee our overdraft. In the prospectus shareholdings had to be paid up in the form of calls extending over six months, so that from the earliest days a joint and several guarantee of the overdraft by the directors was necessary. At first this was a real matter for we could all pay if called upon to do so; later this guarantee rested principally upon Lord Grimthorpe. All I had personally to throw into the pool was my liquidation in bankruptcy, for what that was worth.

By October our bank overdraft was £1,479.

By the beginning of December the design work upon the Ferry was tailing off, so well and quickly had Tiltman done his job, and construction of the first machine was coming on well in the shop. It became important to decide what we should do next. The Ferry was a specialized machine got out to suit Cobham's requirements. It was quite likely that we could sell a few of them to other operators for use on routes where speed was unimportant, and with its ability to land in any field it was perhaps the safest ten-passenger machine produced at that time. Experience, however, has taught me one sad fact – that you can't sell safety. Everybody pays lip service to the safety of aeroplanes, but no one is prepared to pay anything for it. A technical advance in aeroplane design can normally be expressed in various ways: the machine can be made to land more slowly, or it can be made faster for the same landing speed, or it can be made to carry more payload for the same landing speed and cruising speed. No operator ever elects for the lower landing speed. Passengers won't pay extra for that.

It seemed to us that the next thing for the company to do was to design a machine for the commercial market which would be much faster than the Ferry, and a good deal cheaper. Already there were signs that the private owner market was becoming satisfied, in England at any rate. The prospect was that numbers of small airlines would begin operations in the next few years, in England and overseas. Such infant airlines would not have much money and would not require, at first, machines carrying more than four or five passengers and the pilot. The aircraft must be faster than the normal run of civil aircraft at that time but must be capable of operation out of small grass aerodromes; runways were still unknown.

This specification was discussed at length between Cobham, Tiltman, and myself, and Cobham indicated that it was just possible he might be able to produce an order for the first of the new type, as he had with the Ferry. In the drawing office Tiltman and I got down to the consideration of designs. We had already arrived at the conception of a clean, low-wing monoplane six-seater powered with a Lynx radial engine, when a copy of *The Aeroplane* came out showing a very early, rather indistinct picture of the new Lockheed Orion monoplane produced in America, with its retractable undercarriage housed into the wing in flight.

Up to that time no aircraft with a retractable undercarriage had been built in England with the exception of one experimental and little-known Bristol type which had been produced immediately after the first war. Various pundits had pronounced against the retractable undercarriage on the grounds that the added weight and complexity of the device would not be justified by the saving in air resistance, and at the low cruising speeds then in vogue this might well have been true. We were contemplating a big step up in cruising speed, however, and we were fascinated by this picture of the Lockheed, showing that in America this thing had really been achieved. It did not seem so difficult, moreover, when you approached the design with an unbiased mind, and there was no reason to suppose that it would be unreasonably heavy. It was certainly no more difficult than many of the novel design problems we had had to face and solve upon the airship. The whole of Airspeed was a gamble, anyway; there was no future for us in playing safe. We decided to incorporate a retractable undercarriage, hydraulically operated, in the new design.

CHAPTER EIGHT

IF I WERE starting a company like Airspeed over again, and had to begin again to look for risk capital, I should look first for individuals who had recently made a profit out of the sale of land. If I couldn't find them, I should probably abandon the job as hopeless.

In such a quest, it is no good going to any organization such as a bank, or an insurance company with large funds to invest, or even to a government office charged with the development of industry. Such organizations frequently think quite sincerely that they are putting out a portion of their resources in the form of risk capital, but their definition of a risk is different from mine. I never got any of them to touch Airspeed.

In organizations such as that, some one official has to take the responsibility on his own shoulders for hazarding other people's money. If the money is lost, that official will have to stand up to some inquiry by the owners of the money, and say, 'I thought this was a good thing to do with your money, but it wasn't. I'm sorry, but it's lost.' That official may be charged with the duty of laying out investments in risk capital, but in his own interest he will always avoid the more wildcat schemes and will invest preferably in those which, in his view, present a reasonable prospect of security. In this way he modifies and waters down his definition of the word 'risk' to a meaning which others might class as development capital. No man who is responsible for other people's money wilt gamble with it to the extent required by genuine risk capital.

To find risk capital, one must seek for the individual who has recently made a large profit in the nature of an unexpected windfall. Such a man, in general, will invest ninety-five per cent of his profit prudently and safely, and he will gamble with the remaining five per cent in the hope that this small investment will yield a great return and so increase the average income from his total holding. In my view, to find an investor of £1,000 in risk capital one must seek for the individual who has recently made a profit or sold assets for £20,000 and has to do something with that money.

Profits of that order may be made from the sale of a business such as a shop or a chain of shops. Commercial people of that type, however, are not ready investors in genuine risk enterprises; perhaps they know too much. Such profits are, however, made every day from the sale of land in the vicinity of a growing city by landowners who are not primarily commercial people but may be farmers, or politicians, or lawyers, or country gentlemen. In my experience these are the people who will invest a little money in a genuine risk enterprise if they have it to invest, partly no doubt from ignorant cupidity and partly from a far-sighted and altruistic desire to help new industry come into being. In my experience the latter motive is more common than the former, though they may be mixed.

I believe that much of the early capital of Airspeed Ltd. came fundamentally from profit on the sale of land, though the money may have passed through several hands in its journey from the land to our company. Reflecting on these matters, it appears to me that money derived from land sold at a profit on the outskirts of a growing city is probably re-invested in the form of risk capital and development capital in the industries that make the city grow. To put the matter in a simplified and elemental form, the industries of an industrial city may have been capitalized in the past largely from the profit made out of the sale of the land on which the city stands.

If this be true, any restriction on the sale of land for profit which may be imposed by a government will have the effect of cutting off the flow of risk capital and development capital from the industries of that country, and should be approached with the utmost caution. Right-thinking people of all parties will probably agree that it is unjust that the inheritor of a few fields should make a large fortune for doing no work. Yet if that fortune is prevented from passing through the hands of that inheritor, it may well be that no new company will find the capital to start on in the early days of risk. The individual gambler is an essential feature in the provision of risk capital for industry. No organization can replace him, and without him no new industry of any consequence can come to life.

The first Ferry was finished at the end of March and had to be transported to Sherburn-in-Elmet aerodrome for flight trials. Its transport was a bit of a problem. To take it there in bits upon a truck and assemble it over there for flight would have meant weeks of very costly and inefficient work in somewhat primitive surroundings. We decided to tow it there along the road on its own wheels, less the extension planes. Being a three-engined machine it had a span of sixteen feet in this condition, which meant that it had to be moved in the middle of the night with a special police escort. We got as far as Tadcaster by two in the morning, and met the rudder of the Berengaria coming the other way ...

That was sorted out, and we reached the aerodrome at dawn and began assembly and final inspection for flight. I had arranged for the very experienced pilot instructor of the flying club to do the test flying for us; I would have liked nothing better than to take it off myself, but my experience was inadequate and the financial responsibility to the company too great. Worrall made the first flight a couple of days later, and found practically nothing wrong with the machine. It was about five miles an hour slower than we had estimated but it flew, and flew well; there were virtually no modifications needed as a result of the flight trials. It was, of course, a well understood and a conservative design, as was essential to us because we couldn't afford a failure or any long delay in getting through the trials.

Cobham's display was already starting operations for the season, and it was essential to get the machine operating in the minimum of time. We put our case to the Air Ministry and they helped us. All new-type civil aircraft at that time had to be flight tested at Martlesham Heath before a certificate of airworthiness could be issued. The Air Ministry and the RAF pilots got behind the job and the Ferry passed through Martlesham in four days without any trouble, and was operating with National Aviation Day Ltd. in the third week of April. In the first three months the aircraft did six hundred hours of flying and carried 36,000 paying passengers.

So far so good. We had shown that we could do what we set out to do, but the overdraft had risen to £4,223. We set to work to complete the second Ferry for Cobham and to build up two more machines for stock. That month we instituted a premium bonus system in the shop, full early, perhaps, in a concern that boasted only about forty operatives. Output went up, however. We engaged a typist and telephone girl who was a great help, a Miss Brunton.

Some months later, when the work had grown to the point where no one girl could manage the telephone and the letters and the books, we started to look for another girl. Miss Brunton asked if we would consider her sister, who could manage the telephone and do simple clerical work; she had been breeding dogs but the dogs didn't pay. The second Miss Brunton came along and presented me with a problem. Rightly or wrongly I decreed that the girls were not to be called by their Christian names in the office. The new girl was no problem to my staff of shareholders because from the first she was known as Dog-Brunton. An unfortunate extension followed, and the office heard cries of 'Bitch! Where's Bitch? Oh, Bitch, when you've done Mr Norway's letters I've got some for you.' Perhaps Ethel and Joan would have been better, after all.

The success of the Ferry, following on the little success that we had had with the Tern sailplane, acted as a tonic to the company. The Ferry was a sizeable aircraft for those days, and the other firms in the aircraft industry began to take note of our doings. Within the company we began to make plans for establishing the concern on a more permanent basis. Clearly if we were to go on building aeroplanes we should have to move from the bus garage in York to some location on an aerodrome, and I began to visit various cities in England that had set up municipal aerodromes to ascertain what help they would give us if we were to move the company to their aerodrome. York was, unfortunately, rather backward at that time and it was some years before an aerodrome came into being for the city.

By May the overdraft had risen to £5,303. Cobham was paying for his aircraft at the rate of £400 a week from the profits of National Aviation Day Ltd., but these payments were swallowed up as soon as they came in by the ever-increasing costs of the company as we built up two more Ferries as a speculation and proceeded with the design of the monoplane six-seater, soon to be christened the Courier. In the midst of his engagements all over the country with National Aviation Day Ltd., Sir Alan Cobham was working up a novel project, for those days, which would enable him to place an order with us for the new machine.

This project was for the refuelling of aeroplanes in flight. In general, the limitation to the load that an aeroplane can carry is set by its ability to get off the ground with a reasonable length of run and a sufficient rate of climb to clear the obstacles surrounding the aerodrome. Once off the ground and up at its cruising altitude, however, an aeroplane can normally carry a considerably greater load than it can take off the ground. Accordingly, if a bomber or a passenger aircraft could take on board most of its fuel in flight by transferring the liquid to it by a hose from another aeroplane, it could carry a greater load of passengers or bombs off the ground than would be the case if it had to take off with fuel for the whole journey.

Refuelling of one aircraft from another had been carried out before this time in the case of small personal aeroplanes attempting long endurance records; the technique in this case had been to lower two-gallon cans on the end of a rope from one aeroplane to the other. Sir

Alan now proposed a serious programme of research and experiment into this matter which would culminate in a non-stop flight from England to India in our Airspeed Courier, refuelling in the air at three points on the way.

For this purpose he formed a new company, Flight Refuelling Ltd., which is still in existence as a great and powerful research concern. The late Lord Wakefield, who had made a fortune out of lubricating oils, was at that time a generous sponsor of all forms of aviation enterprise, and in the summer of 1932 Cobham was endeavouring to secure support from Lord Wakefield for Flight Refuelling Ltd. while he moved National Aviation Day Ltd. from town to town and piloted joyriders himself for much of the time. On my side, I was endeavouring to secure the order for the Courier from Cobham.

A great deal of this many-sided negotiation took place in fields in the surroundings of the air circus. At Lincoln and Liverpool, at Oxford and at Plymouth, I used to visit Cobham to correct the minor troubles of the Ferries and to try to close the Courier order. While a girl looped and spun a glider over the aerodrome or a clown in a Moth bombed a couple escaping to Gretna Green in a Model T Ford with rolls of toilet paper, Cobham would drink a cup of tea with me in his tent or caravan and discuss the teething troubles of the Ferry, or the Courier order, or the new location for the company. Gradually I was eliminating all the towns but one, and by July our choice had fallen upon Portsmouth for the permanent establishment of the company.

Portsmouth had everything to offer us. It had a new municipal aerodrome upon the outskirts of the town, immediately adjacent to good seaplane water in Langstone harbour. At that time the flying boat was in the ascendant and most of the services of Imperial Airways were about to turn to operation by flying boats. There was a proposal to develop Langstone harbour as a great terminal flying-boat base for services throughout the Commonwealth. Portsmouth was a town with a good reserve of engineering labour normally working in the dockyard. Moreover, Portsmouth was anxious to have us there.

In July 1932 negotiations with Portsmouth were in quite an advanced state, and justified a visit by Lord Grimthorpe to the Lord Mayor. This luncheon and the subsequent negotiations went off well, and we left the Guildhall and went to have tea in a small café while we waited for a train to London. Here my chairman raised a point with me which had been troubling him, and which I think deserves a record.

He had a general arrangement drawing of the Courier which we proposed to build, showing the retractable undercarriage. Already by that time he had a very serious financial commitment in the company, and quite prudently he had shown this drawing to a knowledgeable friend in the aircraft industry to get his opinion on it. This friend had shown the drawing to a great and famous designer.

In the Battle of Britain, eight years later, the brunt of the battle was borne by the Hawker Hurricane and the Supermarine Spitfire fighters, both, of course, with retractable undercarriages. The designer in question designed one of them, and wild horses will not drag from me which. In 1932, however, he held different views. The drawing came back from him with the message that the Courier was a very good design and should fill a place in the commercial market and do well, provided that the designers would forget about the retractable undercarriage and fit a normal undercarriage to the machine. He, the designer, had been attracted by the retractable undercarriage at one time and had gone into it very carefully. It was no good. The device could not be made to work reliably and if it could it would be of little value in an aeroplane design. Over the teacups in that shabby little café Lord Grimthorpe presented this report to me.

I had to think and talk quite hard. To think quite hard, because it was essential that so good a friend to the company should not lose his money by a technical error of our own. If we were wrong and the great designer were right, he would probably do so. To talk quite hard, to convince my chairman of things that he already had vaguely in the back of his mind, that a policy of caution, of doing what everybody else was doing, could never bring us through to an established position in the industry. If we did only what the large, conservative firms of the industry were capable of doing we should inevitably lose to them, for with their great manufacturing capacity they could sell for lower prices than our infant company could hope to manufacture for. Our only hope was to lead the way, to put out something technically ahead of them and so monopolize the market till they had time to catch up.

Lord Grimthorpe thought about it, and decided to allow us to go on with the retractable undercarriage.

The negotiations with the Portsmouth Corporation were brought to a satisfactory conclusion in July; I think the terms that they gave us deserve a record as a model of the sort of encouragement that can be given by an enterprising city to an infant industry. They would build us a factory building on the aerodrome to our own requirements, only stipulating that it should be capable of being used as a hangar if our company were to fail. This building, about 14,000 sq ft in floor area, would cost about £4,000; the Corporation wanted a down payment of £1,000 and the balance on hire purchase spread over ten years with 5% interest on the outstanding loan. For the use of the aerodrome we would

pay a rent of 1% of our sales turnover up to a turnover of £60,000, $1/2$%
from £60,000 to £200,000 and $1/4$% thereafter. In addition there was a
rental of, I think, £50 per acre for the land we occupied. These were
generous terms, which resulted in the establishment of a very
considerable industry on Portsmouth aerodrome.

In August the order for the Courier was confirmed by Cobham, the
move to Portsmouth was definitely decided on as soon as the factory
could be built, and further bank guarantees were entered into by Lord
Grimthorpe and Hewitt. An extra shareholding was taken up by Sir Alan
Cobham. As the autumn drew on I was chiefly occupied, I think, in
progressing the design and construction of the factory at Portsmouth
and in trying to sell the two Ferries we were building as a speculation. It
was essential, of course, that we should keep on building something to
retain our men, yet we had little capital to spare for locking up in stock
and no room for storing any completed aircraft.

That autumn, as Cobham had forecast, some interest began to awaken
in the formation of small private airlines in the British Isles. It came not
from the private owners of aeroplanes, as we had thought it would, but
from the bus operators. In England the late Mr Hillman was beginning
to consider an airline to Paris from his elementary aerodrome at
Romford, and in Scotland Mr John Sword was making plans for a
network of lines joining up Glasgow with Belfast, Edinburgh, Inverness,
and the Western Islands.

I visited Mr Sword several times and found him a hard-headed
business man, but generous and helpful personally. He had worked up
from a modest start after the first war to a wealthy and a powerful
position in the motor-bus world in Scotland; like many such men he was
expert in getting value for his money. He was, however, keenly
interested in Airspeed Ltd. and very sympathetic to the company;
having trod the hard way upwards himself so recently he could
understand our many difficulties. He bought the third Ferry that
autumn and incorporated it in the name of his new company, Midland
and Scottish Air Ferries Ltd.

We made no progress with Mr Hillman, for a reason which caused us
a good deal of concern. De Havillands were after him. Up till that time
the small commercial machine had not attracted this company very
much; they had built small machines for the private owner in great
numbers and they had built large machines for Imperial Airways. When
we had bought engines from them for the Ferries they had indicated
verbally that they were not very likely to compete with us. However,
necessity knows no law. The continuing depression was playing havoc

with the sales of aeroplanes for the private owner, and we were pointing the way to a new market. Early in 1933 de Havillands produced the twin-engined Dragon to the order of Mr Hillman, a machine that was a good deal faster than the Ferry and a good deal cheaper, though not, perhaps, quite so safe. In the design of aircraft a designer studies and analyses the machines that are already flying and then goes one better; the Dragon was produced a year later than the Ferry and was a better aircraft for the job, and was sold for a price which in our smaller works we could not hope to equal. From the day the Dragon appeared we had little hope of selling Ferries.

We sold the fourth Ferry, quite unexpectedly, one day to Mr Sword, who had expertly concealed the fact that he wanted another. He made us take his 6 $1/2$-litre Bentley in for £700 as part of the price of the fourth Ferry; in his first affluence he had bought a fleet of seven very expensive motor cars but he was now coming to the view that a wise man could do with rather fewer vehicles. I drove this magnificent thing from Ayr to London to sell it, the best car that I have ever driven or am ever likely to drive, but in the depression there was no sale for a car like that and we could not afford to keep it till the times improved. I think we only got about £400 for it; even at that price we could none of us afford to buy it in for our own use.

The advent of the Dragon raised a point of policy which was to trouble us throughout the life of the company, till Air Ministry orders were to swamp and obliterate commercial work. We were using de Havilland engines in the Ferry, and were therefore buying engines from our competitors in the same market. However friendly to that company we might be, and our relations with de Havillands were very good throughout, there were obvious commercial dangers in using their engines. We were far too small to think of manufacturing engines for ourselves, besides being inexperienced in such a business, and we began to shape our developments to use, if possible, engines manufactured by an organization that did not make aeroplanes.

In the British aircraft industry at that time such engines were not very easy to find. Lord Nuffield, however, was turning his attention to aero-engines and Wolseley Motors had produced a very attractive little radial engine of about two hundred horsepower which was technically very promising. From that time onwards we began to shape our design policies around the Wolseley engine wherever possible, and as time went on we were to get a good deal of cooperation from that company. Their engines, however, in the winter of 1932-3 were in an early stage of development.

The company's accounts for the first year of working showed a loss, the first of many. I forget the amount of this loss, but I know that it was reached after capitalizing everything that could possibly be capitalized in the accounts, so that the true position of the company was a good deal worse than the stated loss. This result was no surprise to anybody; on the other side was the considerable degree of technical success that had already been achieved. I do not remember that anybody was particularly depressed, though by the end of the year 1932 the position of the company was serious. The issued share capital by that time was £11,800, and the overdraft about £6,000; for the first time we were getting behind in paying the monthly trade invoices. It must have been about this time that I began to defer paying our own monthly salaries, too – a default that was to occur a number of times within the next two years. It did not seem to me quite fair to defer paying our bills for materials and yet to take our salaries in full on the first of each month; if any creditor turned nasty and threatened us with a writ it would add strength to the position if one could say, 'Look, old boy, I'm in this as well as you. If we go into liquidation you and I are both in the same boat. We're both creditors.' And then one could follow up with the story about the businessman in the West Riding who went in to see his bank manager about the overdraft, and asked the manager if he had ever been in the wool trade. The bank manager said, no. The man said, 'Well, you're in it now,' and walked out. Our trade creditors were soon to find themselves involuntarily in the position of debenture holders, and I must say that they were all extraordinarily good about it. In this, of course, they were influenced by the good technical reputation that we were building up.

That winter we built a small monoplane two-seater designed by W S Shackleton and Lee Murray, both firm friends of mine still though rather surprisingly in view of the dispute that we had over what constituted good workmanship. I had taken this job on at a fixed price and in view of the financial situation of the company I well remember the grief and mental anguish that I went through when they called on us to remake a thoroughly bad piece of cowling. The machine was low powered and slow but very delightful to fly in, for it was a parasol monoplane with the pusher engine in the centre section; the fuselage was very low on the ground and the pilot and passenger were out in front ahead of the engine and the wing with a perfect view. Only one machine was ever built, for it came out at a time when the private owner market was dying in England, but it was a good design for club use.

In March 1933 we moved the company from York to Portsmouth, into the new factory built for us by the Portsmouth Corporation. By that time we had over a hundred men employed in the bus garage in York, but of these I think only about fifty elected to make the move south with us. Some of the others were to join us again later on, for we were to find that the Portsmouth area was attractive to labour. As spring came on, men working in the grey industrial towns of the Midlands and the North would begin to think about the sunshine and the seaside, and would take the opportunity of moving down to a job with us thinking that they would go back north in the autumn. When autumn came, they usually stayed on. The transfer of the company to Portsmouth was probably a wise move on those grounds alone; it enabled our struggling little company to get a good staff together more quickly than otherwise we could have done.

For the first time in Portsmouth we were all under one roof, a tremendous help to Tiltman and the design office. We had nearly three times the area to work in, with the aerodrome immediately outside the door, giving promise of lower costs and more effective work. The first Courier for Cobham was practically complete when we left York and only the final erection and inspection before flight remained to be done in the new factory.

This was the first retractable-undercarriage machine to be produced in England for many years, and in the test flying therefore we should be breaking new ground. There were, of course, no proprietary hydraulic components already on the market that we could make use of; Tiltman and his drawing office had had to design the manual hydraulic pump and the jacks and the change-over cocks and the indicator lights entirely from first principles with little expert help because the design was a new conception. It was inevitable that teething troubles would occur, sometimes in flight, and this would mean that the pilot might well find that he could not lower his undercarriage. To meet this point the design was arranged to retract the undercarriage legs completely but to leave half the diameter of the wheels exposed below the under-surface of the wing. In this position the axles were up against a firm abutment and a belly landing could be made upon the wheels with little damage to the aircraft. In fact, a belly landing on the Courier only involved a bent metal propeller and minor damage to fairings, and was normally put right for a repair cost of about twenty pounds.

The choice of a test pilot for the first flights of the Courier was a serious responsibility, complicated by the financial situation of the company. In the first flight trials trouble with the undercarriage was quite likely to arise and if that happened a first-class pilot would be required to use all his experience and skill if the aircraft were to be landed safely, but we had little money to pay the fees of a first-class consultant pilot nor had we any great confidence in the civilian pilots who were available.

In these circumstances we made contact with F/Lt G H Stainforth. George Stainforth was a serving officer in the RAF, employed at that time as a test pilot in the Royal Aircraft Establishment at Farnborough. He was one of the best test pilots in the country; he had been a member of the Schneider Trophy team and held the world's speed record for seaplanes in the Supermarine S6B. George Stainforth was keenly interested in the Courier and wanted to fly it, and I think his superiors in the Royal Air Force wanted him to fly it, too, for they made no objection when he requested permission to carry out this test flying for us while he was on leave. Married flight lieutenants in the RAF are not particularly affluent as a class and George was glad to do the job for us for the pitifully small fee that I could offer him; on our part we could have got no better man.

I have found that it is difficult, if not impossible, to generalize about the mentality of a good test pilot. George Stainforth was a fine character, a big, humorous man, generous to the point of having little sense of money so that he seemed to be in the habit of giving any that came into his hands to his wife lest be should spend it too quickly. When standing a round of beers at the bar he would ask his wife for five shillings, and give her back the change. On the ground he was mentally slow to grasp a technical point, but he had immense tenacity and would never leave a technical matter till he had mastered it in every detail. Before the test flights of the Courier we had the machine supported on trestles and jacks in the hangar in the flying attitude so that the pilot could get the feel of the machine before he left the ground; the open hangar doors in front of the aircraft permitted a full view of the aerodrome, and the undercarriage could be raised and lowered as in flight. In our innocence we had supposed that an hour in the machine in this condition would be sufficient for the pilot, for the Courier was not a very complicated aeroplane, but it was not so. George Stainforth sat in the machine in this condition for five solid hours, all through one working day, with Tom Laing or the chief inspector at his side, asking and re-asking the same questions and receiving the same explanations, or just sitting, feeling the controls and staring at the aerodrome, in an apparent daydream. I think his one deficiency was that he was not a very quick pupil and I think that he was very well aware of it, so that he required this prolonged study before he could feel that he really knew the aircraft to the extent that he would not have to stop and think in an emergency.

In the air he was masterly, of course. So far as I remember he did about five hours' flying on the machine, establishing preliminary performance figures which were practically identical with those established later in the official trials. The undercarriage gave no trouble in these early trials, but he had to cope with an emergency of another sort. Taking off into an easterly wind from Portsmouth aerodrome the mud flats and tidal water of Langstone harbour lie immediately beyond the confines of the aerodrome, with no possibility of landing undamaged. George Stainforth suffered a complete engine failure at an altitude of about three hundred feet just after taking off in this direction, due, I think, to a defect in the petrol system. The machine was climbing steeply with the undercarriage already up when this happened, and I have never seen an aircraft handled so expertly. Within an instant the machine was forty-five degrees nose down to keep up speed, and turning while the undercarriage came out in record time; then she flattened out neither too high nor too low and landed neatly and perfectly back in to the aerodrome down wind. In the hands of a lesser pilot the machine might well have been lost; perhaps the long wearisome hours spent in the cockpit in the hangar had paid off.

George Stainforth was killed in the Second World War flying a Beaufighter in the Western Desert, a great loss to the RAF and to his country.

The Courier went to Martlesham for trials, which were extended, because this first machine to have a practical and a reliable retracting undercarriage was to exercise a considerable influence on the design of military aircraft. The Air Ministry got all the leading aircraft designers in the country down to Martlesham while the machine was in their hands, presumably to rub their noses in it. At Portsmouth we were completing the last Ferry for Mr John Sword and commencing the production of a batch of six Couriers, but the finances were again in a serious condition. By the middle of May the guaranteed overdraft was £8,450 and there was an unsecured overdraft above this limit, making the total debt to the bank well over £10,000. We also owed about £1,700 in the form of trade invoices, some of them going back to January. In spite of our considerable technical successes a cautious man might well have hesitated to support such an unfinancial company further. Yet in the middle of May Lord Grimthorpe turned up, unasked, with a cheque for £1,000 to take up a thousand more shares.

In spite of the financial picture the prospects of the company were encouraging, because when the official performance figures came through, the Courier was seen to be a technical success. With an Armstrong Siddeley Lynx engine of 240 horsepower the machine had a maximum speed at sea level of 163mph, about eight miles an hour faster than our forecast, when carrying a pilot, five passengers, and three and a half hours' fuel. About 20mph of this speed was probably due to the retraction of the undercarriage. In its day this was an outstanding performance, and the prospective orders for the machine were promising, a promise tempered by the fact that most of the small airlines that were then coming into being had little or no money.

By the end of August the overdraft had risen to £12,847, over £4,000 of which was unsecured, and the bank manager was getting very unpleasant. Trade creditors, too, were showing signs that their forbearance was near its end. In these circumstances Lord Grimthorpe came forward again with a personal bank guarantee of a further £5,200, and by this act produced a situation amongst our working shareholders which deserves a record.

These shareholders got together in the office without consulting either Tiltman or myself to debate the financial situation of the company which employed them on their trivial salaries. Most of them had access to a little more money, and they came forward after consultation between themselves with a proposal to support the company further to the extent of £12,000 between them, in the form of 6% debentures or bank guarantees. This offer from officials of the company who were not members of the Board was generous and a great encouragement to the directors, for these men, led by Tom Laing, knew all the seamy side of the business and could not be deceived about its prospects. Accordingly the company took powers to issue the debentures, and with this encouragement went cracking on.

By the beginning of September we had delivered the first production Courier as a demonstrator, paid for, to the Aircraft Exchange and Mart Ltd., to whom we had given the selling agency for the British Isles, and the machine had already made a very fast return flight between London and Edinburgh to demonstrate the possibilities of internal airlines. We must have paid a lot of invoices, because debtors and creditors were about equal at £3,000. Having got the financial situation more or less under control a prudent Board might well have hesitated before a further expansion, but both Board and shareholders were of one mind: the company must get big quickly or it must inevitably perish. It was resolved at the beginning of September to double the floor area of the factory, making the best hire purchase deal we could with the Corporation, to lay down Couriers in batches of not less than six, and to press ahead with the design of a new twin-engined machine based upon the Courier.

This new machine was the result of sales experience. In the provision of aircraft for the little airlines that were coming into being our chief competitors, as always, were our old friends the de Havilland Company. Their Dragon and Dragon Rapide machines were slower than the

Courier and, I think, less economical in operation by virtue of the high performance of our aircraft, but they had twin-engined reliability to offer as well as low price and a first-class servicing organization. Price we could argue about because all speed costs money, and we were making every effort to provide a first-class service for our aircraft, but already the single aeroplane was becoming out of date for airline use; already legislation was in sight to restrain operators from flying paying passengers over sea routes in single-engined aeroplanes. We therefore set ourselves to consider whether we could not develop a twin-engined version of the Courier using the extension planes and many of the other components of the single-engined machine to lower the development costs of the new aircraft, later to be christened the Envoy. We specified Wolseley AR engines for this machine, a very promising new engine of modern design backed by all the resources of the Nuffield organization.

That autumn Sir Alan Cobham was hard at work on his refuelling experiments, using one of the old Handley Page W10 biplanes from National Aviation Day Ltd. as a tanker. Squadron Leader W Helmore was normally his co-pilot on these flights and was to go with him on the projected flight to India, but on one or two occasions I flew with Cobham upon these experiments. The Courier was provided with a hatch in the top of the fuselage which the co-pilot could open in flight and stand up in, his body above the waist exposed to the airstream at about 90mph; a hose was then let down from the tanker flying a hundred feet above the Courier to pass the fuel.

The chief difficulty lay in making the first contact between the machines. The hose could not be lowered at once, for it waved frantically and could have whipped the tail off the Courier if it had hit it. The first method tried was to lower a little bag of sand on the end of a light cod line; Cobham would fly the Courier so that Helmore (or myself) could reach out and catch the line. The cod line was then pulled in to the Courier, pulling down a heavier rope, and finally the hose was pulled down, the nozzle poked into an appropriate funnel leading to the Courier's petrol system, and the juice was turned on. All this demanded very accurate formation flying by Cobham, impossible in bumpy weather, but it worked fairly well till one day the little bag of sand jammed between the aileron and the wing of the Courier and put the machine out of control, and gave Cobham and Helmore a great fright. After that they used a child's toy balloon filled with water as the weight, which would burst if anything of the sort happened again, and it was on the basis of this system that they set out for India early the following year. I shall always remember standing up half-out of the Courier trying to catch this thing as we flew in formation below the Handley Page, and how frightened I was; my respect for Air Commodore Helmore has not diminished with the passing of the years. Now, of course, a totally different system has been developed by Cobham's organization for the refuelling of aeroplanes in flight.

These Courier refuelling flights were valuable to us, because all aeroplanes have initial teething troubles to be rectified by modifications to the design, and with the first Courier operating in Cobham's hands upon short local flights in this way we were able to get through this stage of the development with the minimum of trouble; this was not the least of the many benefits that Airspeed owed to Sir Alan.

That autumn two of our £5 per week working shareholders, Lord Ronaldshay and R D King, formed a small selling company to take the agency for Airspeed and other products in India and Burma. They bought a Courier as a demonstrator fitted with a more powerful engine to improve the take-off of the machine in tropical conditions, an Armstrong Siddeley Cheetah Mark V of about 300 horsepower, and Ronaldshay flew this out to India to set up a sales organization for us in New Delhi while King remained on as our sales manager. In England the Aircraft Exchange and Mart had produced a number of dubious orders for Couriers, most of which were from optimistic newly created airlines with little money who required a hire purchase deal. In the end most of the aircraft that we sold upon these terms found their way to the war which was to break out two and a half years later in Spain.

The second annual general meeting of the company was held in December 1933, and a further loss was announced. This produced no crisis, because the meeting was held in my office in the works at Portsmouth and was attended only by the directors and officials who were working in the company; there were still very few other shareholders. The Air Ministry had just ordered a Courier for experiments with the retractable undercarriage, an earnest of better things to come. The new factory extension was well under way by grace of the Portsmouth Corporation, but already we were talking of another one. Twelve Couriers and six Envoys were under construction at the end of the year.

During that winter both Tiltman and I were elected Fellows of the Royal Aeronautical Society. This is the highest technical distinction that British aviation has to offer and we got it, I think, primarily for the production of the Courier with its retractable undercarriage, though in my case my work upon the R100 had something to do with it as well. The company, too, was marching on to technical distinction. At that time the firms composing the British aircraft manufacturing industry were grouped in a very tight organization, the Society of British Aircraft

Constructors. After the first war when government orders were few and most aircraft firms were running at a loss, an agreement had been reached between the government and this trade Society that, in consideration of the firms remaining in being, when bulk orders came to be placed again no orders would be given to newly created firms until the firms in the existing industry were full to capacity with work. This was a reasonable agreement in 1923 when it was made, but ten years later it bore hardly upon us. For years we were to see less competent firms receiving bulk government orders while we struggled on upon the edge of liquidation. The Society was conscious of this position and were not unfriendly to us; first they made us associate members and permitted us to show the Courier at their annual display in 1933, and after several years we broke into their ring and became full members of the Society.

About this time we engaged our first regular, whole time test pilot; previously we had made do with whatever pilots we could find at the time we wanted a machine flown. Now, however, the work had grown to a point when a full-time pilot was justified. We could not pay more than a poor salary, however, and we were lucky to get so good a man for our £400 a year. When delivering the second Ferry to John Sword at Inverness six months previously I had met F/Lt C H A Colman, a retired young RAF trained officer who was joyriding for John Sword with a Fox Moth. Colman was a merry, apparently irresponsible young man and I would have classed him with a hundred other light-hearted benders of aeroplanes but for one thing. He was flying his little aeroplane out of a pasture field, and before taking off I saw him deliberately pace out the distance to the far hedge to make quite sure that he had enough room to get off. I questioned him about the distance and found he had a very clear and accurate idea of the room that he required to get off safely with varying conditions of load and wind and height of obstacles. In these days this approach may seem elementary, but it showed an attitude of mind that was by no means common amongst ex-RAF pilots in 1933. When he applied for a job with us it seemed to me that our aeroplanes would be safe in his hands, and I was not disappointed. He was killed in 1941 over Northern France, flying a Beaufighter.

In January and February 1934 the question of an issue of shares to the public began to be discussed by the Board. In our continuing quest for fresh capital we had made contact with a City firm who seemed to think that they could place a public issue for us, and in our financial condition the prospect of sixty or seventy thousand pounds of new capital was not one to be treated lightly, whatever the source might be. It was much too early for a public issue. Such orders as we had in hand were mostly from dubious operators on tenuous hire purchase deals; if civil airlines went ahead and these operators prospered the aeroplanes would be paid for in the end, but if the operators failed the aeroplanes would be back on our hands, unsold. It will be understood that the financial houses in the City who announced that they could float us on the public were not the most conservative houses that the City could produce, and even they found our continuing losses something of an obstacle to a successful issue. Our needs, however, were urgent, for the finances of the company had grown to such a scale as to make it impossible for our early loyal supporters to carry the company much farther.

Negotiations for this difficult issue dragged on slowly, but I can find no evidence that the lack of money impaired our resolution to forge ahead. We should get nowhere without building aeroplanes and getting them on to airlines, and at the end of February we negotiated a second extension to the factory, again on a hire purchase agreement with the Portsmouth Corporation, still our staunch supporters. We must have had a nerve, because by the end of March the guaranteed overdraft was again exceeded by £2,267 and the salaries for March were still unpaid. One small airline, as unfinancial as ourselves, had ordered six Couriers and had paid the princely deposit of £5 on each; another had ordered one machine and had defaulted on the first hire purchase payment. There was, however, a prospect that the Air Ministry would place an order with the company for the design of a fighter; we lived mainly on prospects in those days.

Airspeed, however, was now beginning to attract the attention of more conservative City houses. One in particular, a concern of good standing which specialized in shipbuilding and ship-operating finance, had already agreed to advance money to us on firm orders for aeroplanes during construction, though owing to the peculiar character of our orders we had some difficulty with them over a definition of the word 'firm'. This concern was closely linked with the well-known shipbuilders Swan Hunter and Wigham Richardson Ltd., a great and powerful concern established on the Tyne and with ramifications in many other shipbuilding districts. At that time shipbuilding was depressed and many of the slips were empty, and there was a good deal of unemployment in the shipbuilding cities of the North Country. A proposal that they should take an interest in an aircraft manufacturing concern seemed reasonable, especially as flying boats were then in the ascendant for the major commercial airlines of the world and seemed likely to grow rapidly in size, so that the construction of the hulls, at any rate, seemed to be well on the way to similarity with the hulls of ships.

Negotiations with Swan Hunter, who proved to be directed by hard-headed business men, resulted in an offer of finance in April 1934 which involved writing down the value of our shares to 25% in view of the unsatisfactory nature of our company's finances. This came about the middle of the month when we were two months in arrear with salaries and trade creditors for £2,750 were threatening us with writs. I persuaded my Board to turn this offer down flat, though they did not need much persuasion; better to go into liquidation, for such an offer never could have formed a basis for a harmonious partnership. I think it was difficult for the shipbuilders to understand our point of view, which was still one of light-hearted adventure and not wholly monetary; their own concern had been established for over a hundred years and was as stable as a bank, and was administered by directors who had much of the mentality of bankers as is proper to such an organization. I doubt if any of them had personal experience of working up a business through its early difficulties, as we had no personal experience of running a large-scale business to show a commercial profit.

Company finance could only occupy a small part of my energies in those weeks, for we were starting up an organization, which was to prove abortive, to sell Couriers in Canada, and we were starting up sales concessions in China, Siam, Malaya, and Australia. Any spare time left on my hands was spent in analysing the letters from our creditors, some of which were clearly drafted by solicitors, and doling out what money we had to stave off the writs. I found the City house who were the intermediary between Swan Hunter and ourselves to be both helpful and constructive at this time; they were impressed by our technical achievements and appalled by the condition of our business. The passage of the centuries has made shipbuilding and ship operating a solid and a predictable business, very different from aviation as it was in early 1934.

By the beginning of June an agreement bad been reached with Swan Hunter and Wigham Richardson for a public issue of shares in Airspeed Ltd. under their auspices. They would acquire control of the company through an ordinary shareholding, the existing shares would be transferred at par into ordinary shares, the nominal capital of the company would be raised to £220,000, and an issue of £100,000 in preference shares would be offered to the public. This arrangement was acceptable to us. It meant the formation of a new Company to be known as Airspeed (1934) Ltd. After three years substantial capital was at last in sight, and one might say not before time. Our unsecured overdraft was again about £5,000 and the trade creditors totalled no less than £19,712; again the directors led by Lord Grimthorpe came to the rescue with yet another joint and several guarantee for a further overdraft of £5,000. It must be remembered, however, that at this time I was increasing production to the limit of the finance that was in sight; as the prospect of more capital became concrete I was manning up the shop and buying materials to the very limit in order to get our costs down by an increased turnover. If we were to get in capital from the public it was essential that our first year's working under the new conditions should be profitable if humanly possible, and this could only be achieved by pressing on with output. As the new capital drew closer, therefore, our debts mounted up, including the debt to ourselves, for at that time our salaries were two months in arrear.

In the month of June I was a great deal in the City, drafting the new prospectus with our friendly intermediaries and with the issuing house for the new issue of shares to the public.

CHAPTER NINE

TWO EXTRACTS FROM the minutes of Board meetings in the last weeks of the old company are of interest. On June 15th,

> The amendments of the prospectus were read and discussed, particularly the Directors statement as regards profits being payable in the first year. Certain alterations were agreed upon, which Mr Norway undertook to see were made in the next proof.

And on June 22nd,

> Mr Norway reported that considerable delay had been caused in the progress of the issue by the auditors taking very drastic action and views in regard to orders in hand, value of stock, and profits made, and he expressed the opinion that their action had been in no way helpful to the Company.

At this time I was acquiring a reputation with my co-directors and with my City associates for a reckless and unscrupulous optimism that came close to dishonesty. I think this bad reputation was deserved, for having set my hand to Airspeed and brought it so far up the road towards success I was intolerant of obstacles that seemed to me to be based upon an ultra-conservative and pedantic view of business. For three years the wildest business risks had been my daily bread and under this regime the company had grown mightily. A cautious and conservative policy could still kill it stone dead, a fact which I think was better appreciated by my Board than by our new associates. Even so, some of the things I was prepared to do shocked my Board and caused them, very rightly, to impose a tactful brake on my activities from time to time.

Because this is a position that many men in charge of growing companies may find themselves in I am going to discuss it a little. Many men drafting a prospectus have taken a quick glance inside the prison door, and some of them have subsequently entered it, but very few, if any, have written about their dilemma.

In the three years since Airspeed had been founded the capital requirements of the aircraft industry had changed vastly. When we started, thirty or forty thousand pounds would have been an adequate capital on which to achieve a profitable business, and this figure had been substantially constant for ten years previously. We had now attained that amount of capital in the form of shares, debentures, and bank guarantees, but profits still eluded us through circumstances due to basic changes in the industry and largely beyond our control. Each year the units of construction, the aeroplanes, were getting bigger and bigger and so requiring more capital for their production; the private-owner market had dwindled away to nothing and the all-up weight of the Envoy was more than three times the weight of the original three-seater on which our first capital estimates had been based. Each year our competitors with their superior organization lowered the cost of civil aeroplanes, and over all there was now the change from wood construction to metal becoming imminent, with all the vast and incalculable capital expenditure that that change would involve.

A wiser man than I might have foreseen a vast increase in capital requirements looking forward from the year 1931, but I doubt it. I doubt if in 1934 when we went to the public for £100,000 anybody could have foreseen that by 1954 a capital of ten million pounds would be required for any company that hoped to manufacture civil aircraft. All we knew in 1934 was that the capital requirements of a company in the aircraft business were rising very quickly, and that the only safe course was to gather in as much capital as we could get hold of.

Without fresh capital the company would fail, the money that had been put into it would be lost, and everyone employed in it would be thrown out of work. To me it was unthinkable that this should be allowed to happen. I do not think that the loss of the shareholders' money, regarded as money, worried me very much, and certainly the loss of my own money didn't worry me at all, for I had long written it off in my mind. I felt personally responsible for having got the shareholders into Airspeed and I should have felt it keenly as a personal disgrace if they had lost their money. The greater responsibility, however, was to the men working in the shop. We had nearly four hundred men and women employed in the company by that time, and in 1934 unemployment was still bad in England. I had confidence that I could get another job of some kind if Airspeed folded up, and it would have been no hardship to my wife if she had had to take up her profession again for a time, but the men were in a different case. The welfare of four hundred families was the real thing that mattered; at all costs the wheels must be kept turning for them. Airspeed must not fail.

Perhaps it is a good thing that company auditors work in offices remote from the working men and women who are vitally affected by their accountancy decisions. For my part, I had chosen a position for my office close up underneath the roof, so that every time I glanced up from my desk I could look out of a window into the shop and see practically every man at his work. This was good for preventing lost time over the morning tea but not so good for drafting a prospectus, for inevitably the sense of responsibility to the men working down below outweighed one's sense of responsibility to a vague, amorphous body of prospective shareholders. It was my job to state the value of the half-completed aeroplanes now in the factory, most of which were unsold or ordered by impecunious companies. This is an estimate that no one else can make and take responsibility for except the managing director, and it is this estimate of the value of stocks and work in progress which has sent many a managing director to the threshold of the prison door, if not right inside. False statements in the prospectus of a limited company are a criminal offence.

If I certified that every Courier aeroplane half-completed in the shop below me would be sold eventually at the full price for real money, then the value of the stocks was good and it was reasonable to assume that the company would very shortly with increasing turnover be working at a profit. A prospectus drafted on those lines would be attractive to investors, fresh capital would be subscribed, and four hundred families would be safe from unemployment, the families of the men working on the floor below me. If on the other hand I took a prudent and a cautious view and said that the Courier was an obsolescent type, that we must make provision for half the machines that we were building being unsaleable, then we could not make a case for the prosperity of the company which would attract investors, no more capital would be forthcoming, and all those men would very soon find themselves at the labour exchange drawing a pittance of unemployment money. It rested mainly on my word which way it went. If my optimism went too far it might well land me in the dock; if it did not go far enough it would land the men out on the street.

The case of the six Couriers sold to an operating company which had little or no money, on which a hire purchase deposit of only £5 on each machine had been paid, may serve as an example of the dilemma. This company was managed by an able and an energetic man, who was seeking capital hard for his venture. If internal airlines could be run in England profitably he was as likely to succeed as anybody else by reason of his energy and competence. If his venture failed the aeroplanes would come back to us and would lie on our hands until we succeeded in selling them again. Couriers, however, were an obsolescent type and might not be so easy to sell again. I had faith that we would sell them eventually, however, a faith which I think was based upon the growing talk of rearmament and war. I knew instinctively that if war should break out anywhere in the world every civil aeroplane of any size would sell immediately for military transportation or even as an improvised light bomber. I could not feel that these machines would find their way unsold on to the scrap heap and I was determined to resist any attempt on the part of the auditors or anybody else to write down their value in our accounts. To do so might well mean the end of the company and plunge four hundred families into deep distress.

To the auditors and to our shipbuilding associates this sale was no sale at all. The point was an important one, for the six aeroplanes were worth nearly twenty thousand pounds. To write them down to, say, one half their value in our books would be to add ten thousand pounds to our loss, making the financial picture of the company so unattractive as to make it unlikely that the public would invest in it. The auditors, however, took the gravest view of my representation that these aeroplanes were a good asset to be taken at face value. From that time on I think that I was suspect, as an unscrupulous man determined to swindle the investing public by any means within his power.

I do not resent that reputation, for it is part of the price a man must pay for being a managing director. At one time or another one must be prepared to throw one's personal reputation into the scales, when money is at an end. The alternative would be to say, in effect, to four hundred working men, 'I'm sorry, chaps, but you'd better start looking for another job. You may not find it easy, but that's no concern of mine. I could keep this works going and your jobs would be safe if I were to take a chance for you, but I value my reputation and I'm not going to do that. I'm an honest man, and you're out of work. Too bad.' To take that attitude would be the act of a poltroon.

I have dealt with this matter at some length because the ethical points raised seem to me to be so interesting. I have in mind the case of one fraudulent financier in particular who went to prison for a term of years in the early 'thirties. This man had several companies employing many hundreds of people. At the beginning of the depression things started to go badly with these companies. It seemed then that the depression would be over in six months. Rather than see his whole industrial edifice collapse with all the consequent distress to his employees, this man entered on a complicated transfer of property between his own companies at fictitiously inflated prices, which resulted in such glowing prosperity for one company that it could go to the public for more capital, with which it proceeded to assist all the other companies of the group. If, in fact, the depression had come to an end in six months everything would have come right again, the fraud would never have come to light, and many people would have been saved from great distress. In fact, however, the depression went on, the whole card castle fell down, and the man went to prison. I have often wondered what I should have done if I had been in his place. I think I know.

At the same time, it is right and proper that such men should go to prison. All business is based on truth and confidence, and unless certain standards of honest dealing are maintained no industry would be possible. It is the job of company auditors to maintain these standards of rectitude, and they do their job fairly and well in my experience. It is one of the defects of the capitalistic system that a managing director's responsibility to his employees and his responsibility to the investing public may conflict and often do; the resolution of this conflict is a matter to be solved by each man for himself.

In fact, I won my battle over the six Couriers and they went forward at face value in our books, while I lost a good deal of credit. My hunch that this was the right course was justified. They all came back to us when the operating company suspended operations a year later, but shortly after that the Spanish civil war broke out and the machines all sold immediately to various intermediaries for better than the original prices, and all went by devious routes to Spain. I do not think that Airspeed ever failed to sell a speculative aeroplane that we had built for stock at the full price; wars came eventually to clean up the position for us.

The public issue of shares in Airspeed (1934) Ltd. took place in July 1934, and was a great success. Applications for shares from the public were double those offered, a result due perhaps to the fact that the new Envoy happened to appear in public for the first time about the time of the issue, and created a very good impression. Tiltman had made his usual magnificent design job of this machine; even today, twenty years later, the machine looks a modern and a beautiful aeroplane. The first machine had Wolseley engines which were small and smooth running and very quiet with geared-down propellers, and we had very few teething troubles to impede us.

The average shareholding in the new company was £72, a fact which gave me secretly a great deal of satisfaction. So small an average investment seemed to indicate that a great number of people were having a little flutter in Airspeed; we still had gambling money for the most part in the company and not serious investment. This was a great comfort, for in spite of the new capital the company was by no means secure. The buyers of our aeroplanes were no more solvent than they had been. Operators who had real money to spend still went to de Havillands for their aircraft; there was a tendency for us to get as customers the many operators who were too unfinancial for our more powerful competitors to bother about. Yet we were making progress to a better class of business every day.

With our new capital we at once put in hand yet another extension to the factory, and for the first time we were able to buy a few modern machine tools; hitherto most of our machining work had been done by contract with other firms. I started an aeronautical college, a three years' course for a premium of 250 guineas which attracted a good many young men. At that time there was a marked shortage of suitable recruits for the sales and the design side of the aircraft industry; there were plenty of good lads coming forward from the normal trade apprenticeship schemes who would ultimately become good chargehands and ground engineers, but few trained for the office. We aimed to give them a good general training in the theory of aeronautics, in shop practice, and in general business methods, and we turned out a number of young men in the next five years who quickly attained the highest positions in the expanded aircraft industry of the war.

The autumn of 1934 was a very strenuous time. In September Sir Alan Cobham and Squadron Leader Helmore set off on their attempt to fly to India non-stop, refuelling three times in the air on the way. The attempt failed, for one of those trivial little defects that occur to plague so complicated a mechanism as an aeroplane. They took off in the Courier and refuelled in the air, and flew to Malta, where the second refuelling was to take place. This was accomplished satisfactorily over Malta and contact with the tanker was released. Cobham then turned on to course, I think for Amman in Jordan, and as he turned a split pin fell out of a link in the throttle control, the control ceased to function, and the spring-loaded throttle flew fully open, as is usual in aero engines. It was, of course, hopeless to continue and Cobham brought the machine in upon the switch and landed her upon an aerodrome at Malta. We never traced the cause of that defect. It seemed incredible that the split pin should not have been properly opened, for the machine had been inspected by our own inspectors many times, and also by Cobham's staff. It might have been caused by a defective or fatigued split pin; we modified the design of the parts in question as a precautionary measure. It was a great disappointment and one that I felt keenly, for Cobham had done so much to help the company. The flight to India was not attempted again; the rehearsals and the development work done for it had aroused interest at the Air Ministry and contracts were forthcoming for the continuation of the work on service aircraft, so that the demonstration flight to India which was to arouse interest and to secure development contracts was no longer necessary.

In October the MacRobertson race from England to Australia took place. We had taken an order for a special racing model of the Envoy from a very famous pilot, now dead, for this race; an order that had to be upon a hire purchase basis, for the pilot could only produce a deposit of a thousand pounds. The machine was fitted with two of the latest supercharged Armstrong Siddeley Mark VI engines and had a large fuel tank in the fuselage in place of payload; for its day it was a very powerful and advanced racing machine with a long range. It was so much modified from the Envoy that we gave it another type name, and christened it the Viceroy. The pilot, however, had the greatest difficulty in finding the finance for his flight and was an exhausted and a worried man when the race started; bad weather across Europe defeated him in a manner that would never have occurred if he had been himself, so that he landed several times and finally retired at Athens, to commence a legal action against us for the most trivial defects in the machine. He pursued this matter and we had to go to court against him to preserve our reputation, and received a judgement in our favour resulting in the return of the machine to us with a considerable sum of money.

We had another entry in this race, an Airspeed Courier flown by Squadron Leader Stodart. Stodart also had no money and was financed largely by our own directors as a personal gesture because I was resolute in refusing any company money for this venture, since the advertisement value to the company seemed to me to be small. In fact, Stodart and his nephew, a sergeant pilot in the RAF who flew as co-pilot with him, put up a very fine show. They could not hope to compete with the de Havilland Comets or with the Douglas DC2 in speed or range, but they got through to Australia and came in seventh in the race in a remarkably good time considering the character of the machine. Both airframe and engine were borrowed for the race, the airframe being the property of our English distributors the Aircraft Exchange and Mart Ltd. and the engine being supplied by Armstrong Siddeley Motors Ltd.

The subsequent history of the Viceroy is interesting as an indication of the type of business which was to develop in the next few years. The machine came back to us after the lawsuit in the early summer of 1935 and stood in the back of a hangar for some months. In the autumn we were approached by a Croydon aircraft-selling organization managed by a man that I will call Jack Norman, who had a client who wanted to buy the Viceroy. This client, said Jack Norman, was the proprietor of a concern called Yellow Flame Distributors Ltd., whose business was the rapid transport of cinema films between the various capital cities of Europe. For this service our long-range racing aeroplane, the Viceroy, was exactly what they wanted, and they were prepared to pay a good price for the machine.

I was, of course, delighted at the prospect of shifting this white elephant. Jack Norman paid a deposit and we set about reconditioning the Viceroy and preparing it for flight. A few days later Jack Norman turned up in my office and said that cinema films were very inflammable things to carry in an aeroplane and his clients were a bit worried. Could we fit bomb racks underneath the wings to carry the films on?

By that time war had broken out between Italy and Abyssinia, and Mussolini's army was invading the country of the Emperor Haile Selassie and driving back his coloured primitive army towards the capital, Addis Ababa. I told Jack Norman that I was fitting no bomb racks, that I was selling a civil aeroplane to be delivered on our aerodrome at Portsmouth to his company, a British concern. He then asked if I would provide certain lugs under the wings to which they could attach anything they liked, and I agreed to do this.

The next thing was that Jack Norman asked if the pilot for the Viceroy might fly our demonstration Envoy for an hour or two with our test pilot Colman at his side, to familiarize himself with the type. This was a very reasonable request, to which I agreed at once. Jack Norman then said that there was some difficulty about the pilot because he hadn't got a passport. He was a stateless citizen. He was German by birth and his name was, shall we say, Ernst Schrader. Mr Schrader had been a pilot of the German airline Luft Hansa and one day had spoken disrespectfully of Adolf Hitler in a beer tavern. Next day his sister had rung him up at the aerodrome in a great panic, to tell him that the Gestapo had been at the house looking for him. Mr Schrader was about to leave to pilot a machine of the airline to Amsterdam and he made no delay; at Amsterdam he resigned from the Luft Hansa. He was now in Holland with very little chance of getting a German passport. Would we send the demonstration Envoy to Amsterdam for him to fly it there?

I said we wouldn't.

Presently they produced Mr Schrader at Portsmouth aerodrome to fly the Envoy, which he did remarkably well; he was clearly a very fine pilot and a most experienced man. He was spirited away immediately the flight was over, and I had no chance of conversation with him. Colman, however, came into my office directly the party had departed. He had been in Berlin on our business a few weeks before, and there he had met one of the most famous German pilots of the day, whom I shall call Weiss. He was convinced that this man was Weiss.

It seemed to be about time for a showdown with Jack Norman, and I told him that I would go no farther in selling him this aeroplane unless I was taken into his confidence, and perhaps not then. After consultation with his principals I was let into the secret. The army of Haile Selassie had no hope of standing up against the Italian invaders of their country unless modern arms and equipment could reach them. The Emperor had the pitiful sum of £16,000 to spend on modern aircraft with which to defend his country. With this he was buying our Viceroy for £5,000 and the remainder was to be spent on three fighters, Gloster Gladiators I think, to shoot down the Italian planes that were harassing his troops. All four machines would, of course, be flown by soldiers of fortune from Europe. The job of the Viceroy was to bomb the Italian oil-storage tanks at Massawa and so halt their mechanized advance. The Viceroy was a good deal faster than any aircraft the Italians had in Abyssinia, and this mission was well within the capabilities of the machine. It was, however, vital to maintain complete secrecy, because if the Italians were to get to know about the Viceroy they would move a squadron of first-class fighters from Italy to defend Massawa, with the result that the Viceroy would almost certainly be shot down.

At that time military operations in Abyssinia were held up by the rainy season; there was time for the machine to reach Addis Ababa and perform its mission before hostilities could commence again. The Emperor had a little more money to spend and Jack Norman was buying bombs and small arms for him, which were to be shipped in some way to Abyssinia, perhaps through French or British Somaliland. Fuel for the aircraft also had to be provided. Jack Norman visited Finland and bought the bombs and bomb racks there, and also bought a quantity of sub-machine guns to equip the primitive army of the Emperor. I think the Viceroy was to transport most of this stuff to Addis Ababa at some stage in the journey, and in order to evade the notice of the Italians the Viceroy was to fly from England to Abyssinia by night, refuelling once at some secret landing ground in the Mediterranean area.

Accordingly Jack Norman rang me up one day and asked if the pilot might have some further night-flying practice on our demonstration

Envoy. This was reasonable in view of the great hazards of the work that
lay before him and I agreed, stipulating of course that Colman must be
with him. Jack Norman then said, a little coyly, that the pilot had
changed his name.

'I bet he has,' I said. 'What's he changed it to? Weiss?'

'Oh no,' he said hurriedly. 'He's nothing to do with Weiss.' He then
explained that the pilot was now an Abyssinian subject and was
provided with an Abyssinian passport, so that everything was all regular.
In Abyssinia it is usual to put the family name first, so that he had
changed his name from Ernst Schrader to Schrader Ernst.

'That's all right by me,' I said. 'Schrader or Weiss or Ernst, you produce
him here and he can do a couple of hours' night flying with Colman.'

He came and did a couple of hours' landing practice by night in the
light of a flare path, and was whisked away immediately in a fast car in
real cloak-and-dagger style. Next morning at ten o'clock a plain-clothes
officer of the CID was in my office, wanting to know all about an alien
pilot who had been flying one of our aeroplanes over Portsmouth
dockyard by night.

There was nothing to do but to tell him the whole thing; by that time
I had reason to believe that the Foreign Office knew all about the
venture, and were friendly to it. The CID man went away and troubled
us no more, and I was left wondering who had talked and whether the
talk was getting to Italian ears. At that time there was great feeling in
England against Italy and in favour of the Emperor. I do not think that
any obstacle was put forward to impede Jack Norman's activities by any
official body.

After so much effort it was a pity that this bold venture failed. It
proved impossible to get the supplies of bombs and fuel to Abyssinia in
time; hostilities broke out again in January and by the end of April the
Emperor had been defeated; on May 2nd he went on board a British
warship and was conveyed to England while the Italians occupied his
country. The Viceroy never left our works. So far as I can remember, it
was finished and paid for but resting in our works till it was time for it
to fly to Abyssinia, for they did not want it to be seen on public
aerodromes. I think it was left in our hands to be sold on behalf of the
Emperor, who went into exile in England and lived at Cheltenham.

It was sold again quite soon. An air race was announced from London
to Johannesburg in October 1936, and two well-known British pilots,
Max Findlay and Ken Waller, secured finance to take part in this race
and came to us and bought the Viceroy. They made a strong team, for
the machine was very fast and capable of carrying a crew of four
including a radio operator. They were regarded as very likely winners of

the race. In July 1936, however, the civil war in Spain broke out, and an agent of some continental nationality came to them and wanted to buy the Viceroy. They told him that the machine was not for sale.

Between friends, he said, everything could be arranged.

They said they weren't interested in his friendship. They weren't selling.

He said that was no way to talk, between friends. He knew how much they had paid Airspeed for it. They had paid five thousand five hundred pounds.

They said that was nothing to do with him. They were going to fly the Viceroy in the Johannesburg race and win the first prize. The machine was not for sale. Now, would he please go away and stop wasting their time.

He said that the first prize in the race was four thousand pounds. Four thousand and five thousand five hundred made nine thousand five hundred pounds, so they would not have to fly at all and would save the cost of the petrol. He would give them the cheque right away.

They took it, cashed it and saw that it was good, and handed over the Viceroy, which left for France without delay and was never seen again. Ken Waller and Max Findlay got into a Moth and came down to us to order another machine if we could get it ready for them in time for the race. We managed to complete a Cheetah-engined Envoy with long-range tanks for them in time, which had a very similar performance to the Viceroy, so that when they took off in the race they had already won the first prize.

They met disaster, however, at Abercorn, a high-altitude aerodrome in the middle of Africa. The strip was slightly uphill; they had the choice of taking off at maximum load either uphill against the wind or downhill down wind. Local residents advised them to wait an hour or two till the wind dropped, as it would, and take off downhill, but the exigencies of the race prevented that. They got off the ground but failed to clear the trees beyond the strip and crashed, Max Findlay and the radio operator being killed.

All this stemmed from events that happened in the autumn months of the year 1934, immediately after the first public issue of shares. In the formation of the new company Hewitt had been asked to retire from the Board to make room for the new directors; this was a very great loss to the company, for Hewitt was not only an expert on commercial law but also had a wide experience of the growing pains of young companies and so had a full understanding of our difficulties. The two directors of Swan Hunter and Wigham Richardson appointed to our Board were elderly men, experienced in running a great and powerful inherited shipbuilding concern successfully, with little previous experience of such an industry as ours. I think that they had entered into the manufacture of aircraft without a full realization of the difficulties of an industry so different from their own; quantity production was unknown to them and in selling they had always operated under the umbrella of a great and famous name established a hundred years before by their forefathers. They had expected, I think, to see the construction of large all-metal flying boats commence in their shipyards almost immediately, and when they found that many years of gradual development must pass before that result could be achieved they tended to lose interest. The third new director was a young and energetic man, Mr George Wigham Richardson, not at that time a director of the shipbuilding company that bore his name but managing director of the friendly intermediary company in the City to which I have referred. Richardson at that time knew little about aviation but he was hardworking in the interests of the company and very capable of learning; he quickly became a great strength on the Board.

Soon after the public issue the record shows that we were already considering the design of a new and commercial aeroplane, considerably larger than the Envoy, capable of carrying two pilots and twelve to fourteen passengers. With the swift development of airlines larger aircraft were demanded every year by the operators; however inconvenient to our business this might be it seemed necessary to follow the demand. Another factor in these difficult problems concerned the employment of the drawing office: unless we had a big and competent design staff we could hardly hope to secure Air Ministry orders for aircraft of our own design. To keep an adequate design staff we had to give them something to do, however inexpedient it might be for us to launch a new commercial aeroplane before we had recovered the development and design costs on the Courier and the Envoy. Accordingly we were considering the layout of a new machine, a high-wing twin-engined monoplane largely to be built in metal.

In the autumn of 1934 the Douglas DC2 appeared in Europe. This was a very advanced American commercial aeroplane seating about eighteen passengers. It made a great name for itself with an outstanding flight in the race from England to Australia, and began to sell in quantities to major airlines all over Europe. The manufacturing and selling licences for this machine in Europe had been acquired by the Dutch firm colloquially known as Fokker, and Mr Fokker had been very active in selling Douglases in many countries.

I forget who first raised the proposal that we should take a manufacturing licence for Douglas and Fokker aircraft; I doubt if it came from either Tiltman or myself. There was much to be said for and against the proposal. It would provide us with the design and manufacturing licence for a highly successful aeroplane of the size that the market demanded, thus obviating lengthy and expensive development work upon a new design, for the days were rapidly passing when a new-type aircraft could go straight to operations, as the Ferry had done. It would provide a short cut for us into all metal construction. To take these licences we should have to get in more capital from the public, and this in itself was good in view of the rapidly increasing capital requirements of the industry.

On the other hand, it meant the closest technical association with Mr Fokker, an alien, and his alien company. We would not be able to conceal from them the projects upon which we were working, and this might have a serious effect on the orders that we hoped to get from the Air Ministry. With rearmament already in sight, though proceeding at a languid pace, it would be disastrous if the association with Fokker should prevent orders for service aircraft being placed with us. Tiltman was greatly concerned about this aspect of the matter, and rightly so, for he conducted most of the negotiations with the Air Ministry, since the prospect of orders for service aircraft was inextricably involved with the qualities of the designs that we could offer.

For myself, I was for the association with Fokker. It meant a further increase in the capital of the company without which we might well have to cut down the strength of the drawing office; if that became necessary it might be more detrimental to our chance of Air Ministry orders than the presence of Mr Fokker. Given the money, I was convinced that our technical qualities would drive Airspeed through to success; without adequate capital we could do nothing. Though we might never build a Douglas or a Fokker aeroplane, and in fact we did not, I was still in favour of taking this manufacturing licence. Not least was the consideration in my mind that Fokker was a man that the shipbuilders would listen to and whose judgement they would respect, and he was a man who knew the aircraft industry, who had himself built up a small company from the beginning. I knew that he would find little to complain of in the conduct of the business and would understand our problems.

In fact, it was the shipbuilders who controlled our company who really decided this matter. They were puzzled and concerned about the unpredictable and unprofitable business that they had got themselves mixed up in, which seemed to be running upon principles that they considered totally unsound. Within a very few months they had lost confidence in our management, and they welcomed as an adviser to the Board Mr Fokker, who had made money and a great name in the aircraft industry. Perhaps they thought that Mr Fokker could put the whole thing right and cause great flying boats to be laid down in their shipyards in a very short time. In any case, throughout the late autumn and winter of 1934 negotiations with Fokker went on mostly in the hands of Richardson and myself, in Amsterdam, in Newcastle, in London, and in St Moritz.

Fokker at that time, I think, was already a sick man; he was to die in 1939 at the early age of forty-nine. When we first met him he was forty-four but he was no longer fit to fly an aeroplane, nor had he done so for a number of years. I found him to be genial, shrewd, and helpful to us; he was critical of some parts of our organization as was to be expected, but on the whole he approved what we had done. He was a difficult man to deal with, for he had no settled home but travelled constantly; his domestic life was irregular. Matrimonial conventionality is an asset in business in this way; if a man has a settled home you do at least know where you can get hold of him upon the telephone. With Fokker, even in Amsterdam you never knew where he was living; he travelled incessantly and frequently his very efficient legal adviser and secretary could not tell us where he was. He worked at all hours and in strange places: business was frequently commenced in the half-light of an empty restaurant at three o'clock in the afternoon, when Fokker would order lunch for us from resentful waiters and himself consume nothing but a glass of milk. I do not think that such a man is ever himself very efficient, but Fokker was a good chooser of men and had gathered around himself a most efficient staff of Dutchmen and ex-Germans.

In October 1934 we took an order from C P Ulm for a Lynx-engined Envoy. Ulm was a very well-known Australian pilot who had been an associate of Kingsford-Smith on a number of long-distance flights in a three-engined Fokker machine; he had parted from Kingsford-Smith and was now engaged upon a venture to initiate an airline across the Pacific from San Francisco to Sydney. He intended to operate this service with Douglas DC3 machines, but initially he had secured a little capital with which to make a series of demonstration flights in one of our Envoys. I think his intention was to fly the Envoy several times along the route carrying a token load of mail, and then to float a public company for capital with which to buy the Douglases and start the airline. Already we were talking of Fokker and the Douglas licence, so this order was interesting to us in several ways.

Ulm cabled his order from Australia. He wanted the longest possible range when carrying a crew of three, for the distance from San Francisco to Honolulu is about 2,200 nautical miles. I forget what tankage we were able to put into the Envoy but it probably gave him a range of about 3,000 nautical miles at about 170mph. To achieve this it was necessary to build a very large petrol tank in the fuselage filling the cabin section entirely, and this tank, of course, had to be located on the centre of gravity of the machine. The room that was left in the machine forward of this tank was certainly cramped for three men with wireless and navigating gear but it was possible; the navigator had to work upon a folding chart table and there was little elbow room.

There was some urgency about the delivery of the machine: Ulm was an energetic man, usually in a hurry. The construction of the machine was well advanced when he arrived in our works. He at once declared against the seating arrangement that we had prepared: the men were too much on top of each other in his view, with the result that nobody would be able to do his work properly.

There was a large, empty space in the rear fuselage of the machine, behind the great petrol tank. Ulm decided to transfer the navigator from the front to the rear of the tank and to put the wireless with him, as he was also to be the wireless operator. In that position we were able to provide a big chart table with proper facilities for navigation, while there was now ample room for Ulm and the pilot ahead of the tank. We provided a speaking-tube past the tank from Ulm to his navigator. This new arrangement was obviously better in all ways except one. Ulm was the captain of the aircraft, and he could not now see the charts or calculations for himself, or touch the wireless. However, he was the purchaser and that was the arrangement that he wanted.

His crew joined him to take delivery of the machine. Both were, of course, Australians and we were surprised to hear that the navigator had little previous experience of navigating in the air: he was a ship's officer. Perhaps at that time it was not easy to find experienced air navigators in Australia, for that was a new technique and Australia is a small country. However, that was nothing to do with us. Ulm test flew his aeroplane and was satisfied with it. It was then dismantled to be shipped across the Atlantic. It was erected in the United States and flown across the continent to Oakland airport near San Francisco, from which the Pacific flight was to commence.

They took off from Oakland late in the evening, timing their departure so that they would arrive at Honolulu an hour after dawn. The purpose of this was that if they failed to find the islands they would have all the hours of daylight in which to look for them, until their fuel ran out.

And that is what happened. They failed to find the islands, and were heard calling Honolulu on their wireless for five hours after they should have landed. Radio was less developed in those days, and though Honolulu made every effort to help them their signals were too weak through distance for the airport to get a bearing on them; there was no means of telling them which way to fly for a safe landing. All through the forenoon the distressing calls went on as Ulm made visual searches for the islands in every direction, till at last the final message came that fuel was exhausted and they were going down into the sea. No trace of men or the machine was ever found.

Our own analysis of this disaster was based on the position of the navigator. Ulm was the experienced man in air navigation over the ocean, but Ulm could not himself examine either charts or radio log in the air. It seemed to us that the probable course of events was that the machine had had a strong tail wind during the night which the navigator had not appreciated or allowed for, and had overflown Honolulu before dawn and had gone on to the west of the islands. When they started looking for the islands they were probably far beyond them, and going farther away each minute. Their own radio direction-finder might have given them a clue during the hours of darkness, and it seems possible that at some stage they got on to a reciprocal bearing without realizing what had happened. In short, there was clearly a mistake in navigation which Ulm might well have found if he could have taken control, but with the seating arrangements as they were this was impossible. When the navigator got bushed Ulm could not get at him to steady him or to take over. So they died.

CHAPTER TEN

IN JANUARY 1935 Airspeed Ltd. signed an agreement with Fokker and his company by which we took the manufacturing licence for the Douglas DC2 and a number of Fokker types; Mr Fokker was to be consultant to the company for seven years. In connexion with this we made another public issue of shares for about another £100,000. This issue was oversubscribed, though not so much as the first one: the City were justifiably wary of a company that came back for more capital before showing profits made upon the first lot.

In Newcastle Mr Fokker failed to pull the rabbit out of the hat for the shipbuilders, as we had failed before. There would at that time have been no particular technical difficulty in building great flying boats in their shipyards, though more suitable locations for building flying boats could be imagined. The trouble was to find anybody to consider placing an order for boats built in such circumstances: it took a little time for the shipbuilders to appreciate that their great name earned in shipping did not automatically induce Imperial Airways to place orders for flying boats with them. Another difficulty concerned money: conversion of the shipyards to the new type of manufacture would absorb a vast amount of capital which nobody seemed very willing to produce. The negotiations to build flying boats upon the Tyne dragged on for a year or so, and finally expired as increasing Admiralty orders for ships under the rearmament programme made it clear that every shipyard would be fully occupied in its original function.

In the spring of 1935 I spent about three weeks in Athens. The Greek Government wanted to buy fighter aircraft, and the Fokker D17 suited them well; this was a single-seater rather like a Hawker Fury, but built with wooden wings. The Greeks had to place their aircraft orders in Great Britain, however, for currency reasons, and the proposal was that

Airspeed should build these Fokker fighters for Greece. It was a reasonable proposal and might have come off, but it would have taken a better man than I to close the deal. I spent three weeks in Athens with a representative of the Fokker company who was well accustomed to methods of business in the Balkan states; those who want to find out what those methods were may read my novel *Ruined City*. In the end, I don't think the Greeks ordered anything at all. After three weeks I came to the conclusion that I was wasting my time, and came home.

At home, however, orders for Envoys were beginning to come in from reputable concerns who had real money with which to pay for their machines. We sold the manufacturing licence for the Envoy to Mitsubishi, the airline of Japan, with an order for two machines; three months later they came back and ordered four more Envoys making six machines in all. The Japanese were curious little men very active with Leica cameras; when we offered them entertainment at the weekend they usually chose to go and see the *Victory*, Admiral Nelson's old flagship laid up in the middle of Portsmouth dockyard. One of them got drunk one night, and told us a lot about his hatred for Britain and the coming war, which we passed on to the proper quarter.

Two Envoys followed for the Czechoslovak State Air Line and three for North Eastern Airways, an internal airline operating through Britain in which Lord Grimthorpe had an interest. A number of hire purchase orders for less substantial companies were in hand also, some of which came back to us and ultimately found their way to Spain. With these orders in hand and with the increased production that they indicated the company was gradually getting on to a firm basis, though it was still working at a loss.

A very unpleasant part of the duties of a managing director came upon me at this time, due to the growth of the company. In some cases the earliest members of the staff, sometimes considerable shareholders, were proving inadequate in the larger job. In the York days one of the earliest supporters of the company had been appointed Secretary, though he had no qualifications in accountancy. This was all right while the total of the employees did not exceed fifty; he put up a brave show as the numbers rose, but even before we became a public company he had to be replaced by a man with qualifications and put on other, less important work. In turn, in 1937 this second Secretary was to prove incapable of handling the accountancy of what was by that time a great company, and had to be replaced by yet another, higher grade of man.

In the summer of 1935 this process had to touch Tom Laing, our first and best employee and a supporter of the company to the limit of his finances. Tom Laing simply did not know what went on in a works making aeroplanes on the production line; he was a first-class man in the shop, but the technical knowledge required by a works manager employing four hundred men just wasn't there. Tom was the first to admit it and to recommend that we look for someone out of one of the big companies, under whom he would serve loyally as an assistant. We did this and got a first-class man from Avro. Tom Laing worked under him and they became great friends; when in the war a great shadow factory for Airspeed was put up by the Air Ministry at Christchurch Tom Laing became works manager of that and remained so till his death. But it was not always so easy.

I think this is the most miserable part of being the managing director of a growing company. One by one I had to replace our earliest supporters as the job grew too big for them, as the company grew to a size when it could afford properly qualified staff, till in the end the same cup came to me and I was myself replaced. It is a process which is inevitable in a growing business and which takes much of the fun out of it, so that after a few years of sacking one's old friends one grows to feel that success may not be such a good thing after all, that possibly there may be other, less sorry ways of earning a living in this world. When success ultimately came to Airspeed, I was ready to leave the company, having come to the conclusion that I didn't much like my job.

By the end of the first financial year of the new company it was evident that we were still working at a loss, though in the first flush of optimism we had paid one interim dividend. This loss was due primarily to our small turnover coupled with the ever decreasing basic price of small civil aeroplanes dictated by our competitors. At the annual general meeting to announce this loss Lord Grimthorpe resigned from the chairmanship of the company, to my regret. He had seen the company through its earliest days two-thirds of the way to success, but the business now demanded much work from the chairman and was located in the south of England, while he lived in the north. He remained a member of the Board and was succeeded as chairman by Mr Richardson, who enjoyed the confidence of our aged shipbuilding associates, could talk to them like a Dutch uncle, and often did. He worked hard for the company and picked up a knowledge of our peculiar business very quickly, while his reputation in the City probably saved us from a good deal of trouble as we passed our dividends year after year.

By the beginning of 1936 an order for seven Envoys had been received from the South African State Railways. It reflected the condition of the world at that time, that these were civil aeroplanes for use on an airline but they were to be readily convertible to military purposes. Bomb racks and release gear were to be provided, a mounting for a forward firing gun, and the roof of the lavatory was detachable and replaceable by another roof which carried a gun turret. Apart from this and one or two other orders, we had taken subcontract work from other aircraft companies to the value of about £50,000, so that we had orders in hand totalling about £90,000 though no Air Ministry orders for machines of our own design had yet come our way. A further extension to the factory was put in hand to cope with all this work, and with the larger orders which were now certain to come in due course.

A difficult situation now arose over our association with Fokker. The increasing amount of work for the Air Ministry on which we were engaged made it necessary for everyone to sign the Official Secrets Act and precluded any alien from entering our factory without Air Ministry sanction. This not only excluded the Dutchmen from our factory but made it expedient to exclude them from attendance at our Board meetings. It was unfortunate that the drift towards war had developed to this point only a year after we had gone into our association with the Fokker company but there was nothing to be done about it; we made an attempt to carry on the partnership over civil aeroplanes but from this time onwards the association declined, partly, perhaps, because of the increasing ill health of Fokker himself.

By the end of March the orders in hand totalled £117,000 and the employees had risen to nearly six hundred. There were still no direct orders from the Air Ministry, though verbal assurances had been given to us by officials that our factory would be kept full of work for at least three years to come. By this time the proposal to convert the Envoy to a twin-engined military training aircraft, later to become known as the Airspeed Oxford, was well advanced, and the same officials were talking glibly of an initial order of a hundred of these machines, with a total requirement of four hundred.

These prospects, however, were of little value, and the long delays at the Air Ministry in placing orders for the rearmament programme caused a great deal of loss to our shareholders. The layout of a factory for building aeroplanes and the layout of a factory for building small parts of aeroplanes is totally different. Our works was established on an aerodrome and laid out for the construction of complete machines, and in the end the orders were to justify this set-up. While the Air Ministry delayed in placing production orders with us it was necessary to reorganize this unsuitable factory to build small components for more fortunate companies, with a totally different ratio of machine tools to floor area; we entered on this process unwillingly, convinced that in six months the civil servants would have finished drinking their tea and would consent to send out orders for complete aircraft to us, making it necessary for us to rip out all our new installations and reconvert the factory to its original function. This is in fact what was to happen, and involved a totally unnecessary loss to our shareholders in the years 1936 and 1937 due, I think, to ignorance of industry on the part of the politicians and high civil servants in charge of the Air Ministry in those years.

In May we received an order from the Air Ministry for two prototype machines to be known as the Queen Wasp. The Queen Bee was a radio-controlled target aircraft based on the well-known de Havilland Tiger Moth training machine, and the Queen Wasp was to be a better and bigger edition of the Queen Bee. Tiltman had designed a very beautiful little tapered-wing biplane cabin machine with the Wolseley engine for this job, much too good to serve as a target and be shot down, but he had argued very rightly that perfection was the best selling point to senior Air Force officers spending other people's money. The Queen Wasp was fitted alternatively with a landplane and a seaplane undercarriage; for target use it was always fitted with a seaplane undercarriage and was landed on the sea if it remained undamaged after the shoot.

In July our shipbuilding controllers offered us a general manager from their shipyard, an offer which I was glad to accept. Mr Townsley was a genial, friendly man with long experience of labour relations in the shipping industry. He filled a gap in our organization which needed filling, for I had little experience in dealing with trades unions or labour problems on a major scale. By that time we were employing over eight hundred men and the shop was getting slack and out of hand, while the costing and rate-fixing departments on which the whole prosperity of an engineering business must depend needed reorganization with an expert hand. Townsley was gravely handicapped at first by ignorance of aircraft and the peculiar, rapidly changing aircraft industry, but he made up for these deficiencies by his energy and will to learn. From the first he was a great addition to our team, and under his management the business for the first time looked as if it might some day be working at a profit.

Townsley was young enough to learn the aircraft industry, but some of my shipbuilding co-directors were not. In August 1936, when they had had two years' experience upon our Board, the minutes show a bitter comparison of our work with shipbuilding. The design of a ship, it was stated, took eight weeks, and a cruiser 700 feet long could be delivered complete with all details in twenty-seven months: therefore Airspeed was a grossly inefficient organization. Age was no doubt a factor in this unwise expression of opinion; I doubt if many men retain the flexibility of mind required to learn a novel industry after the age of seventy. It did not make our day-to-day conduct of the business of the company any easier when time had to be wasted in trying to educate old men to the basic facts about our industry. We were indebted to Swan Hunter for assistance in our public issues and for giving us a first-class general manager, but for little else.

In July 1936 the Spanish civil war broke out, and by August agents for one side or the other were buying up every civil aeroplane that would fly. We made a bulk sale of practically the whole of our stock of unsold Couriers and Envoys to one British aeroplane sales organization and heard no more of them. One aeroplane was excluded from this deal, our first demonstration Envoy on which we had carried out a large amount of development flying, I think because we could not spare it for a week or two. Then I decided to take the opportunity to shift it. An agent at Croydon aerodrome had a client who wanted to buy it, and for this middle-aged aeroplane with Wolseley engines I quoted the very high price of six thousand pounds; I think we must already have heard about the Viceroy sale. The client did not blench but he insisted on seeing the machine first, and would inspect it nowhere but at Croydon aerodrome.

At that time there was some cheating going on over these aircraft sales to Spain; once the machine was handed over to a British agent it would leave the country usually within an hour and would never be seen again. Cases had occurred where payment for the machine had been omitted, a small formality which somewhat marred the deal from the seller's point of view. I could not spare Colman to wait at Croydon so I sent a young man of our sales staff up in the machine to stay with it until I had received the cheque and our bank had pronounced that it was good. I told him that he was to take sleeping gear with him and that he was not to leave the aeroplane till it was well and truly paid for; he was to stay with it all day and night, and sleep in it, till he received further instructions from me.

They flew to Croydon early in the morning. In the late afternoon I got a message that my young man was coming back upon the evening airline service; with our sales manager I waited for him in the Aero Club, drinking beer. The airline Envoy landed and the young man joined us in the bar. I asked him why he had come back, since no cheque had been received. Without a word, he took out his wallet and spread out on the bar before us six one thousand pound Bank of England notes.

None of us had ever seen one before and nor had our bank, but they proved to be quite good. It was in this machine that General Mola, one of Franco's most successful generals in the early part of the war, was killed by flying into the side of a mountain in bad weather. That was the end of our first Airspeed Envoy, which had produced such a good impression at the SBAC display of 1934 and had, perhaps, made possible our first public issue.

In August 1936 we got another order from the Air Ministry for two small prototype machines called Irving biplanes. These were never in fact built, and are only mentioned as a stage in the development of our order book. The type was to be a small single-seater with a Wolseley engine, carrying no armament but provided with a power-operated winch from which two thousand feet of steel cable could be unreeled in flight. The function was that of barrage balloon cables; the machines were to be flown in large numbers just above a layer of cloud trailing their cables down into the cloud, so that enemy bombers would never know where to expect a barrage. Second-line pilots, or women pilots, were proposed for these little unarmed aircraft. The scheme, however, was abandoned.

By that time we had managed to get the whole of our aeroplane production on to Wolseley engines. This engine was a radial engine of about 250 horsepower, modern in design and with a geared propeller, and a very considerable technical advance on any other British engine in its power range. It was manufactured by the well-known Nuffield motorcar organization who had devoted much effort to its development. They did not, of course, make aeroplanes, so that the use of this engine freed us from our previous trouble of buying engines from our competitors, while in size it suited all the production, present and future, that we had in hand. It was therefore a tremendous blow to Airspeed when, in September 1936, Lord Nuffield stopped production of this engine without notice.

The circumstances that led to the abandoning of this fine little engine deserve record. At that time Britain was at peace but was rearming in preparation for war. The Government were having a rough time from the Opposition over the cost of this rearmament; to placate the country over the rising taxation the Government pronounced that armament manufacturers would be strictly controlled from making excessive profits.

This policy decision, when filtered through the ignorant and over-cautious high officials at the Air Ministry, arrived at the manufacturer in this form. For any given number of machines it was proposed to order, the manufacturer was required to quote a fixed price for the contract. A document called an Instruction to Proceed, or ITP for short, was then sent to him. This document said, in effect, that he might start work and would be paid something some day, when the government accountants had had time to investigate his business. His quoted fixed price would

161

be taken as a maximum, more than which he could not be paid; he would probably be paid a good deal less. Government accountants were to have full access to all the costs of his business and would make their own estimate of his overheads properly chargeable to the contract, and would then announce the price which they would pay.

The aircraft industry, being dependent for their existence upon government orders, had no option but to accept contracts on these lines, while commencing corporate negotiations to eliminate the initial inequities and absurdities of the standard ITP document. Not so the motor car manufacturers. After a good deal of negotiation by Lord Nuffield's aero-engine sales manager his company received an invitation to tender for two hundred engines for installation in machines that it was proposed to order from us. I do not think that even his worst enemy could ever accuse Lord Nuffield of attempting to swindle the British public. The price that they quoted struck me as low at the time though I forget now what it was; on a basis of pounds per horsepower it was much lower than the price we were then paying for competing engines. The Air Ministry responded by sending them an ITP.

Lord Nuffield received this document and spent a morning studying it with Mr Boden, his only co-director at that time. They read it carefully, and noted all the provisions; neither of them had seen or heard of anything like it before. If they were to submit their vast business to this sort of an investigation it would mean a wholesale reorientation of their offices; it would mean engaging an army of chartered accountants on their side with a consequent increase in overheads. They had quoted a price for the engines which might well involve them in a heavy loss, through a genuine sense of patriotism, and they were rewarded by this suspicious nonsense. They were very angry.

They had spent at that time about two hundred thousand pounds upon the Wolseley aero-engine, and it had led only to this. In the scale of their whole business that was not a large amount of money, and as good businessmen they knew when to get out of an unsatisfactory venture. To admit the Air Ministry methods of doing business into their vast enterprise would be like introducing a maggot into an apple; the whole thing might well be brought to ruin in the end. Better to stick to selling motor vehicles for cash to the War Office and the Admiralty who retained the normal methods of buying and selling. They sent the ITP back to the Air Ministry, rejected, and closed down the aero-engine side of their concern.

This was a major disaster to Airspeed, for every type that we were then designing or manufacturing was fitted with the Wolseley engine. It was also a major disaster to Britain, for the engine was technically far ahead of any competitor in its power range. I had a hurried consultation with my chairman and then a telephone conversation with Lord Nuffield's secretary. It was always difficult to see Lord Nuffield personally, but he agreed to see me and I went to Oxford to visit him next day.

My object, briefly, was to induce him to give us the aero-engine business for nothing, for we hadn't got two hundred thousand pounds with which to pay for it, or anything like it. The most we could have offered would have been another public company to take the business over, in which we could have offered him a block of shares. I found Lord Nuffield very courteous, and he listened attentively to what I had to say. He told me that before closing his aero-engine business down he had thought of Airspeed and had ascertained that there was a competing engine that we could use. I said it was a rotten engine compared with his, and he remarked that for that I had to blame the Air Ministry. He was still furious with the Air Ministry. He grew red in the face at the thought of them, and thumped the desk before him. 'I tell you, Norway,' he said, 'I sent that ITP thing back to them, and I told them they could put it where the monkey put the nuts!' How many managing directors must have echoed the thought in those days and, unlike Lord Nuffield, had to swallow their principles with their pride.

Over the aero-engine business he was sympathetic to our wish to take it over and willing to consider any proposal that we could put up; he was in no hurry to dispose of the assets but would require the factory space within two months for other military production. I left with the knowledge that he was genuinely sorry for the trouble he had caused us and he was anxious to assist us if he could.

The opportunity to continue the manufacture of the Wolseley engine was one that Airspeed should have taken; if we had done so, on however insecure a basis, it would have come out all right under the increasing war demand for aero-engines of all powers. It proved impossible, however: the matter was too big for us. Airspeed had never made a profit and so had little power of gathering in the finance that would have been required, and we had nobody within our organization who knew anything about the manufacture of aero-engines. Our shipbuilding controllers, perhaps rightly, were averse to any further adventures till we had shown that we were capable of working at a profit. In the end we had to let this opportunity go, to my great regret; such opportunities do not come very often in the life of a company. The Wolseley engine died and today is hardly remembered, to the great loss of Britain. For this the blame must be laid fairly and squarely on the Air Ministry high civil servants of that day, for all their decorations and their knighthoods.

They should have had the wit to handle the business of the country better than that.

We had not long to grieve over the engine changes that were forced on us, because in October 1936 the company received an ITP for 136 Envoy trainers from the Air Ministry, the type that was to become known later as the Airspeed Oxford and was to become the standard twin-engined training aircraft of the British Commonwealth during the war. The redesign necessary to turn the basic Envoy into a first-class military trainer was very considerable, while the tooling necessary would take many months. The reconversion of the factory to making aeroplanes instead of parts again delayed production, so that it was to be more than a year before the first Oxford could be delivered and production could commence. At last, however, the company had a run of work ahead of it which would result in profits, tenuous though they might be on Government contracts. The success for which we had striven through so many years was now within our grasp, and I cannot recollect now that we found it specially exciting. Perhaps it had come too late, for hope deferred makyth the heart sick.

We lost another opportunity a month later, again through the restrictions of finance and the caution, perhaps justifiable, of the Board. British Continental Airways, the forerunners of the present British European Airways, asked us to tender for the manufacture of a batch of twelve Douglas DC3 aircraft. This was the successor to the DC2 for which we held the manufacturing licence and we could have got the drawings of the DC3 with little trouble; it was the aircraft which was later to be christened the Dakota when in British service. If we had taken this opportunity to go into production on the Dakota it would have had a very far-reaching effect upon the fortunes of the company. First things, however, had to be put first, and we had half a million pounds' worth of Oxfords to build before we should be free to take the opportunities that seemed to pass us every day. We were, however, still struggling to find a means to carry on the Wolseley aero-engine, although hope was gradually dying.

In the year 1936 Watt sold the film rights in my novel *Lonely Road* quite suddenly and unexpectedly to Ealing Studios. In writing the chief character in this book I had visualized him in the person of Clive Brook the well-known actor, and on publication of the novel I had sent a copy to Clive Brook. I had practically forgotten all about it in the pressure of more important business, but now four years later Ealing Studios bought the story for a film starring Clive Brook and Victoria Hopper. The sum paid by this British company for the film rights was not large by

American standards but I had the pleasure of seeing the film made, and the visits to the studio were an interest and a diversion from the frustrations of the growing aircraft business of those days.

With orders in hand which would keep the company busy for years ahead and which must show a profit, even though a small one, I now began to feel less personal responsibility to the shareholders. It no longer seemed necessary to abandon every personal interest to the company, and for recreation in the evenings I began to write again. It was five years since I had touched my typewriter except to write a business letter; now I got it out and gave it a new ribbon and began to write another book which was to be published later under the title of *Ruined City* in England and *Kindling* in the United States. It was a relief to turn to something that would take my mind off Airspeed and its troubles, for by that time I was often at variance with the other members of the Board.

It was a relief, also, to turn a little to domestic life. Since our marriage Airspeed had absorbed the whole of my energies, and in this my wife had been both helpful and cooperative. We had had few holidays in the six years of our marriage beyond weekends of cruising in the Solent on my old ten-tonner *Skerdmore*, and there had been periods when we had been acutely short of money as the salaries remained unpaid. We had two daughters by that time aged five and two and just becoming interesting; I had had little time to get to know them. Not only personal credit must be thrown into the pool by any managing director who dares to start a company like Airspeed Ltd.; domestic life must be thrown in as well. Now I had time, I felt, to get back to a normal life, to confine the business of the company substantially within office hours, and to try to behave more as a father and a husband should.

At the beginning of 1937 war was brewing all over the world, and it was becoming practically impossible to sell a civil aeroplane abroad without finding that it was to be put to a military use. In January we received an order from a British agent in Hong Kong for a civil Envoy for the personal use of the Governor of Kwangsi Province. This order was from a reputable agent and the money was real. I knew little of China at that time and looked at the atlas: Kwangsi was in the south and bisected by a great river which ran out near Hong Kong, which was probably their shopping town. It looked all right, and it still looked all right when the agent told us that the client was in a hurry for his aeroplane and would pay to have it flown out, instead of being crated and shipped.

I gave the job to Colman, with a young man from our college as a ground engineer. My wife went with them for the joyride, getting off at Calcutta. The flight out went without incident until the aircraft landed at Hanoi in Indo-China, to refuel and spend the night before the final stage on to Hong Kong. There the British agent met the machine. He told Colman that the Governor was in a great hurry for his aeroplane and to fly through Hong Kong would be an unnecessary detour; they would fly northwards from Hanoi straight to the client and deliver his machine.

Colman knew that he was urgently needed back at Portsmouth and this seemed to save a couple of days' flying; it did not occur to him that Hong Kong was British territory and that might have something to do with it. They flew north from Hanoi next day over hundreds of miles of mountainous and desolate country, and finally landed at a place called Liuchowfu upon a military aerodrome. It was explained to Colman there that Kwangsi had two Governors, a Military Governor and a Civil Governor, and this machine was for the Military Governor. It was immediately surrounded by Chinese technicians studying it to see where they would attach the bomb racks, and where the machine guns.

Before taking delivery the Governor wanted a flight in the machine. He had a bodyguard of four soldiers armed to the teeth who had to come with him. Each soldier wore a leather belt provided with two hooks, one on each side; from each hook hung a Mills bomb dangling by the safety pin. Colman struck at that, and insisted on the bombs being left behind. After the flight the Governor, very pleased with the machine, gave them a banquet of Chinese food that lasted for nine hours, and sent both Colman and the engineer to bed with acute gastro-enteritis. They were shipped down river to a hospital in Hong Kong, and came home from there.

A week after the delivery of the machine at Liuchowfu an official of the Foreign Office rang me up in my office at Portsmouth. The Chinese Government in Peking had sent a Note to the British Government complaining that they had been supplying arms to a rebel state, to wit, one Airspeed Envoy. The official wanted to know all about it and I told him. Evidently the matter was smoothed over, because we sold another Envoy to the same Military Governor at Kwangsi a couple of months later, with the full knowledge and consent of the Foreign Office. I sent that one out also by air, with George Errington as pilot, who had joined us as a ground engineer and is now one of the best-known test pilots in England.

In March 1937 we were honoured by an order for an Airspeed Envoy for the King's Flight, for the personal use of His Majesty and the Royal Family. This was the largest aeroplane that the King's Flight had acquired to that date, and we made a special effort over the finish of the aircraft, as might be supposed. The machine was painted in deep crimson and royal blue and had seats for four passengers, with accommodation for pilot, wireless operator, and steward. When Wing Commander Fielden, the Captain of the King's Flight, came to see me about the specification of the aircraft I questioned the necessity for carrying a steward in a vehicle that was little larger in accommodation than a motor car, and in which the passengers were unlikely to travel for longer than two or three hours. In explanation I received a brief account of the fatigue that royal personages must endure, a disturbing picture of radiant people who had opened a Town Hall and shaken a thousand hands smiling and waving to the crowd as they got into the aeroplane that was to take them home, and collapsing in a coma of fatigue directly the door was shut, grey-faced and utterly exhausted. I said no more about the steward.

With this order, I think Airspeed reached the peak of its career. Whatever the profit and loss account might show, no company could receive a higher endorsement of the quality of its products than we had received. We might continue to do as well technically; we could hardly do better.

From that time onwards, I think I began to lose interest in the company that I had brought into being. Civil work was coming to an end and all new design projects were of a military nature. None of us had ever served in the Royal Air Force, and though that experience may not be absolutely necessary for the production of a good military aircraft I think that our military designs lacked the touch of genius that had characterized our civil aeroplanes. Personally I could not pump up a great deal of enthusiasm for the military work that came our way, and with the approach of war and the conservative policy of our Board no new adventures were possible. Ahead of us stretched an endless vista of producing Airspeed Oxfords, and in fact the company was to go on producing Oxfords to the limits of its capacity for the next eight years. From this production there was not even the incentive of profit, for essentially the ITP system boiled down to work upon a cost-plus basis with a small margin of profit on whatever the costs happened to be. Ahead of the managing director of Airspeed Ltd. stretched an unknown number of years to be spent in restraining men from spending too much time in the lavatories in order that the aeroplanes might cost the taxpayer less, with the reflection that every hour so saved reduced the profit ultimately payable to the company. In time of war the sense of national effort will galvanize a system of that sort, and does so; in time of peace it tends to make a managing director bloody-minded. I think it did with me.

From this state of affairs stemmed the personal disagreements that began to plague the company about this time, which were to check its growth and ultimately lead to its absorption into a larger concern. Even the finance was now far beyond anything that we could do about it, for Airspeed by that time was a national asset and no bank dare close us down for such a trifle as an overdraft of £104,000, the figure reached by July 1937. With orders in hand for £594,000 of military aircraft we could cash the wages cheque without a thought about the bank manager, who in his turn had no control over the situation; our overdraft, with that of many other aircraft companies, was now a matter for negotiation far over our heads between the Board of the bank and the Secretary of the Air Ministry.

The prices of our shares upon the Stock Exchange reflected something of my own feelings. As success came to the company through Air Ministry contracts, the price of our shares dropped to an all-time low. The shares issued to the public were 5/- Preference shares, and the quotation of these shares upon the Stock Exchange had been buoyant in spite of our continuing losses. In no month did the average of the dealings in our shares represent a price below par until the first order for 136 Oxfords had been received from the Air Ministry, but from that point onwards there was a steady fall in the value of our shares upon the market. I think investors realized that on Air Ministry contracts the margin of profit was so small that there would be little hope of reimbursing shareholders for previous losses. While we retained freedom of action in the field of civil aeroplanes the high quality of our work technically might well bring profits in the end from which past losses might be recovered, but the flooding of the company with military orders meant an end to these financial hopes. We got the first Oxford production order in October 1936 and in November a steady and continuous fall in our shares commenced which was to go so far as a price of 1/6, and few buyers at that, as deliveries of the Oxford commenced in December 1937. The value of our shares was to recover somewhat as the initial absurdities of the ITP procedure were negotiated out, but I do not think they ever recovered much above par value.

A further 52 Oxfords were ordered from us in November 1937, and yet another batch of 140 in April 1938, but these orders did nothing to restore the spirit that had once inspired the company. Perhaps it had all become too easy. For my own part, I was learning what a better man than I had learned before me, that to travel hopefully is a better thing than to arrive, and the true success is to labour.

CHAPTER ELEVEN

IN APRIL 1938 my Board decided to attempt to quell the disputes that were plaguing the company by getting rid of me, and in this they were probably quite right. I would divide the senior executives of the engineering world into two categories, the starters and the runners, the men with a creative instinct who can start a new venture and the men who can run it to make it show a profit. They are very seldom combined in the same person. In Airspeed the time for the starters was over and it was now for the runners to take over the company. I was a starter and useless as a runner; there was nothing now for me to start, and I was not unwilling to go after the first shock to my pride.

The settlement that the Board made with me was a generous one. While we all thought things over they sent me on indefinite leave till the conclusion of my contract with the company fifteen months ahead; when the final settlement was made it gave me enough money to keep myself for five or six years at my then standard of living. I found myself in the totally unaccustomed position in the summer of 1938 of having enough money to live on and no work to do. A holiday abroad to collect my thoughts seemed to be the first thing; my wife and I made arrangements to park the children, and opened the atlas at the map of France. With an unaccustomed sense of freedom I shut my eyes and stabbed the map with a pencil, saying, 'Let's go there.' The point fell on St Claude in the Jura mountains; it could not have fallen on a better place.

Ruined City, known in America as *Kindling*, had been delivered to Watt a few months previously; my American publishers had got very excited about it and had taken an option to buy the film rights for a stated sum within three months. In St Claude, only a few weeks after leaving Airspeed, I got news by cable that this option had been taken up and the film rights sold. My wife and I retired to a small café opposite the post office and read the cable through again, struggling to believe the written words. We had never been affluent, never had more than a pittance in the bank at any time. Now several thousand pounds had dropped into my bank account for doing what to me had been a relaxation from real work. Our security for five or six years had grown to ten. For ten years, if I chose, I could just sit in the sun drinking Pernod, and not bother about work. It seemed incredible, but it was all quite true.

We had another Pernod.

When I left Airspeed the orders in hand were worth £1,262,000 and we employed 1,035 people. In the eight years that I was joint managing director the company never made a profit; I left the company in the ninth month of our financial year and in that year a small, tenuous profit was shown for the first time.

In the month that I left the company an order for 200 Oxfords was placed with de Havillands, so that we had the satisfaction of seeing our old friends and competitors pocketing their pride and building aeroplanes of our design while they prepared to wipe our eye again with the Mosquito, perhaps the most successful day bomber of the war. In turn, and later on, Airspeed was to build Mosquitoes. This close association with de Havillands was to lead in the end to an amalgamation. In all, 8,751 Oxfords were built by four companies, of which 4,961 were built by Airspeed. It was a good twine-engined trainer for its day, and most of the pilots for Bomber Command were trained upon the Oxford.

Two years after I left the company Swan Hunter and Wigham Richardson gave up their venture into aviation and sold their controlling interest in Airspeed Ltd. to the de Havilland Company. By that time the urgent need for ships was absorbing all their energies and was to do so for many years to come; in these circumstances they judged it better to yield control of Airspeed to a company more conversant with the nature of the aircraft industry. I think this transfer was a fitting one, for both Tiltman and I had learned our business with de Havillands; if we could not carry on the company ourselves my own vote would have been to let de Havillands take it over.

At the time of that transfer, in June 1940, only two of the original York working shareholders were left in the company, Tiltman and Tom Laing. The rest had either branched off into other and more profitable jobs arising from their work with us, or, in one or two cases, had left the company feeling that they had had a raw deal, which I regret. I do not think that anybody who invested in the company at par lost money if they held on to their shares, although they may not have made anything commensurate with the risk taken. All shares were finally transformed into share capital of the de Havilland Aircraft Company on favourable terms.

Tiltman resigned from Airspeed shortly after de Havilland assumed control and only Tom Laing was left, our first shareholder. He became works manager of the great Airspeed shadow factory at Christchurch, Hants, where he built a very large number of Oxfords and Mosquitoes. He always retained the appearance of a country gentleman in a changing industry, and his interests were very close to the good earth. Apart from family happiness he was devoted to shooting, fishing, dogs, good company, and Airspeed Ltd.

He died in the service of the company that he had joined as its first employee seventeen years before. He had been to Market Harborough in the Midlands on business and, driving back after dark, he rang up his wife from Newbury to say that he was very tired and he was going to stop there for the night; she was not to wait up for him. Apparently he failed to get a room because an hour later, travelling at a high speed, he hit a railway arch near Whitchurch and was killed instantaneously. Probably he went to sleep.

Airspeed Ltd. has now ceased to exist as a separate entity. It is still known as the Airspeed division of the de Havilland enterprise but the last Airspeed-designed aeroplane has probably taken off and it may well be that in a few years' time the name that I dreamed up in my bedroom of the St Leonards Club in York will be forgotten.

So ended a chapter of my life. I have never gone back to manufacturing and I shall probably not do so now, for that is a young man's game. Industry, which is the life of ordinary people who employ their civil servants and pay their politicians, is a game played to a hard code of rules; I am glad that I had twenty years of it as a young man, and I am equally glad that I have not had to spend my life in it till I was old. My gladness is tempered with regret, for once a man has spent his time in messing about with aeroplanes he can never forget their heartaches and their joys, nor is he likely to find another occupation that will satisfy him so well, even writing novels.

NEVIL SHUTE

THE FAR COUNTRY

A romance telling the story of a young English woman's holiday in the Australian outback just after World War II. Travelling from a cold, rainy country she finds a land of plenty and falls in love with Australia's wild countryside. She meets an older doctor, a displaced person from Europe. Their friendship teaches them about themselves and their adopted home.

LANDFALL

A romantic World War II adventure about the strength of true love and how it can overcome any obstacle. A British air reconnaissance officer falls for a pub waitress, but finds his life in chaos when he accidentally bombs a British U-boat, mistaking it for a German submarine. What begins as a romantic fling develops into true love as Mona fights to present the evidence she has discovered about this tragedy. Her hope is that it will absolve her lover.

Nevil Shute

On the Beach

Australia is one of the last places where life still exists after nuclear war starts in the Northern Hemisphere. A year on, an invisible cloak of radiation has spread almost completely around the world. Darwin is a ghost town, and radiation levels at Ayres Rock are increasing.

An American nuclear-powered submarine has found its way to Australia where its captain has placed the boat under the command of the Australian Navy. Commander Dwight Towers and his Australian liaison officer are sent to the coast of North America to discover whether a stray radio signal originating from near Seattle is a sign of life.

Pied Piper

Elderly John Howard goes off to the Jura in France on a fishing trip, except this is no ordinary time. Germany is at war with Europe. Friends at his hotel ask him to take their children back to England with him to safety as Germany is poised to invade France. Their harrowing journey begins by train and then proceeds on foot.

'Mr Shute not only writes vividly and excitingly of occupied France, but with a delightful understanding of children.' – *Sunday Times*.

NEVIL SHUTE

A TOWN LIKE ALICE

Jean Paget has survived World War II as a prisoner of the Japanese in
Malaya. After the war she comes into an inheritance that enables her to
return to Malaya to repay the villagers who helped her to survive. But
her return visit changes her life again, when she discovers that an
Australian soldier she thought had died has survived. She goes to
Australia in search of him and of the town he described to her. Jean sets
out to apply the same determination that helped her to survive the war,
to turning the community into 'a town like Alice'. She finds both her
soldier and romance.

TRUSTEE FROM THE TOOLROOM

Keith Stewart is a model engineering writer and a humble man with a
big heart. When his sister and brother-in-law yacht to British Columbia,
Keith looks after their young daughter, Janice. A hurricane drowns them
and their illegally concealed valuable stash of diamonds. Keith has to set
off alone to recover the diamonds so he can afford to be Janice's trustee.
Engineers across the world who know him through his construction
articles help him on his voyage.

OTHER TITLES BY NEVIL SHUTE AVAILABLE DIRECT FROM HOUSE OF STRATUS

Quantity		£	$(US)	$(CAN)	€
☐	Beyond the Black Stump	6.99	11.50	15.99	11.50
☐	The Chequer Board	6.99	11.50	15.99	11.50
☐	The Far Country	6.99	11.50	15.99	11.50
☐	In The Wet	6.99	11.50	15.99	11.50
☐	Landfall	6.99	11.50	15.99	11.50
☐	Lonely Road	6.99	11.50	15.99	11.50
☐	Marazan	6.99	11.50	15.99	11.50
☐	Most Secret	6.99	11.50	15.99	11.50
☐	No Highway	6.99	11.50	15.99	11.50
☐	An Old Captivity	6.99	11.50	15.99	11.50
☐	On the Beach	6.99	11.50	15.99	11.50
☐	Pastoral	6.99	11.50	15.99	11.50
☐	Pied Piper	6.99	11.50	15.99	11.50
☐	The Rainbow and the Rose	6.99	11.50	15.99	11.50
☐	Requiem for a Wren	6.99	11.50	15.99	11.50
☐	Round the Bend	6.99	11.50	15.99	11.50
☐	Ruined City	6.99	11.50	15.99	11.50
☐	So Disdained	6.99	11.50	15.99	11.50
☐	Stephen Morris (Incl. Pilotage)	6.99	11.50	15.99	11.50
☐	A Town Like Alice	6.99	11.50	15.99	11.50
☐	Trustee from the Toolroom	6.99	11.50	15.99	11.50
☐	What Happened to the Corbetts	6.99	11.50	15.99	11.50

ALL HOUSE OF STRATUS BOOKS ARE AVAILABLE FROM GOOD BOOKSHOPS OR DIRECT FROM THE PUBLISHER:

Internet: **www.houseofstratus.com** including author interviews, reviews, features.

Email: **sales@houseofstratus.com** please quote author, title, and credit card details.

Hotline: UK ONLY: **0800 169 1780**, please quote author, title and credit card details.

INTERNATIONAL: **+44 (0) 20 7494 6400**, please quote author, title, and credit card details.

Send to: **House of Stratus**
24c Old Burlington Street
London
W1X 1RL
UK

<u>Please allow following postage costs per order:</u>

	£(Sterling)	$(US)	$(CAN)	€(Euros)
UK	1.95	3.20	4.29	3.00
Europe	2.95	4.99	6.49	5.00
North America	2.95	4.99	6.49	5.00
Rest of World	2.95	5.99	7.75	6.00
Free carriage for goods value over:	50	75	100	75

PLEASE SEND CHEQUE, POSTAL ORDER (STERLING ONLY), EUROCHEQUE, OR INTERNATIONAL MONEY ORDER (PLEASE CIRCLE METHOD OF PAYMENT YOU WISH TO USE) MAKE PAYABLE TO: STRATUS HOLDINGS plc

Order total including postage:———Please tick currency you wish to use and add total amount of order:

☐ £ (Sterling)   ☐ $ (US)   ☐ $ (CAN)   ☐ € (EUROS)

VISA, MASTERCARD, SWITCH, AMEX, SOLO, JCB:

☐☐☐☐☐☐☐☐☐☐☐☐☐☐☐☐☐☐☐

Issue number (Switch only):

☐☐☐

Start Date: **Expiry Date:**

☐☐/☐☐   ☐☐/☐☐

Signature: _____

NAME: _____

ADDRESS: _____

_____

POSTCODE: _____

Please allow 28 days for delivery.

Prices subject to change without notice.
Please tick box if you do not wish to receive any additional information. ☐

House of Stratus publishes many other titles in this genre; please check our website (**www.houseofstratus.com**) for more details